Latin Lessons

Ryeland Press
Books by Women For Women

By Maggie McIntyre

2025

This trade paperback is published by Ryeland Press

Cataloging information
ISBN: 978-1-916927-10-0
CREDITS
Editor: Nicci Robinson
Cover Design: Nicci Robinson
Production Design: Global Wordsmiths

Acknowledgements

Many thanks to Nicci Robinson of Global Wordsmiths, who has done sterling work, editing and formatting this book. I recommend Global Wordsmiths as a superb little publishing company, who always go the extra mile to turn rough cut stories into polished prose. Nicci also designed the cover for Latin Lessons and, I hope you agree, has done a superb job.

Dedication

This book is dedicated to the memory of my first Latin teacher, Elizabeth Miles, who introduced me to the joys of grammar and the works of poets like Virgil and always made the subject fun and fascinating.

Dear readers,

A word of explanation...
Latin Lessons is a special book for me. It's the sixth and final novel in my series, Isabel and Friends which I started back in 2020, with Isabel's Healing. It was a year when none of us knew what would happen to the world, as COVID kept us locked down at home, but gave us more time to write and read.

Since then, through four further novels in the same series, I have tried to combine tender love stories between two women, with plots that reflects tough realities of contemporary life. *A Girl on the Plane* includes an account of sex-trafficking. *Into the Rough* focusses on the work of Isabel's fictional aid agency, "Righteous Anger." *Love under Lockdown* spotlights the heroic work of NHS staff coupled with a visit to three couples' lives from the previous books. Then a more light-hearted romance, *Olivia's Pirate*, takes Isabel's publisher friend Olivia to Ireland, where she discovers love for the first time.

Now, in *Latin Lessons*, Olivia introduces us to Fenella, a literary editor and grammarian who is bowled over by a young American student. Susie bounces in from the States and totally disrupts her life. Fenella and Susie's story completes "Isabel and Friends," and I hope you love them as much as I do.

But *Latin Lessons* is also a crossover book linking the above UK based novels to another series, Behind the Camera, which is based in the USA and Ireland. Susie first appeared as a young teenager in the second of these novels, *Wildfire*, set in 2019. So meeting up with her again at age twenty, we are invited back to Hollywood to meet the strong and talented women working in television.

I do hope you enjoy this book, and if you do, please leave me a positive short review on both Goodreads and on Amazon. Times are pretty tough right now for all writers, and we can only flourish if people decide to open our books and settle in for a good long read!

A full list of all my Sapphic novels appears at the end of the book. Each one is available on Amazon, in paperback and eBook, and are "free" to read on Kndle Unlimited. You can also follow me on Facebook and through my website, maggiemcintyreauthor.com

With thanks to every precious reader!
Maggie McIntyre.

Chapter One

September 2024

Olivia Massie watched a flock of pigeons swoop past her office window across the London skyline and felt pretty good. This last year had seen her transform from frigid snow queen to flamboyant floozie. It had been a hell of a ride, but she'd loved every moment. In the month since her wedding, she'd changed from tidy to tidal, and her hormones were surging. Outwardly little may have changed, but appearances could be deceptive. She still favoured crisp white shirts, black stockings, tight-fitted suits, and very high heels and still wore her hair sleek and short. She continued to run Barnstorm Books with a firm hand and enjoyed the view from her office on the top floor of their central London premises.

But since her wedding to Niamh, Olivia felt like a new woman. Niamh, who possessed all the talents and spell-casting abilities of a witch, had turned her from a bookish loner into a sensual animal: warm, physical, and sexually rampant. Niamh could bring her to orgasm any time of day or night, simply by giving her "the look" and tossing her head of flying auburn curls. So Olivia approached her fifth decade with as much libido as a twenty-one-year-old and had rediscovered an enormous passion for life. Her energy almost outmatched the five young nieces and nephews who shared their Hampstead home.

This afternoon, though, Olivia stifled a yawn. It was past three p.m., and she'd been awake for over twelve hours, ever since Niamh had accosted her in the middle of her dreams, demanding they make love to celebrate their wedding anniversary. That irresistible invitation had led to two straight hours of sex. In bed, whenever Niamh commanded, Olivia obeyed.

Her friend Bel Bridgford had been right, if somewhat vulgar, when she'd said, "There's nothing in the world that feels as great as a good shag in the middle of the night!" Olivia had blushed to her ears, but now she owned the truth of it.

However, too much sex could make one feel lazy the following day. She turned away from the window and looked down at her on-screen diary to see what appointments her assistant had added since lunch. There was only one name: *Fenella Carlton.*

That should be fun. She and Fenella had been friends for twenty-five years. They had missed each other at Oxford by a college generation, as Fenella was about three years her junior, but when they'd met as young editors at the same publishers, they'd hit it off and stayed on good terms ever since.

Now Fenella edited *Perceptions*, one of the UK's most respected literary journals, and was one of few people left in London who shared Olivia's devotion to fine grammar. She fought a one-woman war against Americanisms taking over British English and pursued Zs, as in memorize or subsidize, with as much fury as she might have chased cockroaches crawling across her immaculate office carpets.

Fenella's office was a penthouse, an idea she'd blatantly copied from Olivia, but of course, Fenella's was the size of a loft conversion. She was one of those women who always expected the best, and as a result, usually got it. She was one scary woman, and even Olivia, who was no wimp, knew not to contradict her unless she was very sure of her ground.

Fenella was also a known man-eater who had already munched her way through two husbands, with a potential third only managing to escape before they tied the knot. Crueller friends nicknamed Fenella "the Mantis." Fenella might be a pedant on paper, but in relationships, she was reckless, or she had been in the past.

Olivia hadn't met up with Fenella for a whole year, since before her wedding to Niamh, which Fenella couldn't attend due to her children being ill. Professionally, they lived parallel lives, as Olivia sometimes sought reviews for her authors' latest books in the lofty columns of Fenella's journal, but she hadn't asked her for one recently.

She wondered what Fenella would make of her new way of life and didn't want to be teased or berated about it. But it would be fun to catch up with her, whatever she wanted. A get-together where she could introduce her to Niamh was long overdue. But why had Fenella made the appointment to see her today? She pressed the intercom into Selena's office. "When Fenella arrives, could we have some tea, please? And a good half hour free from interruption."

"She's here already," said Selena. "I'll send her up now."

Olivia quickly looked in the mirror, smoothed down her fringe from its annoying habit of bouncing up like a lapwing's feather, and sat behind her desk. She tried to think about publishing deadlines instead of the delicious curve of her wife's bottom, but the little smile that played across her face gave her away. A sharp tap on her door stopped her daydreaming. "Come on in, Fenella. What a nice surprise!" Olivia's normally impeccable manners deserted her when Fenella strode into the room. "My God, Nellie, what the hell's happened to you? You look dreadful."

Fenella flung down her bag and crashed onto Olivia's black leather sofa. She kicked off her heels and closed her eyes. Then she pushed her fingers through her mop of dark auburn curls and shuddered. "Thanks. That's made me feel much better! But you're right. I haven't slept properly in more than a week, and I can't concentrate on anything. I feel like lions are crawling up my back, and rabid wolves are chewing their way through my stomach. I'm a total mess."

"But why? Are you having a breakdown? Overwork? Bankruptcy looming?"

"No." Fenella sighed. "And don't call me Nellie. You know I hate it."

"Okay. So why are you here, Fen?"

"That makes me sound like some Cambridgeshire bog. I'm here because this is all your fault, and you have to get me out of it."

Fenella looked so fierce that, for a moment, Olivia felt almost guilty, though she knew she'd done nothing wrong. "My fault? What have I done?"

"Because you had the nerve to come out at forty-eight, run off with someone half your age, and then marry her and flaunt your happiness all over London."

"So?" Olivia wasn't going to apologise for being happy.

"Well, you give me hope where there shouldn't be any. And hope is a horrible thing. It won't let me rest."

"I still don't see—"

"Don't be so dense, Olivia. Can't you tell? I've fallen for someone. But the object of my affection is totally impossible. A twenty-year-old female and, if you can believe it, an American to boot! And because of you, I made the foolish mistake of confessing to her some of what I felt. It was horrible, humiliating, and the worst idea in the world."

"Oh, dear Lord, and she rejected you? You poor thing." Olivia thought she now understood, and prepared to provide sympathy along with the tea, but Fenella shook her head.

"Rejected? No, such a thing would have been far too easy. The young idiot says she's lusted after me from the first moment we met. She wants us to start a relationship for God's sake, only of course she puts it more vulgarly. She's incapable of understatement, or any restraint."

"Wow. So why isn't that good news then? If you like her, then follow it up. Let her in."

"Oh, don't be so stupid!"

"But wouldn't that be the logical next step? Why don't you start by simply asking her out for a coffee?"

Fenella turned pink beneath her makeup, and Olivia was tempted to laugh, but she managed to keep a straight face. She did sympathise. Falling in love was a shock at any age, and Niamh's enthusiasm had certainly taken some getting used to. But if Fenella's advances had already been accepted, Olivia still didn't see what the problem was.

Fenella put her right. "Darling, I'm forty-five, going on sixty, especially the way I feel right now. She's twenty, only four years older than Nathan. My body is a creased, saggy old thing, and my face, well…"

"Fen, shut up. Your face is lovely. Don't pretend."

There was a tap on the door, and Selena entered with a tray of tea and biscuits, set it on the coffee table between them and discreetly disappeared. The arrival of tea broke the tension and Olivia moved to sit closer to Fenella on the sofa.

"Shall I be mother? You'll no doubt be pleased to see how we still do things properly here."

She was shocked to see tears appear in those glamorously made-up eyes as Fenella gripped her fingers, clutching her hand like someone about to drown.

"You don't understand, Liv. For her, this is a simple, crazy crush on an older woman, a temporary fixation from which she'll recover tout de suite. The first time she sees my body, I shouldn't wonder! But for me, it's more like a terminal illness. The most obsessive love of my life. A ludicrous passion, and one I can't shake off."

Olivia stirred the pot, poured the tea through a strainer, and passed Fenella a bone china cup and saucer, a vintage ritual she retained from her childhood in the previous century.

"Here, drink this and do try to calm down. Tell me all about this young woman and why you're so smitten."

Fenella took the tea, her hand trembling as she did so before taking a deep breath. "When we first met, I was horrified. She was appalling, with a terrible accent, non-existent dress-sense. Just totally annoying."

"So, tell me about it."

As she continued to tell her story, Olivia began to understand the depth of Fenella's problem. Her friend hadn't exaggerated. She was irrevocably smitten. No doubt about it, Fenella had fallen in love.

Chapter Two

One week earlier

For Fenella, the first day of her problem had started much like any other. On arrival at her London office, she'd hung up her coat, changed from sensible flats into the pair of killer heels she kept under her desk, and opened her large retro desk diary, a blue cluttered hardbound affair, full of colour-coded deadlines.

It reminded her she had a lunch appointment with two women from her journal's new design company, so she added in a half-hour slot to make an online grocery order. Then her sons would have something to eat when they opened the fridge. She'd spend the rest of the day working on the next edition, and, if the trains ran on time, might get home to Oxford by seven to receive the food delivery and reach for her first G&T. She must remember to add another bottle of gin to her shopping list. Since Maurice, the man she'd expected to become her third husband, had abruptly departed back in the spring, her evening snifter had become more than a casual habit, and her drinks were getting stronger. She'd add a few more tonic water bottles to her grocery order to balance things out.

Fenella pressed the intercom to call in unflappable, capable Greta, who did more of her grunt work than either of them let on to the outside world. "Greta? Come on through, please."

"Right you are. In a minute," Greta said, her voice hoarse.

"Are you quite well?"

"Oh, yes."

But when Greta did enter, not one, but a full five minutes later, it was obvious she wasn't well at all. Her eyes were almost closed, and her nose was red. Clutching a paper tissue, she sneezed explosively.

Fenella gestured her to move backwards against the doorway. "Why are you here in that state? You should've stayed home."

"Not the best idea. The women from Farlane are coming today. I've finished prepping the brief for them, and I've booked us all in for lunch at Carluccio's."

"I'll go alone. I think I can cope with two teenagers over a bowl of linguine."

"Not teenagers. Madeleine Farlane's in her mid-thirties, and she's bringing her top graphics person with her."

Greta always put in the necessary preparation for any meeting. Fenella relied on her for all the support work so she could function as the journal's editor. She smiled a silent thank you. But she didn't want them to share the same room for a moment longer. "Good work. But now I want you to turn around, leave the premises, and stay home until you're free of whatever you've been incubating."

"It's only a cold."

"Probably, but what if it's not? And even if it is, I can't afford to catch it. I'm giving a talk at the Weston Library on Friday, and I need to be in good voice." Living in Oxford, and so commuting by train three days a week, Fenella reckoned she already had enough health hazards to deal with. Her chest wasn't strong after COVID, and she couldn't risk another infection. She glared at her older assistant, but Greta could be an immovable object if she chose and normally ignored hard stares.

"Oh, okay. But text me if you need to know anything more. I think I'm losing my voice."

She must be feeling grim to give in so quickly. Fenella felt sorry for her.

"Please, go back home, put yourself to bed, and stay there."

" I will. I'm sure I'll be well by Monday though."

Having had the last word, Greta vanished. Another enormous sneeze erupted from the outer office as the door opened and shut. Fenella went to the windows behind her desk and opened them as wide as they'd go. Three recurrences of COVID had proved her health worries to be justified.

She thought about the task Greta had left her. Setting on a new graphic design team to revamp her journal was a big thing. The lunch, on neutral territory at a nearby Italian restaurant, was something Greta had booked to not so subtly push Fenella into considering new ideas. She had found Farlane Designs online, and so naturally Fenella had insisted Greta join the party.

She read through the brief with Greta's suggested questions and then scrolled through Farlane's website to look at their recent projects. Black, gold, and purple spikes and squares with ridiculous, unconnected images seemed to dominate the designs. Fluorescent colours that almost hurt her eyes hit her from the screen. These wouldn't do at all. Whatever had Greta seen in this design team?

Chapter Three

By the time Fenella left the office, she had quite decided that Farlane Designs was a non-starter. Far too modern and trendy. Lunch with them would be another wasted hour of her life. But it was now too late to cancel, and she supposed she could endure their company for a quick meal.

Carluccio's was in walking distance of the office and was one of her favourite eating places. It was so close that she arrived early, and a waitress showed her to a booth seat against the inner wall.

"Something to drink, madam?"

"I'd like some sparkling water, thanks."

The waitress passed Fenella some menus and left. She took a moment to settle herself and rehearse the polite brush-off. She would listen to their pitch, appear interested, smile nicely, and mention tight budgets. Then she'd skip dessert and send the women on their way.

For ten minutes, Fenella sipped her sparkling water with half an eye on the restaurant doorway. Two confident, well-dressed young women bearing portfolios under their arms came through the door, prompt to the minute. But they were followed by a third, much younger female. Her nymph-like body was both hidden and exposed in the most appalling get-up Fenella had ever set eyes on. Designer-inspired slashes and rips, or maybe the result of a quarrel with a barbed wire fence, revealed far too much thigh through her black jeans, and a magenta striped topknot tumbled over her ears, around a face covered in gothic make-up. She looked like an escaped cat from a travelling circus. Beneath the make-up and costume, her skin was a golden apricot colour, and she had a wary, feral look in her eye that reminded Fenella of a lynx kitten. And despite Fenella not wanting to pay them any attention, she couldn't fail to see the woman's long eyelashes, framing eyes as blue as a spring sky.

Fenella stood up to shake hands with the adults and tried to concentrate.

"Fenella Carlton? I'm Madeleine Farlane and this is Carla Browne, our head of graphic design. Thank you so much for agreeing to meet. I know it's not professional, but I hope you don't mind that we've brought Carla's cousin, Susannah, along with us. We just collected her from the airport, but I promise she won't bother you. She can sit at another table if you'd prefer."

Fenella stared openly at the youngster, then became aware of how rude she must seem. "No, that's fine. There is room at the table. How do you do?"

"I'm doing fine, thanks. Love your accent. Straight out of Downton Abbey. Cool," the walking ragbag said, her West Coast accent emerging from a generous mouth with curvy lips.

Fenella tried not to shudder.

"Susannah is from the States," Madeleine said.

"Really, I wouldn't have known." Sarcasm was never nice, but in situations like this, Fenella simply couldn't help herself.

Carla had the grace to blush. "Susannah's here in England to start a degree, and she's staying with me for two weeks before her term begins."

"At art college, I presume. She's also into graphic design?"

"Heck, no," Susannah said. "I'm a nerd from darkest Nerdsville. Classics. You know, Latin and Greek. I'm headed to a little college at Oxford University called St Hilary's."

Astounded and silenced, Fenella gestured for them to join her in the red leather booth. Madeleine and Carla placed themselves opposite her, while Susannah plonked herself down next to Fenella, effectively pinning her against the wall.

"Don't mind me," Susannah said. "I'm so jetlagged, I'll probably pass out. I watched four films back-to-back coming over here."

"From where, exactly?" Fenella found her voice and asked, though she wondered why she cared to know.

"Portland, Oregon."

The waitress returned to take orders. Madeleine and Carla asked to share a thin crusted pizza and green salad. Fenella almost asked for a salad as well, but she suddenly felt hungry. For what, she wasn't sure. She turned to Susannah. "Would you like to share a pizza with me?"

"No, better not. I'm so starving that you wouldn't get any of it. The airline food was gross. I'll take a bowl of pasta puttanesca, please."

"Slut's spaghetti?" Fenella asked before she could stop herself. Susannah batted her luxuriant eyelashes. If she hadn't inspected them so closely, Fenella would have thought they were false.

"Yeah, with extra olives, please."

The lunch proceeded on two levels. Madeleine and Carla talked through their ideas and options, while Fenella responded between mouthfuls of spaghetti. For some reason, she'd ended up choosing the same dish as Susannah. Frankly, they could have been talking about anything for all she made of it, for on another level, Fenella was fighting a silent battle with her hormones.

Something weird was happening to her mind and body, way beyond logic and words. The dreadful young woman beside her, with clothes mainly held together by safety pins and knotted string, was attracting her with pheromones, making her palms sweat and a sensation growing between her thighs, which had intensified from a slight tickle into a blazing fire. What the hell was going on?

The lunch didn't end the way she'd intended either. Instead of rising from the table after forty minutes and before they could even look at the dessert menu, Fenella found herself ordering desserts and coffee for all. The pair opposite consumed copious amounts of tiramisu, as they became progressively more excited about the brilliance of their own ideas for relaunching Fenella's journal.

The young thing next to her, on the other hand, seemed to be sinking into sleep, clearly succumbing to her jetlag. Her chirpy chatter morphed into silence, thank God, but then she had the temerity to invade what little space she'd left on the bench and slumped sideways against Fenella. She tried to nudge Susannah away, but she was fast asleep, her head leaning on Fenella's shoulder.

Well at least she wouldn't have to endure the horrible accent any longer. She let the girl's multi-coloured head rest where it lay and managed to lift her coffee cup with her left hand.

"Oh, I'm so sorry," Carla said, finally noticing. "We'd better get Susannah home and put her to bed. But thank you for such a productive meeting. I'll draw up a response to your brief and drop it off by the end of the week. Would that be okay?"

"Er, well, budgets are tight right now," Fenella said.

Madeleine smiled. "Don't worry. We're very competitive. This commission is a huge deal for us, and we want to make sure you're completely satisfied."

Fenella tried to protest, but her mouth went dry as the words took on a completely different meaning to the one Madeleine intended. When had she ever been satisfied? She was unable to concentrate on anything with this Gothic horror nymphet pressed against her ribs. Carla came around the table and hauled Susannah awake as Madeleine gathered up their papers.

Susannah's face turned pink beneath her make-up as she awoke. "Oh, shit, sorry. What a bummer! Have I dribbled on your jacket?"

Fenella had no words. She simply stared into those eyes, which were as clear blue as a Siamese cat's behind all the smudged mascara. She eventually rallied. "No, it's fine. No dribbling. You simply need to get some sleep, young lady."

"Sure. But can I come to see you again? I'm sorry I messed up today. I really want to get to know you better."

"No, you can't come to see me." Fenella smoothed her skirt and shifted even closer to the wall. "Why would you want to know me better?"

"Carla looked you up on Google and says you're a classics buff. You smell wonderful as well, by the way. I think you should know. What is it?"

What impertinence. "I believe it's J'adore by Dior."

"Is that so? Well, I sure do adore it. So can I come to see you? I'd love to know everything about you."

Fenella frowned at their increasingly bizarre exchange. "No. I'm far too busy right now."

"Okay, then I'll get Carla to give me your email address. I'm sure you'll find a time later when you can fit me into your busy schedule."

"Come on," said Carla. "Mrs Carlton said no. We have to go

now."

Everyone was standing. Fenella beckoned the waitress to get the bill and rifled through her purse for her credit card. The design duo pushed Susannah towards the door, thanking Fenella for the lunch and apologising as they went. Release and relief swept through her, but deeper inside there was a strange pang of sudden loss. Without really thinking, she pulled a business card from her purse and scribbled her private number on the back. "Here, Carla," she called after the designers. "Take this and give it to your cousin. We might be able to arrange something."

Then they were gone. Fenella stood by the bar and tried to recentre herself. What had made her so sexually aroused? It must be the perimenopause, maybe the foretaste of a few dreadful years to come. She remembered having a compulsion to eat tinned salmon while she was pregnant. Maybe this strange hunger originated from a similar hormonal imbalance. She should start dating again. Find a new man. But for some unknown reason, a man was the last thing she wanted, or needed, right now.

***

"So when did all this happen?" asked Olivia, when Fenella leaned back against the sofa and closed her eyes, exhausted. "How long was it before she was back in touch with you?

"Four hours. Now she won't let me alone. And it was only a week ago! I'll be dead within a month if things carry on at this pace. I need you to get me back to normal. Come up with a solution. Tell me how to escape. Find me a way out."

"I'm going to have to meet her first," said Olivia. "Invite Niamh and me over for supper next weekend to Oxford and include the girl Susannah. Would she join us if you asked?"

"You don't understand," said Fenella. "She's already moved in. She's living in my attic."

"Why?"

"Because… It's hard to explain. I suppose I invited her."

Olivia's jaw dropped.

"It is only temporary," Fenella said hastily, "until next week when she can move into her college. But…"

Fenella seemed defeated, as though she'd been diagnosed with a deadly virus.

Olivia took pity on her. "When you've recovered, and feel fit enough, you need to tell me the rest. Why don't I send down for more tea?"

Fenella began to tell some more of her story. When she finished, Olivia looked at her with new understanding. Her friend could certainly hold one's attention, but her abilities at telling a tale didn't obscure the inner turmoil this unexpected new friendship was exacting on her. "It's gone six," Olivia said gently. "We both need to get home to our families. Niamh and I will definitely come to Oxford next Sunday, and you can introduce us to Susannah then. Your young American sounds like a bright spark."

"Bright enough to set fire to the world," said Fenella. "But you'll understand my problem when you meet her. She's a little witch."

"But you think you love her, as I do Niamh?"

"Yes, I guess I must do, unless I'm simply under a spell."

"Well, let's find the source of the enchantment. And then, if you want it lifted, I'm sure we can help. What are old friends for?"

Olivia ushered Fenella out of her office, while wondering who else she could invite to help. On their own, she wasn't sure she and Niamh could offer any easy solution. Fenella's disease might be incurable.

Chapter Four

Susie slumped in the backseat of Madeleine's car, eyes mostly shut, trying not to puke as they tore through one London suburb after another like it was a race. The twelve-hour flight hadn't wrecked her, but this wild ride to Carla's apartment just might. The car kept jerking and swerving, and when she cracked one eye open, she saw Madeleine dodging speed bumps like they were landmines.

She hadn't slept in over a day, and her stomach was officially staging a protest. Why had she gone all-in on that massive bowl of spaghetti at lunch? And worse, she'd dumped it into a belly that was otherwise running on nothing but a few cans of Diet Pepsi she'd downed at cruising altitude.

Honestly, Carla could've given her a heads-up about the whole Fenella Carlton situation. The only thing her dad's second cousin had said when they picked her up at the airport was, "Thank God they finally let you go. We're heading straight to a business lunch with a major client. No time to drop you off or clean you up. Just… stay in the background. Don't cause drama or say anything dumb."

Madeleine, Carla's boss, had chimed in, "*Perspectives* might not have a huge circulation, but it's a big deal in literary circles. Fenella Carlton knows everyone in London publishing. If she likes our designs and hires us to redo her magazine, we bounce up several notches."

Drama? Why would Carla think she'd cause drama? Maybe her dad had spilled a little too much about her past. But that was ancient history. She was totally chill now. Reformed. Mostly.

Still, she regretted the whole goth make-up, ripped jeans, and biker jacket look she'd rocked for the flight. She didn't even own a motorcycle. She'd just wanted to mess with the airport officials a little, see if they'd judge her based on the eyeliner and attitude. They did. Big time.

She got flagged at Portland airport, had her bags torn apart, and ended up being the last person to board. Everyone in economy had stared her down like she was a criminal. Her carry-on got tossed in the hold. Then Heathrow doubled down. The immigration grilled her, customs brought out a suspiciously friendly, drug-sniffing spaniel, and by the time she made it to arrivals, the place was practically deserted except for Carla and Madeleine, waving a cardboard sign like they were waiting for a visiting diplomat.

Carla had approached, still looking unsure. "Are you Susannah?"

"Yeah."

"Thank God. We're super late. Let's go!"

Classic. Susie was borderline obsessive about organizing her stuff for travel, but had somehow still managed to sabotage herself like a pro. No time to clean up, no time to change; she just headed straight into a lunch with the most intimidatingly perfect woman she'd ever seen.

Now that the lunch was over, she was dying of embarrassment. She replayed every dumb thing she'd said: something about Downton Abbey (why?), refusing to split a pizza (rude), ordering Puttanesca (which Fenella also ordered, awkward). No wonder Fenella had looked through her like she was invisible, then spent the rest of the meal studying her like she was some insect or an alien life form.

Fenella Carlton was a total goddess. Smart, stunning, and everything Susie had ever dreamed of. And Susie had acted like a total trainwreck. She'd even begged to see her again like some clingy fangirl. Then, to top it off, she'd passed out on her. Literally. On her. Probably snored in her face too.

She rolled down the window, desperate for air. Was her whole trip to the UK going to be this much of a disaster? Her head spun with regret. "Are we almost there?" she asked, sounding like a whiny kid.

"Ten more minutes," Madeleine said. "Hang in there."

Carla turned around from the passenger seat and gave her a soft smile. "Oh, I forgot. After you left the restaurant, Fenella gave me this for you." She handed Susie a small card.

Susie took it and flipped it over. It was a business card for *Perspectives*, super old-school, with curly fonts and a faded red rose over some open pages. It had the office address, a phone number, and an email. But on the back, in neat black ink, was a handwritten cell number.

Susie stared at it, stunned. "What does this mean?" she asked, not ready to believe it meant what she wanted it to.

Carla rolled her eyes. "Well, let's see. Mrs. Carlton said, 'Give it to your cousin. We might arrange something.' So…maybe she wants you to call her?"

"Oh."

"Wasn't that what you were practically begging her for back there?"

"Yeah, I guess."

"Then be happy. You were granted your wish. Now put it away somewhere safe and come with us. This is my place."

Madeleine parked in front of a medium-sized apartment block in a quiet, boring kind of street lined with similar buildings. There seemed to be a few little stores at the far end, but the rest of the street was mainly residential housing. Susie pulled her carry-on from the trunk of the Mini, while Carla lifted out her bigger suitcase for her.

"I'll be off back to the office now, and start work on a draft proposal for Fenella," Madeleine said.

Carla nodded. "Thanks so much for bringing us both home. I'll settle Susie in, and then we can Zoom. We have to think up something spectacular for Fenella. She isn't going to be easily satisfied."

"No, but pleasing her and winning this commission could make our fortune. We have to think of the right magic ingredient."

They both turned and looked at her. Susie could tell they were both mentally sighing and only hoped she hadn't ruined the lunch for them. She could read their minds. She was the opposite of the magic ingredient they were after.

"Come on, little cuz, you need a hot shower and a quiet bed," Carla said and led Susie inside.

There was an elevator, thank God, but it was tiny.

Carla pushed Susie inside with her suitcases. "Press the button for four. I'll meet you up there."

Susie counted five stages, but when the door opened, she heard

Carla pounding up the stairs. "You live on the fifth floor. Why did the elevator say four?"

Carla caught her breath. "It's an English thing. Our first floor is what you call the second in the US. And we call this a lift, not an elevator. We tend to like short, sharp words over here. Follow me. My place is around the corner."

Carla's small apartment was at the back of the block, and she showed Susie into a tiny guest room overlooking an area for parking and a maintenance yard. The window faced west, and the afternoon sun shone through the casement. There was a single bed and a small closet.

"Better not open the wardrobe. It's full of my junk. But the bathroom is next door, and I've made the bed up with fresh sheets. Here, have a bath towel and face flannel as well."

"Thanks for letting me stay. I know we don't really know each other, so...yeah, it's super nice of you," Susie said.

Carla shrugged. "It's fine, really. I'm glad to help. I'll be out most of the time though, so you'll have to figure London out on your own. Good news is we're close to the Tube station, and it's just two stops to Paddington. That's where you'll catch the train to Oxford."

"Paddington? Like the bear?" Susie squinted. "Tube?" she added, still trying to decode British.

"The Underground," Carla said. "And yeah, Paddington Station. We've got five major train stations, but that's the one you'll need."

"Oh, cool. I saw the movie," Susie said and gave a half laugh.

"Exactly. The bear's named after the station. But don't stress. It'll all make more sense tomorrow after you've slept."

Carla led her into the lounge, and Susie scanned the walls. The art was bold, abstract, and kind of intense. She liked it. It wasn't as wild as Abbie's stuff but still cool. "Did you paint these?"

"Yeah. It's mostly student work. But painting doesn't pay the rent, so I did a master's in graphic and digital design. Madeleine gave me my first real break. Things are tight, and this shot with *Perspectives* means everything to her—and to me."

"I totally get it," Susie said.

Carla hesitated. "Just saying…if you reach out to Fenella, please don't say anything that could mess things up. She seemed to like you, but she's super high-end and crazy smart. So if you meet her again, just…be careful."

Susie's heart did a little happy dance. So Fenella liked her? That was wild.

"Want anything? Tea? Coffee? I've got to work for a few more hours."

"I'm good, thanks. But could I get your Wi-Fi password? I want to message Dad and Abbie, and let them know I made it. They're eight hours behind. Dad's probably unlocking the school right now. Abbie's an artist too. I think you'd get along great."

"Well, I hope we can meet one day. But for now, here you go." Carla handed her a little plastic token from the router. "Just put it back when you're done. You look wiped. After you send your message, take a shower and crash for a bit. I'll wake you at seven, and we'll grab dinner."

"Do you live here alone?"

"Mostly. I've got a guy. Richie. He teaches art at a college in Cornwall. It's four hours away by train, so we don't see each other much. We co-own the flat though, otherwise, I couldn't afford it."

So Carla wasn't like her in *that* way. Susie took the Wi-Fi token and headed to the bedroom. But exhaustion hit hard, and before she could text, shower, or unpack, she collapsed onto the bed…still clutching Fenella's little white card.

Chapter Five

For Fenella, the rest of that afternoon passed in a haze. She felt sure she was about to go down with flu. Her temperature had spiked at the restaurant and refused to settle. She shivered with the sudden onset of the fever and seemed unable to concentrate. Maybe she'd caught Greta's cold, though she doubted the incubation period could be so swift.

By four, she knew she'd achieve nothing more by staying at work, so she left for home on an earlier train than usual. When it drew into Oxford station, she sighed deeply. Somehow, putting fifty miles between her and the little American sprite helped settle her nerves. For once, she could get home before the boys and surprise them with dinner.

But after she'd collected her car from the station car park, she realised that she'd forgotten to complete her online grocery order. Damn it. She hated shopping in person, surrounded by all the hoi polloi. But there was nothing for it. If they were to eat, she needed to drop by a supermarket on the way. And she definitely needed to replenish the drinks cabinet.

She stood in line by one of the staffed tills, refusing to use the self-service option. People needed jobs, for heaven's sake. Her phone vibrated with an incoming call. Only a few people had her private number, and she didn't recognise the caller. But she answered it, worried it might be someone informing her the boys were in trouble or injured.

"Hey, Ms Carlton, it's me. Is this a good time?"

"Susannah? No, it's not a good time. I'm waiting in line at the supermarket. How did you get my private number?" Fenella's shock at hearing that accent again made her tetchy. She was sinking under the waves already and angry at both herself and Susannah.

"You wrote it on the back of the business card, remember? I love your handwriting."

"Stop this at once. You Americans are so hyperbolic. Don't say you love this or that about me. How can you when you don't know me at all?"

"Which is why I called you. I want to change that. I want to know you. Can I come and see you?"

"Of course not. Besides, I live in Oxford. It's fifty miles from London." Fenella didn't add that she lived less than a mile from St Hilary's College.

"But it'll work out great," Susannah said, seemingly undaunted. "I need to come to Oxford to sign in and register, sort out a bank account and see my dorm room. You must know everything about the place. I'm so excited about studying there. Can I come home with you when you leave London tomorrow?"

That was cheeky, bordering on inappropriate. "No, I'm not even in London tomorrow. I'm staying home to prepare a public lecture I'm giving at the Bodleian Library on Friday."

"Wow, that sounds so cool. No worries. I'll come on a train on Friday and listen to your lecture. Carla will be tired of me by then."

Fenella emptied her trolley onto the cashier's conveyor belt with one hand. "Look, I really can't talk now. Phone me later." She hated people who carried on inane private phone conversations in public. So rude. She ended the call before Susannah could respond and pushed the phone deep into her bag.

She looked over her impromptu shopping choices and estimated the likely cost as she always did. There had been an offer on the gin, so four bottles clunked against each other on the belt, followed by a collection of the appallingly unhealthy food favoured by her two teenagers. She especially regretted adding four tins of spaghetti hoops and tried to ignore the resulting loud sniff coming from behind her. A large woman stood there, looking sternly down at the frozen chicken nuggets and Pop-Tarts moving forwards, and Fenella's normal hauteur faltered. Three bags of baby spinach and a net of easy peelers didn't seem to do much to repair her reputation. An image of the curve of Susannah's lip as she'd sucked up the slut's spaghetti came into her mind, and she smiled, despite despising herself for conjuring the vision.

If Susannah did come to visit, she could probably feed her similar junk food to the boys. After all, the kid was barely out of her teens. She had the usual American set of perfect white teeth though, which had contradicted her vagabond clothing. Someone must care for her and had raised her to have enough intelligence to get into Oxford. Most Americans stood no chance until they'd already completed a first degree in the States. Perhaps the exorbitant fees charged to overseas students had oiled the wheels. But who was sponsoring her? Someone seriously wealthy must be funding Susannah's trip to the UK, and Fenella was sure it couldn't be Carla. Maybe she had a rich daddy. Someone out there certainly loved her.

"Forty-seven eighty-nine." The laconic voice of the cashier broke into her reverie. "Cash or card?"

"Card." Fenella paid up and hurriedly repacked her trolley. She scooted over to her car and loaded the bags into her boot. Then, as a good customer who could be trusted to return it, she walked back to the trolley park and fed hers in behind the others.

The woman who had clearly judged her at the till suddenly appeared in Fenella's path and thrust a pamphlet into her hand. "Here you are, love. There are better ways, you know, however bad things seem right now. You shouldn't be drinking so much with your kiddies at home. Our church runs a programme. Think about joining in our weekly meetings, and if you need a babysitter, we can provide one while you come along. Whatever problems you have, however far you've fallen, Jesus loves you."

She backed off quickly, perhaps intimidated by the sudden ferocity in Fenella's eyes, and disappeared across the car park. Fenella screwed the pamphlet up and pushed it into her pocket.

Shocked to the core, she sat in her car and trembled for several minutes before she had the courage to drive home. So, she'd been seen as a hopeless alcoholic and a terrible wastrel of a parent by the random evangelical grandma. Rightly so probably, given that she was now lusting after a ridiculously young, badly spoken American woman, and had been caught bulk-buying cheap gin.

Surely the day couldn't get any worse. When she got home, she was definitely going to pour herself a nice, long G&T and recover her sangfroid. She was Fenella Carlton, after all, and today had merely been a sudden and transitory episode of insanity.

Her sons, Nathan and Freddy, would roll home around six-thirty after soccer practice. Born two years apart and from different fathers, they were day-boys at an expensive private school in north Oxford, with the fees shared between Fenella and two ex-husbands. The half-brothers got on well together most of the time and, apart from the normal level of scrapping and bickering of all young puppies, they stayed fiercely loyal to each other and to her.

Only when she'd wanted six-pack Maurice to join the family had they ganged up on her and objected forcibly. So forcibly in fact that the wimpy character had fled from her bed and all their lives only a few days before the planned wedding day six months earlier.

At the time, Fenella had been furious with the boys, but now, if she was honest, they'd been right about Maurice, and their family soon stabilised once more. The affair had taught her a lesson about the tender feelings of adolescent sons, and she'd decided never to marry again.

Chapter Six

Hi, Mum," Freddy called out as he banged through the front door. He threw his sports bag and school coat noisily down on the floor of the hallway before coming along the corridor into the kitchen.

Fenella stood by the table, still unpacking her bad-mother groceries. "Is Nate with you?"

"Same bus, but he's talking to Alice Markham down by the corner. They're a thing. You know that, right?"

"Yes, I know it. There's no harm in it. She's a nice girl." Fenella had already discreetly checked out Alice, whose name had been peppering Nate's conversations since before the summer holidays.

"Why are you home this early? I thought you were in London today," Freddy asked, before reluctantly allowing her to hug his lanky fourteen-year-old body, though he turned his cheek away to avoid the proffered lipsticky kiss. All arms and legs, he was now as tall as her at five foot eight, and he was still growing.

He slid away and inspected the shopping on the table. "What's for tea? I'm starving."

"I was thinking of a risotto, maybe with prawns and spinach—"

"Yuck, no thanks. There's some tinned spaghetti on the table. I'll have that to keep me going."

He grabbed two tins, emptied them into a plastic soup bowl, and pushed them into the microwave. Fenella sighed. Her half-drunk stiff gin and tonic was on the kitchen counter for all to see, setting such a bad example for her poor child as he cooked his own junk food. Mrs Disapproving from the supermarket would be delighted to be proved so right.

"Okay. But we'll all sit down and eat dinner properly at seven-thirty. Swill out those cans and put them in the recycling bin."

"Sure."

He did as she said, retrieved his microwaved hoops and headed out of the room, probably to play on his gaming tablet. Another brain waster. Fenella sighed again, this time with more feeling. "How about prep?"

"Did most of it in last period. We had a substitute teacher who had no idea, so I finished the physics assignment in his class. He never noticed."

"Darling, you must take school more seriously. This new term is important. What was the subject in last period?"

"Latin. So boring! Mrs Clark's not coming back all year, and this new guy doesn't know anything. He can't teach for nuts."

"What a shame. I loved Latin when I was your age. Once you've got your head around the grammar, it can be fascinating." Freddy pulled a face. "No way. Latin's the worst. I'm dropping it as soon as I can."

All energy left her. "I totally disagree, but we can talk about it some other time."

She looked at his shock of dark curly hair, his dimples, and his sweet smile. He was a handsome but lazy child. He followed her in looks but his father in temperament. Patrick Carlton had skimmed through life with minimum effort and always expected other people to work for him and to pick up the tab.

Fenella had married her second husband on the rebound from Nathan's father, truculent Trevor, who had made a lot of money selling cars and, despite being a serial adulterer, had been a good provider. But by the time Freddy turned three and Nathan was five, she realised she and her meagre salary as the editor of an unprofitable literary journal couldn't support three financial dependents. Patrick, a purely decorative item with no practical purpose, needed to leave.

He took some persuading, however, and went around all their friends bad-mouthing her. With his good looks and superficial charm, he eventually found a new sinecure and landed on his feet with a sugar mama, the widow of a Texas oil magnate. He promptly left England permanently for America's lush southern shores.

Apart from the school fees and spasmodic contact with his son, Patrick faded from their lives. Freddy had visited him only once in the summer down in Houston, but he spent more time with the grandchildren of his father's new partner than with him.

Fenella's phone vibrated loudly against her hip. She looked at it and clenched her jaw. "Work," she lied. "I need to take this."

"Okay. See ya," Freddy said and drifted away, slurping down spaghetti hoops as he went.

"You again? I do wish you'd stop bothering me."

"I'm sure you don't really mean it. You told me to call you later, and this is later. Have you gotten home yet? What are you doing right now?"

Fenella looked out of the window. She really had no idea what she was doing. "I was talking to my younger son until you interrupted."

"I'm sorry. Carla told me not to annoy you. But you sound worried. What's wrong?"

The kid sounded sincere. Fenella decided to speak truthfully, as far as was decent. "It's a new term at his school and he already wants to drop Latin. Their teacher has gone on maternity leave, and the substitute doesn't know how to teach, let alone how to keep adolescent boys motivated to study the classics."

"I could do it," Susannah said, sounding like she was bouncing on the other end of the phone. "Teach Latin, I mean. Tell the school I'll go in as a sub until they find a proper replacement."

"What utter nonsense!" Fenella could imagine how kindly the boys' formal school would take to Susannah's unique gothic-meets-ragamuffin appearance. She was the last person Fenella could recommend as a suitable role model for young minds.

"Hey, no need to be quite so mean. It's not nonsense. I'm serious. I worked at my dad's school as a teaching assistant. I taught myself Latin after I dropped out of high school. I'd already skipped two grades and graduated early. Then I went to UC Davis where they have a Latin and Greek programme. They said I was like a brain on rollerblades."

"Susannah, shh, dear. You may be clever, but I don't think you understand our British education system. You would need a teaching credential, and if you are going to study at an Oxford college yourself, you'll have no spare time for anything else."

"Oh, but I need to get a job to help pay my fees. In the States, we all work to get through college."

"That's not the way at Oxford University. Well, not in my day, at least." And she doubted things had changed very much in the last twenty-five years.

"So you studied at Oxford too? How cool. Oh, please let me come and see you on Friday. Then you can explain things better for me. I'd love to meet your family as well. Are you married? How many sons do you have?"

"I'm not married anymore. And I have two sons." Fenella didn't want to explain any further about her various husbands or the details of her family. She only half believed Susannah's academic achievements could be for real but if her story *was* true, then she'd still need some immediate coaching on how to approach life at St Hilary's.

Even by today's low standards of dress and decorum, she would stand out as outlandish. And she was also far too young to pass as a teacher. Throwing her into a classroom of sixteen-year-old boys would be like tossing an unarmed Christian child into a pit of lions in the Colosseum. "Look. You have my work email address on my business card," she said, relenting a little. "Email me tonight, and I'll send you instructions on how to get from Oxford Central to the Bodleian for six p.m. on Friday."

"Wow, thanks so much. I'll look for an Airbnb in Oxford for the weekend."

"No, don't do that," Fenella said after a half second of thought. "It'll be much easier if you stay with us. Most college offices are closed over the weekend, so you should stay until next Monday. Pick up a student railcard at Paddington station, and that will take a third off the train fare."

"Oh, you're the best. Thanks so much! I won't be any bother, I promise. I'll tiptoe around like a mouse."

"Now—"

"I know. You have to go. Bye, Mrs Carlton until Friday. Or can I call you Fenella?"

"You should know the difference between *can* and *may* by now. Well, I suppose you may."

"Gee, you're really sexy when you talk like that. Bye then,

Fenella."

And she was gone.

Fenella sat down for a full ten minutes' recovery time to finish her drink. Then Nathan came home, equally famished and equally loved. She talked to him and then started to prepare a cheese risotto, in deference to Freddy. She hoped all the necessary stirring might steady her nerves.

Chapter Seven

Fenella worried more about her upcoming lecture than any she had given over the last fifteen years. Normally, she was an assured public speaker, always well-prepared and with a solid body of knowledge on any subject she chose to speak on. But today, she felt almost tongue-tied by the thought of dreadful Susannah smirking at her from the front row. For some reason, Fenella felt personally responsible for the young American, who was bound to make a spectacle of herself if she turned up.

The lecture, sponsored by the Oxford Wollstonecraft Society, would be open to the public. The Wollstonecraft group comprised some of the brightest women in Oxford, and they often invited Fenella, a member for twenty years, to speak at their meetings and then lead a discussion.

She'd promised to talk tonight on Hildegard of Bingen, a multi-talented, twelfth-century mystic nun, and a woman of huge learning, a visionary, healer, and musician. Fenella had been inspired by Hildegard since her undergraduate days, even though she couldn't share her belief system. The nun's ability with language especially fascinated her, and the new language Hildegarde created was Fenella's lecture topic today. The talk would be followed by drinks and snacks, and she'd been looking forward to it.

Until Susannah crashed into her life, that was. Any residual positive anticipation was matched by acute anxiety over the extra member of the audience who was likely to raise more than a few eyebrows. Mercifully, Susannah hadn't called again, but she had replied to Fenella's emailed travel advice with lots of over-enthusiastic exclamation marks and a request for the name of the boys' school. It was a request Fenella chose to ignore.

The Victor Hall lecture theatre inside the Weston Library was almost full by 5:45 p.m., but there was still no sign of Susannah. Perversely, Fenella acknowledged a stab of disappointment, but she reached in her bag for her reading glasses and applied her attention to her prepared script. She should be pleased Susannah wouldn't be there to embarrass her.

The chairwoman of the society introduced her to polite applause, and she stepped forward to the lectern. The lights over the audience dimmed, and Fenella began to speak. Once she'd settled her unexpected nerves, the talk went well. She talked especially about the structure of Lingua Ignota, the language which Hildegard had developed and had taught to her fellow nuns, the women within her care. Most people in the room had sufficient knowledge of Latin to understand the gist of her analysis, and she enjoyed bringing fresh insights into the understanding of one of the most original minds in early medieval Europe. After forty-five minutes, she drew to a close and asked for any questions. The hall lights came up, and she took off her glasses so she could see her audience once again.

Several hands went up, and her colleagues asked her to expand on several points, which she happily did. Then a voice she recognised chipped in from the back.

"Did Hildegard invent a new language to conceal what she really thought from public scrutiny? And did she write much about her personal relationships with other women?"

Fenella's heart sank at the American accent. Heads turned to see the speaker on the back row. Fenella hardly dared look, expecting the worst, but she did a double take as Susannah's voice was coming from a slim, smart-suited brunette whose short pixie cut flattered a fresh little face wearing horn-rimmed glasses. Not a hint of Goth anywhere. But still, there was no need to introduce a hint of sexuality in the life and works of the renowned and revered abbess.

"Hildegard claimed her invention of a new language came not from any desire for secrecy, but to reflect the glory of the vision of light she experienced from the divine."

Fenella ignored Susie's second question. No way was she going to bring up the controversies over Hildegard's sexuality. She spoke calmly, but inside she was angry to have her own sexual ambivalence somehow brought into her mind in this public arena.

The meeting broke up, and everyone moved from the lecture hall into the atrium to gather around the buffet tables. Fenella marched over to Susannah. "I hardly recognised you. Why such an abrupt change of look?"

Susannah had bamboozled Fenella with her change of dress, although whether it had been when they'd met in London or now, she wasn't at all sure.

Susannah embraced her in an inappropriate hug, which was much too affectionate and lasted far too long. "Hi, I thought your talk was amazing, and I hope you didn't mind my question. I'd like to pretend this outfit was for you alone, to please you. I could tell you didn't approve of my look when we met before. But I needed to dress up for my interview at St Martin's School. That's why I was late. I got here just as they were introducing you."

"St Martin's? The school where my sons—?"

"I know. You forgot to tell me its name. But I called around all the high schools in Oxford to ask if they needed Latin teachers until I found the right one. The principal called me back when he saw my resumé, and after the interview this afternoon, I think I've been hired."

"What? Impossible." Fenella failed to keep the shock from her voice.

"Well, they say they need to do a criminal background check before I can start. I hope they don't dig out the time I spent in rehab. But as soon as it's through, the principal said he'll set me on with a temporary half-time contract. For now, they say I can go in and teach under supervision with another teacher sitting in. But he approved the sample lessons I gave this afternoon."

"You've already been standing in front of a class?"

Susannah shrugged. "You bet, and it was fun. Their textbook is out of the ark though. I recommended a new one, which has cartoons. And I met both your sons. They are so like you, Fenella: mega goodlooking. And super pleased when I told them I was coming tonight. Thanks so much for getting me the job. I wouldn't have even thought about it without you."

Fenella had done nothing, of course, but Susannah seemed to assume differently. They stood locked in a silent bubble for a few seconds as Fenella thought of all the things she wanted to say but wouldn't. Marcia Harris, the chair of the society, invaded their space and urged Fenella to accept a glass of something and introduce her "young friend" to the rest of the committee.

Susannah was soon swept up by other women who asked her questions about her knowledge of Hildegard of Bingen and how she'd come to Oxford, and it wasn't until the end of the meeting when she and Fenella reconnected.

Susannah unnecessarily tried to help Fenella into her jacket and moved in to grab her briefcase and purse.

Fenella shook her off. "I'm perfectly capable of carrying my own possessions."

Susannah handed the briefcase and purse back with a grin and grasped the handle of her own battered carry-on. "Sorry. Just trying to be useful."

They left the building and walked into the bustle of Broad Street. Oxford was perhaps at its loveliest in September, and the warm evening air was filled with the chatter and laughter of new students walking about with their proud parents, searching for places to eat.

Susannah gazed across the wide street and then up at Fenella with shining eyes. "This is really Oxford. Beyond cool. I'm so mega excited, you don't understand, Fenella. It's a dream come true for me."

Fenella remembered her first week at Oxford and shook her head. "Oh, but yes, I do understand," she said softly. "I think everyone who comes up for their first Michaelmas term must feel the same way. One stands on tiptoe at the threshold of immense unknowable possibilities. When you get your reading card for the Bodleian library, you'll feel like the whole world will be at your fingertips. All the glories of the internet can't beat the feeling of turning the pages, being given all the time in the world to read, and to read whatever you like. It's partly why I disapproved of you trying to get paid work as well."

"Kate said it would be like this. She knew Oxford was the right place for me to study, even if it is halfway around the world."

"Kate?" The name hit Fenella like a thunderbolt. Perhaps Susannah already had a woman in her life. Why was that a thought she didn't enjoy?

"Yes, Kate. Katherine Konrad. Everyone used to call her Kat, but she's changed her first name to avoid being mixed up with Catriona, or Cat, her wife, who's my best friend and stepsister. Kate's paying my fees, and she paid for my travel. She's my sponsor. I owe her everything. That's why I want to get work to help cover some of the costs."

"Your sponsor must be wealthy."

"Heck, yes. Richer than God. She owns and runs Montpellier Media."

The Katherine Konrad! The double M logo for Montpellier was almost as well known as the logos for CNN or the frightful Fox News. Even Fenella had sometimes tuned to its news channel to get an unbiased view of the bizarre goings-on across the pond. Katherine Konrad was also one of the most high-profile lesbians in the world, a famous, or infamous to the right wingers, influencer. "And how did you meet such impressive friends?"

"It's kind of complicated. My dad got married to Abbie, Cat's mom, earlier this year, so now Kate and I are stepsisters-in-law. She's much older than me of course though, maybe around your age. She has three daughters. The oldest, Alice, is eighteen and we're also really good friends."

That wasn't encouraging. Susannah was emphasising they belonged to different generations. Fenella might easily have had a daughter her age. That reminded her she had teenage sons home alone, and it was time to return there. "Follow me," she said. "You can tell me more about your friends tomorrow. But for now, we need to settle you in at home. Nathan and Freddy are there alone, and I promised them I wouldn't be too late. I've put you in the attic."

"Cool."

Fenella refused to pander to the use of banal and meaningless metaphors and sighed. "No, it isn't. We have sufficient heating right through the house."

"You're such a tease. I mean, living in an attic sounds so romantic." Susannah sighed almost wistfully.

Fenella pressed her lips together tightly. This was a very different side to Susannah's nature than the hint of feral savagery simmering when they'd first met in the restaurant. Her latest comment could have come straight from the pages of *Anne of Green Gables*. Fenella realized yet again she was dealing with a very young adult, whose life experience was presumably minimal.

Despite her exceptional intellect and strange ability to somehow shapeshift from wildcat to Miss Priss, Susannah was clearly somewhat naive. That made her all the more vulnerable. Fenella would have to control her own baser impulses and make sure she acted only in the girl's best interests. She certainly didn't want the great and powerful Katherine Konrad bearing down on her from California, breathing fire and accusing her of seducing her protégée.

"Don't be silly. Anyway, you won't be living up there permanently, only visiting temporarily. But you'll have your own bathroom, a good view over the rooftops towards the centre of Oxford, and you'll be able to study in peace." Fenella led the way briskly into a nearby multi-storey car park. She certainly wasn't going to reveal how long she'd pondered on where to accommodate Susannah in her large Victorian house. Nor would she be sharing the insane fantasy she'd had of Susannah curled up with her in her king-sized bed, semi-naked under the sheets, and smelling sweetly of J'adore. She felt thoroughly ashamed and smutty even recalling it.

Chapter Eight

Fenella's new electric car, a post-Maurice present to herself, was a top of the range VW, roomy enough to accommodate two large teenagers and their sports gear, but also zippy enough to match her own image of polished pizzazz. Not that she matched up to her car this evening. She felt more like a beached seal, barely able to flap its flippers.

Having Susannah sit beside her as she drove her through the city gave Fenella the strangest of feelings. She was excited and happy, two emotions she hadn't felt strongly in ages. She navigated the silent car out of the car park, and they headed through the one-way system that circled the central area of the city. She hoped and prayed the young woman possessed no mind-reading abilities, but Susannah seemed preoccupied with staring out of the window at the lights of the shops, which illuminated the streets, and at the crowds of people walking back and forth and spilling out from the pavements into the road.

"You certainly showed initiative in securing an interview at St Martin's School," Fenella broke the silence as the shops and colleges slid behind them. "Well done. Did you take a taxi to the school from the station?"

"No, I walked all the way. I was so nervous, I needed the fresh air to calm me down and the time to work out what I would say. I've never gone for a job interview before, and you, Carla, and Madeleine are the only British people I've met so far, I mean, as people to speak to. I was shit-scared by the headmaster guy when I met him and wondered what the hell I thought I was doing."

"But you must have impressed them at the school," Fenella said.

Dr Warner, the stuffy and slightly pompous head of St Martin's, would have been satisfied he had nothing to fear from this new job applicant and had probably been quite charmed.

"I suppose so, though I guess they were pretty desperate. But thank you."

Fenella frowned. That wasn't the bouncy, self-opinionated response she had expected. Susannah's mood seemed to have changed to match her neat but boring little black office suit, though Fenella tried not to focus on those slim legs encased in sheer black tights. Carla must have taken her shopping in London.

Fenella, however, retained her very different memory of the feral kitten at Carluccio's. Kittens could grow into tigresses. How soon would Susannah become bored by St Martin's fusty regime and staffroom protocols? How long before she disrupted their steady working routine by breaking out into her goth alter ego, replete with safety pins and leather, slashed jeans and body piercings? A tingle of nostalgia for that outfit rippled through Fenella, and she shook it off.

The drive home was short, and she swung the car up the drive as the garage door automatically slid upwards and welcomed them inside. The car clock said ten thirty p.m. That was quite late, but the boys would still be up. Fenella smiled at Susie and said, "I know you've met Nathan and Freddy briefly, but it's time to be properly introduced."

Her sons were seated at the kitchen table, hoovering up the pasta casserole she'd left out for them. It looked more than a little dried up. No doubt they'd ignored it for most of the evening and then shoved it into the microwave at the last minute. But at least they were eating together at the table, and tomato sauce almost counted as a vegetable, didn't it? They were also drinking from cans of Coke and not the beer she suspected they sometimes sneaked in when she wasn't on guard.

Nathan and Freddy both jumped to their feet, and Fenella was reassured by how embarrassed they were, seeing a potential teacher in their midst. They towered over her.

"Hi guys, it's great to see you again!" Susannah beamed. "How's it going? Gearing up for the weekend?"

"Hey," Freddy said. "I've already looked up the guy you talked about in class."

Susannah raised her eyebrows. "Caligula?"

"Him." Freddy nodded and almost bounced on the spot. "Super

cool. I didn't know life in Rome back then could be so wild."

Susannah smiled. "Right? Learn some more Latin, and you'll soon be able to read the original stuff for yourself."

Fenella gave a small inward smirk. Maybe Freddy wouldn't be dropping Latin at the first opportunity after all.

"Would you like me to show you up to your room, Miss?" Nathan asked in a disconcertingly gooey way Fenella didn't like at all.

"No need to be so formal, Nate. Here we can all be on first names terms. Boys, our guest is Susannah…" Fenella floundered, realising she had no idea of Susannah's last name.

"Webster."

At least that part of her was reassuringly normal. "Susannah, these are my boys. Nathan and Frederick, or Nate, and Freddy. They answer to their own names usually and sometimes call me Mum."

Susannah grinned at them both. "Well, guys, you can call me Susie, like my friends do. I was named Susannah after my maternal grandmother. My grandfather came from Alabama and played the banjo."

Fenella picked up on the little joke about that old song she couldn't quite remember, but she doubted the boys would.

"Thanks for the offer," Susannah said to Nate. "I'd love to see my room and wash up. If it's okay with you, Fenella?"

Fenella nodded and watched them leave together before she sat down at the table, hoping to control the fluttering in her stomach.

"You okay, Mum?" asked Freddy. "D'you want me to heat up the pasta for you?"

"No, thanks, darling. You should get off to bed. And don't stay up too late playing on your game console."

He made a move to go but then turned back to her. "Well, don't stay up too late yourself. And lay off the booze, okay?"

It was the first time he'd warned her so openly about her drinking, and it jolted Fenella to the core. So he had noticed. They probably had both seen how rapidly the empty gin bottles piled up in the recycling bin. Maybe that busybody in the grocery store car park had been right; she should cut back and try to be a much better role model for her boys.

"So how did you get to meet Susie? She's nice," Freddy asked after he'd allowed her to pull him in for a goodnight kiss.

Fenella shrugged. "Oh, we met through her cousin in London, someone I'm thinking of hiring to redesign *Perceptions*. It's no one you know," she said and sent him off to bed with a glass of water.

She looked again at the gin bottle but then put it firmly away in a cupboard and grabbed a packet of hot chocolate powder instead. Susannah would be downstairs again in a very short time and might prefer something sweet and creamy to alcohol. She agreed with Freddy. Susannah Webster, Susie, whoever, was nice. Alarmingly dangerous to be around. But yes, nice.

The door opened again within a few minutes, and Susie entered. Gone was the professional dress, patent black pumps, and black tights, and now Susie wore pyjamas with Snoopy on them and a pashmina thrown around her neck and shoulders. Her feet were bare, and she hopped about on the cold tiles of the kitchen floor.

Fenella pulled a clean pair of Nathan's socks from a pile of laundry and tossed them lightly across the room. "Here, put these on."

Susie caught them and sat down. "Thanks. I don't have any slippers with me."

"Keep the socks for now then. Just don't slip on the stairs."

"I didn't want to disappear and go to bed without thanking you again, for everything, for letting me stay. I know I've been behaving like a brat. There's so much I want to learn from you, and you're such a great model for a mom."

"You certainly don't know me at all then!" Fenella laughed, genuinely amused, and trying not to be too hurt by another reminder of their age difference.

"No, I mean it. I lost my mom to breast cancer a while back, and I went off the rails through my teens. I dropped out of school and got into drugs. I gave my dad hell, which he never deserved. I even ran away, for months. But since getting to know Kate and Catriona and their kids, I've seen what a happy family can look like. And now I'm here with you, I can see what a great relationship you have with your sons. I envy them."

Fenella didn't know how to respond. So the kid was looking for a mother figure, nothing more. That should be a relief, of course.

But it threw her salacious lusts and sudden longings right back solely into her court to deal with in private. "Would you care for a nightcap of hot chocolate?"

"Oh, gee. Yes, please!"

"Good. Let's take them through into the snug where it's warmer, and you can tell me more about your family. I'm so sorry to hear about the loss of your mother."

"She was the most wonderful person in the world, but she died seven years ago now. I should be over it."

"No. Our mothers stay with us our whole lives in one way or another, and even when they die, they remain in our heads and hearts."

Fenella hoped she had successfully managed to say this without revealing her own lingering heartache. She hadn't mentioned losing her own mother to the same disease when she'd been only three years older than Susie, so she had walked the same walk, worn similar moccasins. But this time wasn't for her; it was for Susie.

She whisked up two mugs of foaming hot chocolate, and passed one over, then led the way from the kitchen into the snug. She would normally choose a winged chair by the fire, but instead, she sat down on the two-seater sofa and patted the cushion beside her.

"Come here and talk to me. I know I've been abrupt with you since we met, and I'm sorry for not taking you more seriously. I want to hear your story and why you've come all the way to England to study classical languages. Tell me about your mom. I may not be a very good mother myself, but I've learned to listen to youngsters when they have things they need to share. So spill the beans, kid." Fenella fell into a mock American accent with her final sentence, trying to lighten the mood. But as Susie sipped her hot chocolate, Fenella was startled to see how her eyes shone with unshed tears.

Susie swallowed and took a deep breath. "Okay, if you're sure I'm not being a total pain."

Slowly and falteringly, Susie shared her story of losing her mother and how her life had unravelled, her blue eyes turning as dark as pansies in the lamplight. And as she listened, Fenella began to understand the complexities of the young woman staying under her roof.

Chapter Nine

Susie wondered where to begin. She wanted to tell Fenella everything, but her years between twelve and eighteen had been so full of bad decisions and misadventures, of looking for solutions to pain and problems in quite the wrong way, that she was mortified. She'd driven her dad half-crazy with worry and nearly ruined his chance of happiness with Abbie, her stepmother now and one of her very best friends. But she plunged in.

"So, here goes. Both my parents were high school teachers. They met in college, both doing their teaching credentials. Dad's thing was biology, especially genetics, and Mom was all about English and French Lit. She grew up in the Deep South, but her family were originally Cajun, from Quebec, so she was bilingual. After college, they started out in Kansas City but eventually moved northwest, ending up in Oregon. I came along three years later, but of course, even my arrival had to be dramatic. I was a breech birth, feet first, which was kind of a taster of how I do most things the wrong way around. Mom had to have an emergency C-section, and she was really ill for a while. She said I wouldn't let go of her once she was able to hold me, like a little monkey. Apparently, she carried me everywhere, wrapped up in a blanket sling—a trick she picked up volunteering in Africa."

Susie pulled her pashmina more tightly across her shoulders and snuggled up in it.

"I think I remember how it felt, hanging behind her. It was a red blanket, and very soft, just like this one."

"You remember being a baby? That's remarkable," Fenella said.

"Is it?" Susie shrugged. "Well, I remember the warmth, and the closeness, and the swaying as she walked. I loved my mom very much."

"Maybe she told you about it later," Fenella said. "Very few people remember anything before the age of three or four."

Maggie McIntyre

"I don't think she still carried me in a blanket when I was three! Honestly, I think I remember the feeling of that blanket: the softness, the warmth, and being so close to her. Maybe it's just something she told me later, or maybe I really do remember it. Either way, that closeness was always there. After all the complications with me, my parents decided not to have another child, but we were genuinely happy. I never heard them argue. When I was about five, Dad got offered the principal's job at a small high school in Cropton Falls, on the Oregon-Washington border. We moved to a farmhouse just outside town. We had fields, an ancient barn, and, best of all, my first pony. From then on, I was outdoors every chance I got, riding, wandering in the woods, losing myself in nature. Mom homeschooled me for kindergarten, but when I was eight, she went back to teaching, and I started elementary school."

"I remember my own urban upbringing in London, navigating the Underground on my way to Greycoats girls' school in the heart of Westminster," said Fenella. "But yours sounds an idyllic childhood."

Susie nodded. "It was. I was ready, but school itself was a letdown. At school, the other kids were just learning to read, while I'd been reading great since four and was tackling *Oliver Twist*. And math was 'two plus four equals six' territory, but Mom had already taught me basic algebra. I never fitted in with my age group, and when they bumped me up a grade, the older kids made fun of me for knowing about words like Dickensian. I was so lonely; a bit of a Matilda situation, I guess, but my parents were brilliant. I just never found my crowd at school. My best friend was my mom; we read together, talked about everything. Dad was always busy with school, but we had some great summers, kayaking up in Canada, hiking the trails, and fishing." She smiled at the memory, though fishing had always grossed her out. "Then, everything changed when I started seventh grade. Mom got sick. She had all sorts of tests and then told me she'd need a double mastectomy. The cancer didn't go away though; she had more chemo, and by Christmas, she'd lost her hair and wore those bright scarves all the time. But her face was grey with exhaustion, and eventually, she needed a wheelchair. I'd sit with her and read her favourite books, but she soon had to go into hospice care. Dad and I visited every evening until she died…on my twelfth birthday the following month. She was only thirty-five.”

Fenella leaned forward and gently took the mug from Susie's hand, which she then held lightly. “I'm so sorry. It must be very hard to talk about.”

Susie tried to keep her voice steady and brave, not to break into tears. But the memories of that final day, when her mom had slipped into a coma from which she never woke up, were etched into her skull in bright jagged technicolour.

“I remember the sound of my dad sobbing, his head on the pillow beside Mom's, but I still have no memory of how we got home, or what happened in the days leading up to the funeral. I remember the pain in my heart, a sense of loss so bad that the only way to stop it was to give myself even sharper pain. When I cut my arm on a piece of barbed wire behind the barn, I felt better. So I started doing it again with one of Dad's razor blades, little cuts up my arms and the tops of my legs, where no one could see. I found it hard to stop. No one knew, only Benji and Maple, my two horses. Dad was like a zombie, so grief-stricken that he couldn't help me. We just stumbled on together in the same house.”

Fenella pulled her closer, cradled her against her chest and rocked Susie like a baby. “You poor people. It must've been such a time of grief for you. There's no need to tell me anymore for now. I understand how hard this is for you.”

Susie sighed deeply. She'd been gearing up to tell the whole stupid story of her complete breakdown, but maybe Fenella should never know the depths to which she'd fallen and how horrible she'd been. They stayed in the embrace for several long seconds until Susie thought this must just be getting too embarrassing for Fenella.

“Thank you”, she whispered. “I should give you some peace and go up to bed. I have to look over my lesson schedule for next week.” And Susie peeled herself away from Fenella's hug, gathered up her shawl and disappeared from the room, hoping her story hadn't scared Fenella off for good.

Chapter Ten

Fenella took the cocoa mugs back to the kitchen and still felt Susie's presence in their residual warmth, even as she added them to the dishwasher, stacked it with all the remaining crockery, and turned it on to an ecological overnight wash. How strange that all one's deepest feelings and encounters were most often framed by the daily domestic routines of everyday life. Having Susie sleep under her roof might be life-changing, but the kitchen still needed tidying. Like an old Zen proverb said, *"Before enlightenment, chopping wood. After enlightenment, chopping wood."*

It was midnight before Fenella fell into her own bed, her mind still in a whirl. Her American guest had blown in like a wild gentian with her own sweet perfume, and her story about losing her mother had intrinsically connected them.

She heard the creaking of the floorboards in the attic above her head and imagined Susie unwrapping her pashmina and taking off the cosy socks. Or maybe she wouldn't. Maybe she'd keep them on, warming those pretty little feet. Fenella groaned in self-disgust, pulled the pillow over her head and willed herself to sleep.

The following dawn came all too quickly. Fenella lay in bed, worrying. Why had she offered to host Susie for the whole weekend? She had surely sabotaged her own sanity by keeping in her company longer than necessary. A sane woman would have taken her to the train station straight after breakfast, back to her cousin in London.

But Fenella no longer qualified as sane. St Hilary's College was less than twenty minutes' walk away, and Susie wanted to visit it and learn about her room ahead of the start of the Michaelmas term in two weeks. Fenella had always thought the Oxford academic eight-week terms ridiculously short for all they needed to pack in. But the college was open to the new cohort of students from the week before, so they'd be free to look around.

Fenella's college had been Somerville, but she always enjoyed exploring the different college atmospheres, the intimacy of the smaller ones, the libraries, and the common rooms that had housed so many great scholars. St Hilary's had one of the biggest college libraries, and she decided to check whether they stocked *Perceptions*.

Having listened to Susie's story, Fenella could well understand why Katherine Konrad had agreed to sponsor her. She was a very gifted young woman but also a fragile and sensitive little person who had taken her mother's loss very badly indeed. She was someone Fenella wanted to help, to mentor, and to encourage. And there was nothing wrong in that. She simply had to cure herself of this bizarre physical obsession first. Determined to conquer it, she pulled herself out of bed and padded to her bathroom.

When she entered the kitchen thirty minutes later, having showered and applied as much make-up as she thought suitable for home, she found Susie sitting at the long table, one leg tucked under her. She was reading *The Oxford History of Roman Britain,* a hefty book she'd taken from the long bookcase by the door and seemed absorbed in it.

"Hello there," Fenella said. "Sleep well?"

Susie's head shot up, and she blushed. Fenella was worried she'd disturbed her upstairs with her own restlessness. But it wasn't that at all. "Oh, I'm sorry! I shouldn't have pulled this book from your shelf without asking."

"Not at all. It's a good read, especially if you're not sure of the timeline of the Roman occupation. Borrow it if you like. There's no rush to return it."

"Thanks." Susie closed the book and approached Fenella. "Would it bug you if I give you a big fat hug right now?"

"What? No! Yes! I mean, it would bother me!" Fenella took a step back. "Why do you want to do that?"

"You were so good last night, not judging me. I hoped you'd be sympathetic, but you were lovely, and then I slept fine in your gorgeous guest bed."

"You said nothing to judge you on. You can always talk to me. I don't mind." Fenella was trapped, caught by the table. She made some inarticulate noise as Susie came closer, but she was powerless to prevent Susie moving into her space and wrapping her arms tightly around Fenella. Her own arms moved of their own accord and circled Susie's back, instantly feeling the bones of her spine under her sweatshirt. There was no weight to her at all. Fenella let Susie press hard into her chest, as she seemed to need to draw on her energy.

Susie pulled back a little, looked up into Fenella's eyes and swallowed. "Oh, shit. I'm so sorry. I can't help myself."

Fenella's mouth went dry. She had a horrible suspicion Susie was about to kiss her, and even worse, maybe she was going to confess her own feelings. She put up a hand and smoothed down the tousled waves under her fingers. There was no neat little Latin teacher this morning, nor a Gothic ragamuffin. Here was some sort of baby witch, sent to torment her. "No, this is so, so wrong. I'm old enough to be your mother, for God's sake."

Susie's hug tightened. "I had a mom, and I loved her very much. But what I feel for you is way, way different. I've had the biggest crush since I first saw you in the restaurant, Ms Carlton. I'll do anything for you, if you'll let me… If you'll only let me in to love you."

Fenella used every gram of willpower to stop herself enveloping Susie's curly mouth with her own. But she managed somehow to regain self-control.

Instead, she placed her forefinger gently against those lips and said, "Shh. My dear girl, you are adrift in a strange land, and it's turned your head. I'm already very fond of you, and I'd like to be your friend. But you must see that I can't possibly be your lover."

"Why not?"

"Because… Well, for a start, I'm a sharp-tongued, self-opinionated fox, not to say, a lush. One of my ex-husbands called me a praying mantis, which made him very popular on Facebook. He may have been right. I have been known to devour people. I am not right for you as anything more than a guide and mentor to help you settle into Oxford."

"Foxy Fenella. I love it. You look something of a fox with your wonderful copper hair. But you look so unhappy. And I can make you happy. I know I can. You do like me back, though, don't you? I know you do."

Fenella tried to shake her head, but she couldn't physically seem to do it. "No… Yes… Well, all right, if you must. We scarcely know each other, but you've somehow managed to creep under my skin. Maybe if I was twenty-five years younger."

Susie looked triumphant, even though her eyes were wet with tears. "So it's simply the dumb age-gap thing?"

"Along with a pile of other reasons."

"But an age-gap is nothing! We've met in our own lifetimes, haven't we? If we were born two hundred years apart, maybe you'd have a point. But what's a couple of decades like? Zilch!"

Susie had clearly read too many fantasy novels. Fenella was reminded she was barely out of her teens. She could handle Susie's overexuberance without succumbing to it, surely. "When you've lived a bit longer, I think you'll understand the answer to that question a little better." She pulled at Susie's grip around her back and managed to peel her away. "Now, we won't talk about this again. If you want us to be friends, then we can have a civilised breakfast, and afterwards, I will escort you to your new alma mater. No other nonsense. Anything remotely sexual is completely off the table. Understood?"

Susie looked downcast and a little sulky. "I never eat breakfast."

"Well, you will today. I'm going to walk you off your feet as we explore Oxford together, and you'll need some protein inside you. Did you bring any flat shoes or boots?"

Susie waggled her feet, still in Nate's socks. "I've got some trainers upstairs."

"Good. Nathan and Freddy are usually in their bedrooms until midday on Saturdays. So we'll have the morning to ourselves. Are you excited about seeing your college?"

"Yes, of course."

"Then cheer up and prepare to have some fun. Don't wish for the moon, Susie. Enjoy what you've already been given."

Fenella silently vowed to follow her own advice as she clattered about, moving bowls and plates from the cupboard. She broke some eggs in a basin and pushed them towards Susie. "Here, be useful and whip these up."

Susie bit her lip but obeyed without question. She obviously wanted to say more, but Fenella's firmness seemed to have silenced her for now. Fenella had done a decent enough job of pretending to be a responsible adult, but inside, her heart was thumping like a baby rabbit's. She was in deep, deep trouble.

Chapter Eleven

Despite having claimed she never ate breakfast, Susie demolished a large plate of scrambled eggs, two slices of sourdough toast, and a glass of freshly squeezed orange juice. Afterwards Fenella left her to go upstairs to talk to the boys, urging them to get out of their beds, tidy their rooms, and look at their homework before going to the football match they wanted to attend.

"There's masses of food in the fridge, if you can be bothered to open the door. Choose something healthy. Don't live on cereal."

"What are you up to today, Mum? Is Susie staying another night?" asked Nate, who was deep into some game on his computer screen.

"Yes, she'll be with us until Sunday afternoon, when she'll be collecting the rest of her things from London. But I'm taking her on a walking tour of Oxford this morning to show her St Hilary's, the college where she has a place. Then we'll walk down into the centre to visit some of the sights. We may grab a sandwich lunch somewhere, but I'm planning on roasting a chicken for this evening's dinner. So I want you and Freddy back here by six."

"Okay. You head off and have fun. We'll muck along by ourselves for the morning."

"Thanks, Nate. Remember to lock the front door if you go out." She ruffled his hair and kissed him. Nate was the only positive thing to come out of her first marriage, and he was well worth all the pain and angst, someone she was allowed to love as fiercely as she wanted. Thank goodness maternal love was uncontroversial, uncomplicated, and universally approved of.

Going back downstairs, she had to brush past Susie.

"I've stacked the dishwasher and wiped down the counter. I'm going to get ready for our visit to St Hilary's."

"Thanks. Only no string and safety pins today, all right?"

Susie grinned, clearly understanding Fenella meant to be

humorous. "No, I'm going to blend right in. You won't even notice me."

Unlikely. As they stood together on the same step, Fenella's pulse thumped away in her ear, and her fingers tingled as if desperate to touch Susie. "I'm not saying you can't have your own style, though I'm still puzzled as to what that is yet."

"Not too sure myself, if I'm honest," said Susie. "But I'll put on trainers and build up from there. You did say we're going to do a lot of walking?"

"I did," said Fenella and quickly descended the stairs to gain some much-needed breathing space.

They shared a good morning together in Oxford. As soon as she saw St Hilary's College, Susie jumped up and down with joy, which reminded Fenella so much of her younger self.

Founded in the 1890s, modern by Oxford standards, it must have seemed an ancient establishment in Susie's young eyes, and she was clearly enthralled to see it in reality, after only experiencing it through pictures on its website.

Susie had told Fenella she hadn't had a physical interview but submitted some work online. She'd then taken the entrance examination under supervision at her previous university at UC Davis and finally had a Zoom interview with the admissions tutor, so Fenella assumed her grades and references must have been outstanding.

They walked through the gates up the drive, and Fenella noticed how much new building had gone on since she'd last visited.

"I wonder who St Hilary was," said Susie, looking at the red-brick building, set in its ten acres of gardens.

"Some bishop, I expect."

"Why couldn't they find a female saint to name it after?"

"To make it sound respectable, and there aren't that many female saints compared to the men. Allowing young women into Oxford was considered quite scandalous in the 1890s," Fenella said, dredging her memories of the college's history. "They could attend lectures only after a struggle, and it was more than thirty years later before they were awarded degrees.."

"I didn't know that," said Susie. "The prospectus said it was co-ed."

"It is now. All the Oxford woman's colleges agreed to admit men by 2008, just as the men's colleges had reluctantly begun to take women. Come on, let's go to the porter's lodge and apply for a visitor's pass."

"What's a porter's lodge?"

Fenella led Susie onwards, explaining all the old terminology and Oxfordisms that would seem quaint, if not bizarre, to the first-time student, especially an American one.

While they waited at the desk for the porter on duty to come off his phone, Susie looked down at her paperwork. "It says here I have to book in by October first for Freshers' week, in week zero, whatever this means."

"It's just Oxford jargon." Fenella put an arm around her and read the paper over her shoulder. "Week zero is next week. Then full term starts the week after."

"How weird." Susie wrinkled her nose. "Why is it called Michaelmas Term? And why is a term only eight weeks long? Won't it mean I'll spend more time on vacation than I will studying?"

"You'll be able to read right through the year beyond full term, but lectures and tutorials only take place in eight-week blocks. It's why they call it reading for a degree. You're supposed to do most of the work yourself." Fenella smiled when Susie rolled her eyes. "I know it sounds like a rip-off, especially given the huge tuition costs for international students. Part of the reason for such short terms is that most university academic staff treat teaching undergraduates as a boring necessity that interferes with their research. Only a hundred and fifty undergraduate students study Classics, so you'll soon get to know everybody."

"Only a hundred and fifty? That's tiny! How do you know?"

"Because I studied Classics myself, remember? And I have really good friends on the staff. It may seem like a small number, but Oxford still has one of the largest Classics departments in the world."

"Kate's been so generous with her funding. The costs of visas, teaching fees, and accommodation are something I don't have to worry about, especially if I keep the teaching post going. I checked online, and my student visa says I'm allowed to work up to twenty hours a week."

The porter handed them visitors' passes and a little plan of the college. "I can tell you which will be your allocated room, miss, if you bear with me. Then you can walk up and see it. That block isn't occupied with a conference this week, but the decorators are in."

"My own room? You mean I won't be sharing a dorm? Wow!"

He gave them a room number, a set of keys, and a map of the campus. "Bring the keys back when you leave. Then we'll issue you them properly next week." They left the porter's lodge and walked to the building he'd marked with a cross. When they reached the room allocated to her, Susie smiled with apparent satisfaction as she looked through the open door. It was as simple as a nun's cell, but clean, with a bed, chair, bookcase, and desk, and a large window with a good view over the rooftops.

"A room of one's own! Like Virginia Woolf said. And a lock." Susie turned to Fenella and grinned. "Hey, so I can invite you in here for coffee or cuddles, and no one will interrupt us."

"That may be theoretically possible," said Fenella, "but in practice, I won't have any time for coffee-drinking and certainly none for any other nonsense. Neither will you. You'll either be at lectures or in the library studying, or running off to St Martin's to teach, and of course, I work in London most of the week. As soon as you start here, I'm sure we'll hardly see anything of each other."

Susie sighed. "You do talk a load of bull at times, Fenella. 'Scuse my French. That's not how it's going to be, and you know it. I'm going to come visit you as often as I can until I convince you we're meant for each other."

"Then I'll have you arrested for stalking," said Fenella, only half-joking. "Now, hurry up, you little monster. We need to go down into town and get you fitted with a gown and sub fusc for matriculation."

"Yeah. Isn't sub fusc a funky term? Super crazy. I suppose my black suit will do."

"You'll need a commoner's gown and a mortar board as well. I know where we can buy them." Fenella kept them a few treads' distance apart as they walked back down the winding staircase.

Susie turned back towards her. "I think I need a different sort of black gown from a commoner. They've given me a scholarship. I didn't like to mention it before in case you thought I was blowing my own horn."

Fenella didn't often feel outclassed, but she did now. Only la crème de la crème of applicants ever gained a scholarship. Ms Webster was getting more interesting by the hour.

They went shopping for academic dress, then Fenella walked Susie down St Giles to the Classics Faculty buildings next to the Ashmolean Museum. That visit brought out more excitement from her companion. Facing the modern entrance of the department behind their façade, Susie looked as though she'd died and gone to heaven. Her joy was contagious, and Fenella felt almost young again. Taken as a whole, her years at Oxford had been some of the happiest times of her life, despite all the heartache around a certain woman whom she had vowed never to think of again.

"My very best friend at the time, Dr Stephanie Mayfield, is a leading Professor here. I thought she might even be here at the weekend. She stayed on to do a D.Phil., the Oxford equivalent of a PhD."

Fenella took Susie back to Broad Street, opposite the Bodleian Library, where Blackwells stood, which was arguably one of the best bookshops in the English-speaking world and a cornucopia of knowledge. Susie's eyes fired up with a true bibliophile's lust as they entered. She seemed to have more than enough money to buy books and practically shivered with excitement. Going to the main desk, she asked an assistant where the Latin textbooks and Roman history were, and then she dragged Fenella downstairs to where they took up a bookshelf on the lower floor back wall.

"I want to show these to the headmaster at St Martin's," she said. "The ones they're using go back to the last century. They're ancient."

"You make it sound as though it was barely after the Romans left."

"Pretty much." Susie laughed. "BMB, anyway."

"What do you mean? Here, let me take these off your hands." Fenella grabbed some of the books threatening to slide out of

Susie's arms.

"Before my birth."

"Which was when?"

"2004."

Fenella gulped. It seemed only yesterday, confirmation that Susie was inviting her to grab her straight out of her pram. "Let's get out of here and find some food," she said quickly, the heat rising in her cheeks.

They took a sandwich lunch in one of the many nearby bistros and walked as far as the river, where they sat on a bench to watch several sets of rowers, in boats of fours and eights out on the water, skimming along in the early autumn sunshine.

Susie had insisted on buying a couple of large vanilla slices for their dessert. These were impossible to eat politely, and Fenella succumbed to laughter when Susie decorated her face with cream and chocolate.

"You're ridiculous," she said, pretending to be serious. "Here, take a Kleenex and wipe it all off."

"You're a woman who keeps Kleenex in her purse? Gee, what a mom."

Fenella's heart thumped again as it dropped. For a moment, she'd relaxed and forgotten the decades between them. But here she was passing over paper tissues, when what she really wanted to do was to lick every drop of chocolate and cream and every pastry flake from Susie's wicked little face. The pain of inappropriate desire was almost visceral.

She prayed for deliverance, and it came in the shape of a chilly little wind blowing off the river. "Let's go," she said, jumping to her feet. "There's rain in the air, and we need to get home with all our packages."

Their journey home was almost a forced march, as she strode ahead of Susie. This was ostensibly to avoid the rainclouds building to the south, but really because Fenella's nerves were stretched to their limits. She found it the hardest thing to act normally, to be sensible. Something very dangerous was playing with her hormones, and she didn't like it. But Susie trotted beside her, happy with her load of books, and apparently oblivious to all Fenella's angst. And worse, by the time they returned home mid-afternoon, she simply couldn't deny that Susie was good company. Everything interested her, and she never stopped asking questions.

"I'm looking forward to roast chicken," Susie said after she'd deposited her books in the attic. "Can I help by prepping the veggies for you?"

Perfect little houseguest. Fenella wanted to scream.

The rest of Saturday calmed things down. Fenella was careful never to be alone with Susie, and the boys were more than happy to entertain her. The chicken dinner pleased everyone, and Susie's abilities with a paring knife and potato peeler had produced three pans of vegetables, all neatly diced ready for steaming.

Fenella decided to make an old-fashioned apple and blackberry pie, a good dessert for September. Susie took two helpings.

"Gee, you're like Martha Stewart," she said afterwards, wiping custard from her mouth. "Better looking, of course."

"I believe Martha Stewart is over eighty," said Fenella and tightened her jaw. She wasn't sure if she wanted the comparison to go as far as that. "You need to get an earlier train tomorrow to fetch all your belongings from London. Then you can return here later in the evening."

"Yeah, thanks so much. I have three classes to take at the school on Monday, so I'd better do some more lesson planning tonight."

"The boys have an evening of prep ahead of them. Why don't you all sit at the table in the dining room to work together. I have laundry to fold, boys' shirts to iron, and proofs to read."

They all seemed happy with the idea. Susie stacked the dishwasher, and the boys helped her. It was all very amiable and normal. But as soon as she could decently retire for the night, Fenella retreated upstairs and locked her bedroom door. Then she fell on her bed and curled up like a small child. It had been a day of unacknowledged passion gnawing at her insides. And what tormented her the most was knowing Susie would leap on her if she so much as gave a hint of encouragement.

By midnight, she needed relief, so she reached for the little drawstring bag in her night drawer. The gentle hum of the vibrator began to soothe her, and as she pressed it harder and harder inside herself and turned up the power, she finally managed a hip-thrusting orgasm. It wasn't the real thing, of course, but it was physically effective.

Only when she lay back on the pillows and stared at the ceiling did she have a horrible thought. A floorboard creaked above her head. Was Susie still awake upstairs? And had she heard Fenella's battery-powered desperation? God, she hoped not.

Chapter Twelve

The following Monday evening, Fenella emerged from Olivia's office back out into the publishing heartland of London, full of tea and biscuits, and comforted by the simple fact that she'd confessed her stupid obsession. She felt better for getting it all off her chest, and Olivia had understood at least some of what she'd been going through.

Fenella took a taxi to Paddington station and collapsed into her reserved seat on the six thirty p.m. Oxford train. She ached in every bone from nervous exhaustion, as though she'd had the flu. She hoped that her sudden yearning for Susie would surely disappear as quickly as it had come from nowhere to attack her.

Her commute three days a week to and from London was normally when Fenella caught up with reading the Sunday papers. Once she settled on the train, she opened a colour supplement she'd pushed into her briefcase and dived into an article on some newly discovered Roman gravestones. After reading it with increasing interest, she extracted the pages and folded them over. It was something Susie would love to know about, so she tucked it into her bag as a little present. Epitaphs on gravestones were also an easy way to engage young scholars in the learning of Latin.

As the train moved smoothly on through Reading and up towards Oxford Parkway, Fenella thought more and more about how she could help Susie both in her own studies and in her teaching. But then her phone pinged with a new message.

I've been thinking. When we meet for lunch at your place next Sunday, why don't we invite Bel Bridgford and her wife Bryony to join us as well? They only live ten miles from Oxford, and they're ace people, and will help you untangle yourself from Susannah if it's what you want. I can call Bel if you like. I need to talk to her about her next book, anyway.

Olivia's text sent a mini nuclear missile into Fenella's temporary calm. She stared at the phone and tried not to panic. Bel Bridgford. Brilliant Bel Bridgford, who had been a post-grad research student at Somerville when Fenella had been a fresher. Bel Bridgford, notorious Bel Bridgford, the heart-breaker. Memory of her had once been almost too painful to think about, and something Fenella had buried deep in the back of her closet.

But it had been over twenty-five years ago. Their paths had never crossed since, and Bel probably wouldn't even remember her now. Fenella had read about her in a few *Sunday Times'* articles over the years, as a distant observer. Her fingers fluttered over her message keypad. *Yes, to lunch with you and Niamh. I can't wait to meet her. About Bel and Bryony Bridgford, if you like, do ask them. But it's such short notice I'm sure they won't be able to come.*

She metaphorically crossed her fingers as she hit *send,* hoping it would be true. By the time the train drew into Oxford, she'd calmed down enough to have forgotten to treat Susie as some sort of infection and was looking forward to hearing about her first day of teaching.

The house rang with loud music and laughter as she walked through the front door. An aroma of something tasty emanated from the kitchen, where she found Susie and the boys. They were halfway through eating a freshly cooked Mexican dish of enchiladas, accompanied by a large green salad.

Susie, who had changed out of the teaching clothes she'd donned first thing in the morning, wore figure-hugging workout gear that emphasized her neat little ass. Over her black leggings and top, she'd wrapped herself up in one of Fenella's chef's aprons, and her face, warmed by the exertions in the kitchen and no doubt by the Mexican food, flushed even pinker when Fenella walked in, dropping her briefcase and coat onto the kitchen's leather sofa.

Susie's eyes were adoring when she looked up to greet her. The naked intensity of her gaze almost took Fenella off her feet. Never mind the food: the kid herself looked edible.

"So sorry we started without you," Susie said, "but the boys said you wouldn't mind."

"Not at all. Never wait for me. I'm usually late. This looks inviting."

"Enchiladas, Mum," Freddy said. "I had them in Texas when I went to visit Dad. They're great. I didn't know you could get them over here, but Susie went to the local supermarket to get the things to make them."

"You can cook." It was a statement more than a question, and Susie seemed a little uncomfortable at being complimented.

"Sort of. I cooked for my dad after Mom died, until Abbie came along. He would've lived on sandwiches if I hadn't. I'm not really anything special." She spooned out a helping of enchiladas for Fenella. "Come and sit down, and let me fix you a drink. You must be whacked out. Would you like a gin and tonic? The boys say it's your favourite."

Mom the lush. Thanks, boys. "No, thanks. I've decided that what's left of this month is going to be sobriety September. I'll have a glass of sparkling water, maybe with a squeeze of lime." Fenella sat at the table opposite her sons and took the plate of hot food. Susie filled a glass from the bottle of sparkling water in the fridge and slipped in a few ice cubes. The simple act entranced her so much, Fenella felt lightheaded. "I'll never understand why Americans never serve a drink without at least seven ice cubes," she muttered to counter the feeling.

"Do we? I guess so. Gee. I'm sorry."

Fenella shook off her ungracious attitude and smiled. "Don't apologise. It's no problem. This food looks delicious." She took a bite. "And it tastes as good as it looks. Thank you. You're very kind to have cooked this for us all. But now, tell me about your day at the school. How did the teaching go?"

"She was great," said Nate. "She took us for double Latin, and we actually learned some stuff. Did you know that when Romulus wanted to start a new city, after he murdered his brother, he gathered together a group of real scumbags and ruffians from other places to start the thing going, but they couldn't get any women to join them because they were all so horrible. So they went off and grabbed a whole group of them from the local towns. It was called the rape of the Sabine women."

"I have heard something of the same," said Fenella, wondering how graphic Susie's account had been. "Did you get into any Latin grammar along the way?"

Nate nodded. "Yep, I've got a whole page of this guy Livy to translate by Wednesday."

Fenella caught Susie's eye and rewarded her with an honest smile of appreciation. She whispered, "Well done," and was pleased to see Susie's ardent little face turn a deeper shade of pink.

Later, when generous bowls of vanilla ice cream had calmed down the heat from the Mexican sauce, the boys stacked the dishwasher, without being asked for once, and then disappeared to do their homework upstairs.

"Come through to the family room," Fenella said to Susie. She sat on the sofa, where Susie joined her. Fenella remembered the article on Romano-British gravestones in the Sunday supplement and went to retrieve it. She returned from the kitchen with her bag and pulled out the page she'd torn from the magazine. "Here's some reading material for you. England is full of Roman remains, and people are still finding new ones." She sat down again, thinking about how complicated it might be to unwind Susie from her chef's apron and feel her way closer into those soft curves.

Susie took the page and read it intently. "Wow. This is so cool. I finished your book on Roman Britain, and I'm reading another on the lives of Roman women. People seem to think they had no power and did nothing, but it can't be true. Half the population, big fat silence. It'd be fascinating uncovering some more of it."

"Well, if you're interested, I'll have to introduce you to my friend Stevie. She's recently published a new book."

"Great."

"Oh, yes, and I have other friends I'd like you to meet first. I've invited a couple called Olivia and Niamh to lunch next Sunday. I've known Olivia since our Oxford days. She read English though, not Classics. Her wife's an art historian currently completing a PhD on Irish women artists. Olivia is contacting friends of hers, who live even nearer. Bel is an eminent climate campaigner and writer, and I believe her wife, Bryony, is a surgeon here in Oxford at the John Radcliffe Infirmary."

"Wives? So they're two lesbian couples? Gee, that's way cool."

Oh, damn it. Fenella had been a complete fool to think inviting all these gay women to meet Susie would help dislodge her. Rather than be dissuaded, Susie would only see them as living proof that a huge age-gap, mismatch of backgrounds, and total power imbalance could produce a good outcome. For whatever else she'd learn from meeting them, Susie couldn't fail to see Olivia and Niamh were bonkers about each other, and Bel and Bryony were now several years into married bliss. Fenella had done a great job at self-sabotaging there. *Well done*. She looked at Susie, and her mouth went dry. "Next Sunday will be your last day staying here with us."

"I know. What a bummer. It already feels like home."

"Please don't use such a vulgar expression. But I'm thinking, after tonight's excellent dinner, would you like to cook lunch for us all, something different, an American speciality? On Sundays most British people eat their main meal at lunch time."

Susie frowned. "Sure, if you're okay with that."

"I'll give you my credit card. You could shop at Waitrose on Saturday to get your ingredients." Fenella didn't want to set foot in the supermarket again, especially after the gin bottles and spaghetti hoops encounter with the woman in the pink cardigan. "I can collect you in the car after you shop for what you want."

"Great. But I'm thinking I should also maybe learn to ride a bicycle. Everyone seems to have one here, and I can use it to get around to lectures and the libraries. I was going to go look for one downtown."

"Good idea. But there's no need to buy a new one. I have my old one in the garage. It probably simply needs servicing and the tyres pumping up."

"Wow, Fenella. You are so good to me. I don't deserve all this. How can I ever pay you back?" Susie batted her feathery eyelashes.

You little minx. "I'll tell you how. Your use of words is appalling. I can't understand how a person of your intelligence and linguistic talents can have such an impoverished vocabulary. If we are to be friends, you need to make radical improvements to the way you speak. I admit that you have made some much-needed adjustments to your dress, which has been good to observe."

Susie actually fell back on the sofa and began to laugh out loud.

When she'd stopped giggling, she leaned in. "Fenella, you wanna say all it again so I can write it down? You crack me up."

"I mean it."

"Sure you do. It's what's so cool about you. I can't wait to hear what you say in bed. I bet you have some real way-out pillow talk." Susie jumped up, narrowly avoiding a whack from Fenella's outstretched hand, and ran for the door. At the doorjamb, she looked back and smirked. "Gotta dash. Lessons to prepare. See ya"

"Good Lord," Fenella muttered through gritted teeth. Then she thought some more about her oversized apron and how good Susie would look just wearing that alone…

Chapter Thirteen

Susie's overnight trip back to North London had confirmed how much she preferred Oxford for reasons besides Fenella. London was too huge and impersonal, and she'd needed all the help Google maps could give her to find her way back to Carla's on Sunday.

Carla was out but had sent her a text. *I'll be back tonight. Food's in the fridge. BTW, your dad called expecting you to be here. Give him a call or Facetime him. He says you haven't been in touch with them since last Tuesday.*

Suitably guilt-ridden, she dropped her gear onto the floor, flopped down on Carla's sofa and opened her iPad. She was learning the time difference now. Eight hours from four p.m. would make it eight a.m. in Oregon. But on a Sunday, that'd be fine. Her dad and Abbie should be sitting in the kitchen, enjoying a leisurely breakfast of coffee and French toast.

Abbie was an authentic, original hippie, and a talented painter. Susie had accused her of seducing her dad when they'd first started dating. Susie had been a nasty nightmare to them both nearly derailing their chance of love. But her bad behaviour taught her a lesson when all the negative, mean things she'd done rebounded straight back on her. She was now a new person: reformed and truly repentant. She loved Abbie a lot, as well as her stepmother's family, especially Cat, Abbie's daughter, and Kate, Cat's wife.

By finally growing up and accepting that life is in constant flux, she'd also been given her own best future. She was about to start studying at the best university in the world *and* had met the fabulous Fenella Carlton.

Susie hit call on FaceTime and two happy faces immediately appeared. She choked up as she saw them. It had only been a few days, but she'd moved five thousand miles into another world. Perversely, seeing them so close up and personal emphasized her isolation from all the familiarity of home.

"Honey! How's it going? What have you been up to? Carla said you aren't staying with her anymore."

"No worries, Dad. I'm back here now, but I've made a great friend in Oxford, and she's looking after me until I start at the college."

He didn't seem to pick up on her mention of Fenella. "How's Oxford? Is it all you dreamed of? It's a place your mom and I always wanted to see."

"Everything's very weird but totally wonderful, and I've met the best people and seen my college. I've landed a part-time job in a local prep school teaching Latin too. My friend Fenella told me about it, so I applied by calling the school."

"Then they can't have met you yet. Do they know what they'll be getting?"

"Dad! Thanks a whole bunch for the endorsement."

"You know I'm kidding, right? You'll be great. Have you asked them for a box to stand on so you can see over the teacher's podium?"

"Haha. Actually, don't freak out, but I *have* bought a pair of heels. The woman I'm staying with, Fenella, who is the absolute best, almost lives in heels, and she's the coolest dresser. She's showing me how to walk in them and look older."

"I've never worn heels in my life," Abbie said, "and the only person I know who does is Cat's Kate. It sounds as if your friend and her might hit it off."

"They probably would. Except Kate is across the Atlantic, and Fenella's not even out, here in Oxford. Oh shit, I shouldn't have said that. Forget I said it."

"But it sounds like you've been discussing sexuality with her already, have you?" Abbie asked.

Her dad said nothing. Susie's preferences had never been an overt topic of conversation with her dad, but Abbie was a lot less embarrassed about his daughter's love life—or lack of it—and had been happy to talk. But everything to do with Fenella was still so new, so fragile and tender and wonderful, that Susie didn't want to spread it out all over the table yet. She shook her head and steered the conversation away from sex. "Um, not really, but you'd love

Fenella if you ever met her, I know you would, and so would Cat and Kate. She lives in a great big redbrick house in Oxford and has two teenage boys, and she edits a big-time magazine in the UK."

"How did you meet her so soon after landing?" her dad asked. "I hope she didn't see you in the crazy outfit you put on for the flight."

Susie laughed, remembering how her dad had baulked at her idea of travel gear when he'd taken her to the airport. "Carla introduced us. She's trying to land Fenella as a client of the design company she works for. And Fenella likes me despite the rips in my jeans. But I'm learning a lot from her, and she's mega, mega respectable. A really good influence, honest." Why was she protesting far too much? She had nothing to feel guilty about yet, tragically.

"Make sure you keep off the weed," her dad said, sounding less than convinced, "or anything else while you're over there. Every college town's the same—"

"Dad!" Her face flamed. "I've been clean for two years. Can't you give me a break?"

His kind eyes crinkled as he stared at her through the screen. "Honey, I'm sorry. I only worry so much because I love you. You're my pet lamb, and—"

"I know, I know. I put you through hell when I got wasted and ran away. But I promise you, the only thing tempting me now are all the shiny books in the stores over here. I've got to thank Kate for the cash she sent through to my account so I can afford them."

Her dad frowned and glanced away briefly. "We're not penniless, and you're my only child. I should be paying the fees, and your expenses."

Abbie leaned in, her hand on his arm. "It's okay, Chris. Kate wanted to do it, and she can afford it. There'll be plenty of opportunities for us to spoil our Susie when we visit in the summer."

Susie looked at her watch. "Anyway, oldsters, I have to call Kate and Cat. Do you want me to say anything to them from you?"

"Only send our best love," Abbie said. "We haven't seen them in a while. Cat is up to her eyes in her new documentary project, and Kate is battling on every front to drum up support for the Dems. But call us again next Sunday. We love seeing your face, and we miss you very much."

Susie blew them a virtual kiss across the airwaves. " Ditto. I miss you, and the animals, and everything Oregon. By the way, did you know *ditto* comes from the Latin *dicere,* to speak?"

Her dad rolled his eyes. "Get on, you little monster. Call us next Sunday, okay?"

"Bye." Susie swiped their faces away from her screen and tried to shove the homesick ache in her stomach away. She fixed herself a sandwich, then went back to the sofa to call Cat, Kate, and their three girls, her "second" family in Pasadena.

Cat picked up and told her Kate was out, already at her studio preparing for her Sunday morning political hour's round table discussion with local Californian politicians. That wouldn't be easy. Susie knew how mean and nasty political debates could get as the election loomed nearer. But Cat was at home with the girls, having a lazy Sunday, so Susie had a lovely half hour Facetiming with them all and hearing about their doings over the recent days. Then she suddenly remembered she needed to put in a few hours work preparing lessons for the coming week.

"Yep, us too," Cat said. "We all need to study. But keep giving us updates. We miss you, kiddo, and Kate's threatening to take the new Montpellier jet over to England to see you if you don't stay out in touch. We all love you. You know this, right?"

The blanket of family warmth wrapped around her shoulders, even across the ocean. "Of course, and I miss you gals loads too."

Cat squinted through the screen at her, then she shooed the girls away. "There's something else?"

Susie sighed, trying to figure out if she should open up or not. Within seconds though, she'd told Cat all about Fenella and how wonderful she was before her embarrassment kicked in, and she ground to a halt.

"So you *like* your new landlady?"

"You're teasing!"

"Of course. But as long as she's worthy of you, I heartily approve."

Susie grinned widely. "I love you, Cat. No one else in my life would quote Jane Austen at me…except maybe Fenella."

"You can always rely on me to be weird. I know all her novels almost by heart. Maybe we could visit Jane's house when we come out to check up on you. But watch out for yourself, kid. And hey, send me a photo of 'la Fenella,' and I'll give you some in-depth feedback as to her suitability. Now I *really* have to go. Bye, honey."

They finished their call, and Susie gathered her thoughts. A picture of Fenella was one thing she didn't yet have. She had to fix that as soon as she was back in Oxford later that night.

Susie turned to the textbooks she'd brought from the school and sat down to plan two or three sets of Latin grammar lessons for the coming week. In her trial lessons, she'd acted as though she was fearless in front of the students, all of whom were taller than her. But every time she entered the classroom, her heart thumped against her ribs, and she couldn't bear to prove Fenella right and admit that teaching was beyond her.

Chapter Fourteen

It was Friday before Fenella had the time to go into the back of the garage and pull out her old bike. She hadn't ridden it since before Nathan was born, and it looked a poor old thing, with totally flat tires and a rusty chain. Perhaps offering it to Susie hadn't been the best idea, but maybe it would clean up nicely. The first thing it needed was a trip to the bike shop for a complete overhaul and service.

In the garage on Friday afternoon however, Susie hung by her side and seemed enthralled. "Wow. It's a proper cool Oxford bike. Was it really yours? Did you sit your bum on this saddle?" She gave a vaguely vulgar smirk.

Fenella tried to quell the rising heat in her cheeks. "Of course. Don't be facetious. But the bike was really a *she*. I called her Charlotte, and all through my student years here, we went everywhere together. My father gave her to me when I came up, and she certainly made my life much easier."

"Did you get along with your dad?"

"I certainly did. He was a darling. He died when I was twenty-five though. I was the youngest of the family, and he was nearly sixty when I was born."

"What about your mom?"

Fenella wondered whether it was wise to tell her. "I lost my mother to breast cancer, like you, but I was a little older. She died when I was fifteen."

"Why didn't you say? You let me go on and on about my mom, and all the time, yours died of the same horrible illness. So we're in the same team. Do you think we'll get breast cancer like our mothers? I couldn't bear to lose you."

Fenella clutched her hand to her heart. She had regular tests but didn't worry too much about inheriting her mother's cancer gene. But Susie's implication that they would somehow be together for years to come was something she hadn't even dreamed of. And if Susie was at risk of cancer, Fenella would move heaven and earth to protect her. She sucked in a sharp breath at the intensity of this sudden painful thought, and she bent over slightly as though she had a stitch.

Tonight, Susie was once again wearing those dreadful ripped jeans, while her school-mistress get-up was getting the benefit of a short cycle wash in the utility room. On her top half, she wore a work-out bra under a loose pink T-shirt. Fenella felt like pulling off both skimpy items of clothing and licking those breasts. A quick change of subject was essential.

Nathan and Freddy had parked their bikes inside the garage as well, and they needed to be pulled out in order to extricate Charlotte. Fenella hoped that the effort to do this would account for her flushed cheeks and sudden lack of balance.

With Susie's help, she moved the old bike outside, and they both looked at it. Fenella pulled herself together. "Can you really not ride a bike? You'd better learn fast before we get Charlotte back from the repair shop."

Susie shrugged. "I really can't. Home is up the side of a mountain, and I always had horses instead of a bike. I'm good with horses, and I could ride them from the age of three."

Fenella crushed the image burning into her inner eye of Susie astride a galloping horse. "Then I'll call Freddy to come down. He'll take you out around the avenues and teach you how to stay upright. You can practise up and down these quiet back roads on Nathan's bike. Meanwhile I'll call the cycle shop and ask them to come to pick up Charlotte."

Susie threw her arms around Fenella and drew her in for a hug. "Thank you, Fenny. I love you madly 'cos you're so good to me. Can I kiss you now to show how much?"

"No, stop it, silly girl! Do grow up! You're making me very cross."

Susie smirked and squeezed her even tighter. "No, I'm not. You love it when I come on to you. I know you do."

"The boys will notice something if you don't start behaving better. I'm your landlady, not your plaything. No, no! Oh, for God's sake…" Fenella tried to put some real force into her voice, but it was no good. In the semi-darkness of her garage, between the boys' bikes, the lawn mower, and a whole pile of assorted paint tins, she allowed herself to be kissed full on the mouth. And she responded like a starving woman desperate for nourishment.

Susie's mouth was as wide, as sweet, and as irresistible as she'd imagined it would be. Once connected, Fenella wanted more of it. She surprised herself by how quickly she took control, pushing Susie back towards the wall and holding them together, locked in an old-fashioned cinch. She devoured Susie's mouth, taking her breath, feeling her lips, teeth, and tongue. She nearly bit the poor girl, she was so ravenous for her. It was madness. It was absurd. But Susie's slim body heaving against hers was heavenly. Who would've thought that the smell of old paint and oil cans could be seductive? But they added to the fun and the silly, childish delight she took in being adored by someone whom she yearned for so badly.

Neither of her husbands, nor any of their predecessors, had aroused her in the way this eccentric young American did. For the next few moments, Fenella lost her sense of decorum and dignity. She wanted to stay in the garage for ever, "making out" like a teenager, and if she and Susie had been alone in the house, she would have dragged her upstairs and stayed in bed for the rest of the weekend.

She never wanted it to stop but, at the same time, knew in some depth of her sanity that it had to. It had to be cancelled, forbidden, deleted as soon as it was over.

But for now…

Eventually, Susie pulled away after one last sweet tug on Fenella's swollen lower lip. "We sure let out the dragon, didn't we?" she whispered and shivered. "I'm sorry. Now you'll hate me. I should never have tempted you so much. Forgive me."

"For what?" Fenella asked sharply. Was Susie playing games? Had she been teasing Fenella to see how far she could go? Did she now regret making the kiss happen? A turmoil of contradictions tumbled around her head. Ecstasy, self-loathing, and inbred, latent homophobia swirled together in an uncontrollable tension that made it quite difficult to breathe. It was all too, too much to bear, let alone analyse.

Susie seemed to sense her sudden insecurity and pulled Fenella back in closer. "It's never happened to me like this before. I always knew I was into girls, and I'm super queer. But it's never been as strong as this. You're like a drug. Way, way better than anything I've ever taken. I've been craving you every minute since we met. There's nothing I wouldn't do for you."

Fenella turned away slightly and began to slowly swim back up towards the surface of this, whatever this was, regaining her breath and searching for some common sense. She softly pushed back Susie's floating curls and cupped her face. So it seemed they were both struck down by the same disease. She said, "If it's true that you feel much the same as I do, then I'm going to ask you—no, insist that we both do a very hard thing."

"Wha—"

"No, Susie, stop!" Fenella blocked the beginning of what sounded like a little cry, no more than a whimper. "We can't let this go any further. You must see. I'm more than twice your age, and I have two teenage boys in the house to consider. It would be a scandal if we had an affair, and they've already gone through enough with what happened between me and their fathers. Whatever's happening here, we've got to put it straight into the freezer. You are far too young and inexperienced, and besides, I refuse to break your heart as I inevitably would if we got involved." It was as pathetic an excuse as it sounded, and she hated herself for every word, for every syllable. But Susie let her talk until her words dried up, and the silence hung in the air between them.

Susie still had her arms pressed tightly around Fenella, but she averted her eyes and simply buried her head against Fenella's breasts and gave one last small squeeze. Then she drew back. "Okay. You're right, I know. I can see we aren't playing games here. It's real, and we've got the hots for each other. But I guess it's wrong, if you say so. You keep saying you're too old for me, so maybe that makes you wiser. So if you want to say what happened didn't happen, that's okay. If it's what you really want."

Fenella, perversely, almost wished Susie had protested more, but she was relieved there'd been no sobbing, no tears, no scene. Susie was behaving perfectly for someone who had been rejected, and for the sake of what? Well, for her own cowardice in the face of conventional, straight public opinion, she supposed, and her reluctance to disrupt her sons' lives. A deeper, more honest reason was the very idea of loving someone, anyone, so much, with no guard rails or boundaries scared the living daylights out of her. "We'll still be good friends," she said. "And you can still have the bicycle, with Freddy's services thrown in to get you going on these British roads."

Susie managed a grin. "Oh gee, I get to keep the bike? It makes everything fine then. Thanks so much."

Sarky kid. But there was no malice in her tone.

"Please just do one more thing for me, Susie."

"What?"

"Stop thanking me for everything all the time. I admit having you around makes me happy. I want to do things to help you settle in. I love your company, and I don't want you to be a stranger."

"But what happened in the garage stays in the garage, right? Okay, I get it. So we should go ask Freddy if he has time to give me my first bike-riding lesson?"

Fenella nodded in relief, hoping her own flushed face and rumpled clothes wouldn't give her away. She smoothed back her hair and released Susie from the wall. "Very well, and by the way, I've noticed you've started calling me Fen, or even worse, Fenny."

"Yeah. Do you mind?"

"Maybe not. To be honest, I've never cared much for Fenella."

Then they left the magic, darkly romantic imaginings of the garage and went back to the house together.

Chapter Fifteen

Susie's heart jumped up and down so hard that she worried Fenella would see it bouncing out of her sports bra. And why not?

Her first orgasm, *ever*, and it had come from one simple kiss, from being pushed up against the rough, damp brickwork of a dark garage. It hadn't come through any penetration other than Fen's powerful, thrusting tongue and through her own exploding libido.

She walked behind Fenella the few yards through the garden into the house, ogling those exquisite shoulders, the glorious dark auburn shock of wavy hair, and the effortless style of the woman who was her destiny—maybe her downfall, but certainly, her personal goddess. Susie could hardly walk straight, and she stumbled in over the back doorstep like a drunk neophyte.

Susie was quite proud of her response to Fen's lecture, and that she hadn't laughed out loud. Sure, she understood Fen's problems. She wasn't an idiot. In fact, the longer she'd lived with the Carlton family, the more sensitive she was becoming to the conventional niceties and constraints of suburban British life. More importantly, she already loved those two boys and was close enough in age to them to understand that any thoughts of their mother having sexual feelings for anybody, let alone her, would gross them out. Susie knew how she'd pushed and wormed her way without any shame into Fen's life, what an aggressive American brat she'd been. So she really deserved nothing in return for all her flirting.

But her acceptance of Fen's demand, to stop everything as soon as it had started hadn't been a strategic ploy to deceive nor simply to keep the peace. What'd happened in the garage had been like Julius Caesar crossing the Rubicon River. It had taken them into a whole new reality from which there was no means of retreat. It didn't matter what boundaries Fen might erect, whatever pledges they might give each other, what idea they might make to be nothing but friends. They wouldn't change things. Susie knew deep in her guts that this was it, totally *It*.

Beyond any doubt, she'd never love anyone else but Fenella Carlton. Her feelings were so deep, so acute, that she could hardly bear to look at Fen's beautiful, slightly tempered profile without melting into a puddle. She hadn't lied when she'd said their age-gap was irrelevant. They were alive together, on earth at the same time, weren't they? And that was enough. Susie would now live on hope. She'd wait and trust in the Universe.

So she wouldn't whine or try to seduce Fen any further. The orgasmic kiss in the garage had taught her that there was no need. *That* kiss had told her how much Fen loved her back in a hot, uncontrolled, carnal, and vulnerable way. And one day they would be together. When or how didn't matter. They would. Maybe it would take a year. Maybe five, or ten, or even twenty, but one day, it would happen. So she could wait.

But for now, she needed to learn to ride a bike.

"Freddy. Freddy, dear!" Fen called to her younger son.

A door opened and shut on the second storey, and footsteps thumped down the stairs.

"You've never ridden a bike?" Freddy looked sceptical as he walked her back to the garage and pulled out his and Nathan's.

"I can drive any kind of vehicle up to and including an RV and horse truck," Susie said, "but nope, not a bike."

"Not even once, never sat on one?" He put Nathan's saddle down five inches.

"No. I went from scuffing along on my behind in the dirt to sitting on the back of a horse." She supposed it was hard to believe, coming as she did from the land where every kid was supposed to be given bikes. "Backwoods Oregon roads aren't really suited to little kid's bikes. And I didn't live in suburbia. Our place was on a dirt road, halfway up a mountain."

"No worries, then." Freddy shrugged. "You'll soon pick it up. The key is to keep moving forward. If you go too slow and stop pedalling without putting your foot down on the road, you'll fall over. It's simple."

Susie smiled. When she was fourteen, she'd had the same

catchphrase when talking to adults. In reality, she'd worried all the time. She remembered the very first time Kate and Catriona had been to her dad's house, when he'd told them Susie would look after all their animals rescued from the fire. She'd tried to appear competent and okay about it. But they weren't to know that ten minutes earlier, she'd been weeping incoherently in her room and was barely able to think straight. Looking after the Sinclairs' animals, along with her own two horses, had helped her through those months. Then when Cat's grandparents had moved in and taken back the care of the animals, Susie's grief had re-erupted. Everything got too much, and things had unravelled further.

But now, in the September dusk, she was going to concentrate on the present, keep moving forward, learn this thing. How hard could it be?

"We'll go around the corner to start with. It's a cul-de-sac."

Susie wrinkled her nose. "What?"

"A road with no exit. It'll be quieter, without any cars hurtling through it."

"Oh, a dead-end street."

"That's right." Freddy lowered his own saddle by several inches, as he was already taller than her. "We'll just take my bike to start with, and I'll run alongside you. You're such a little squit, Nate's bike will be way too big for you. You should be able to comfortably sit on the saddle with your toes touching the ground on either side."

They walked the bike fifty yards around the corner of the street into a very quiet road with no traffic, then he handed the bike over to her.

"Climb aboard, miss."

She looked at him, and they exchanged grins. "Well, here goes!"

"Right, now press down hard and keep pedalling!"

And she set off, wobbling crazily across the centre of the road for all of four yards before she fell off.

"You have to steer as well," he said and helped her up.

"Sure. Steering. Got it." She guessed there were some things her IQ of 160 didn't help with.

"Try again. And this time, push off firmly with your right foot, and when you start to move forward, keep pedalling and look straight ahead."

"Okay." She tried but soon wobbled to a halt again.

"Shit. It's harder than it looks."

"Not bad. Keep going, You'll soon get the hang of it," he said as he ran alongside her, keeping a safe distance. "Yes, better."

When they returned, half an hour later, Fen came outside to meet them. "It's getting dark. Freddy, you should have given Susie your cycle helmet," she said and frowned.

"Next time, okay?" He gestured toward Susie. "Aren't you going to congratulate me on getting her going? She pedalled all the way down the avenue and back without falling over. Not bad for a kid of five."

Susie hit him on his arm, hard. "Lay off. It's way harder than it looks. But yeah, you're a good teacher." She limped where her knee had hit the tarmac. It wasn't anything, but a little trickle of blood had come through one of the slashes in her jeans.

Fen looked at it though as if she'd severed an artery. "You're hurt. It needs washing. Let me—"

"No, it's nothing but an owie. I'll sort it." Feeling like the queen of the pedals, Susie stopped Fen before she could go any further. No physical contact, no nestling up in the bathroom and stripping off her jeans so Fen could bathe her wounds. She could imagine where it might lead. Fenella had set the rules of the game, but Susie didn't think she had any hope of following them.

Freddy put the bikes back into the garage and locked it up before they went inside together.

"You want another lesson tomorrow morning?" Freddy asked.

"Yes, please!" It had been fun, and tomorrow, she'd be better and not fall off so many times. She'd also seen the look on Fen's face as she'd thought the scratch was worse than it was. The woman was hers, totally hers. And it felt wonderful. And while Susie might not have won the battle today, she knew her campaign had only just begun. She was not only going to improve her cycling skills, but also her skills at Fenella-hunting.

Chapter Sixteen

On Saturday morning, Susie sat down with Fen at the kitchen table. They were about to write a list for Sunday's lunch party on a torn-off back section of an envelope. She liked Fen's odd little traits of frugality, like cutting the backs of used envelopes and hanging them up from a clip to use as note paper. The saved envelopes reminded Susie of Abbie's mother, Deirdre, who had lived in their holiday rental for twelve months and was now her step-granny. Homesickness for Oregon still lurked, but she would die rather than admit it.

Fen shook her head. "No, I've been rethinking this. You can't cook tomorrow's lunch for all eight of us. It was thoughtless of me to suggest it, especially when this is your last weekend. You have to pack up your clothes and books to move down to the college early on Monday."

"But I want to cook lunch," Susie said. "You've looked after me so great, and this is one thing I can do to say thanks. Besides, I enjoy it. Please…"

"Well, if you insist. But what do you have in mind? Something else Mexican?"

"No, I thought more Cajun, if that's okay. Would your boys eat shrimp jambalaya? And would your friends like it? Could they cope with heat?"

"If you cooked it, I'm sure they would. But over here, shrimps are tiny. When you shop, you need to ask for king prawns, or even better, langoustines. But I don't know if Bel and Bryony are vegetarian."

"Not a problem. All of Abbie's family are too. I've got a few recipes good for this time of year. I could even do a vegan enchilada, with summer squash sauce and black beans." Susie began to scribble a list of ingredients. "You said you'd take me to the supermarket, so why not come inside with me?"

Fenella pulled a wry face. "I'll tell you when we get there."

"Tell me now," Susie said, but Fen wouldn't say anymore. When she was done with the list, Fen checked it over and crossed off a few things already in the pantry and then wrote down a few more items. Susie wished her handwriting was as elegant. She'd save the list in her growing collection of Fen-themed objects of veneration. "What are those things for?"

"You'll need a few staples to keep in your college room. I expect there'll be a fridge in a kitchen on your floor. You know, coffee, tea, sugar, milk, those sorts of things. I'll organise you a starter box. Maybe throw in some chocolate biscuits—cookies to you—so you can entertain your new college friends."

"Thanks. I hadn't thought of that."

"I'll drive you to town until your cycling skills improve enough to manage a bike with a heavily laden basket. You don't want to be heaving food bags on and off the bus or walking a mile with a backpack either."

"Freddy and I are having another lesson later."

"I know. But you must wear a cycling helmet at all times from now on. How's the knee?"

"Oh fine," Susie said. The scrape was actually worse than she'd thought. It was her own fault for wearing those ripped jeans Fenella had liked so much. She wasn't that bothered though; they'd done the trick. But Fenella acting so like a caring mom made Susie almost weepy for quite different reasons. She still missed her mom so much, and she would've loved being here, seeing her crazy daughter start life as an Oxford student. It would have cracked her up.

As it was, she could only send daily reports back home through Instagram videos to her dad and Abbie to show them what it was like here in Oxford. She'd talked to her dad twice in the last week too. Maybe she could get Fenella to film her as she went through the portals of St Hilary's for the first time as a proper student on Monday morning. She also wanted to film Fenella for fantasy purposes when she was in her little dorm room and to show her off to everyone in the States.

The front doorbell rang. Fenella rose from the table. "This will be someone from the bike shop. I asked them to pick up Charlotte. I'll attend to it, then let's go shopping."

Susie surreptitiously raided the first-aid tin above the kitchen sink and extracted two large Band-Aids. She was finding her way around Fenella's house and feeling quite at home. Too much at home for her own good, probably.

Fenella returned after ten minutes, wiping grime and cobwebs off her hands. "They've taken Charlotte away for servicing, and she will be back in a week, so you have seven days to perfect your cycling skills. I can't let you loose on the roads until I'm completely satisfied that you're safe.

Susie gave a mock salute. "Ye, ma'am." With luck, her bashed-up leg would be good by then. It didn't look too brilliant now though, so she'd better avoid shorts around Fenella.

When Fenella was finally ready to leave, looking as chic as ever, Susie met her by the door, dressed in her loosest pants and a sweatshirt from UC Davis. Susie carried a few of Fenella's recycled shopping bags to the car and sniffed the air as Fenella bent to uncouple the electric charger. "It's not J'adore."

"No, it isn't. Hold this and wind it back up."

"What is it?" She took the long charging cable and wound it neatly back up to hang by the garage door.

"Only something I was given for Christmas. By Jo Malone, I believe."

"It suits you. For mornings, anyhow."

"Hmm. You have a good nose, but why do perfumes interest you so much?"

"My mom was a great one for different scents and perfumes. She taught me about them when I was young."

"What were her favourites?"

"Super old stuff. Madame Rochas, Givenchy, and Chanel No. 5, of course."

Fenella looked thoughtful. "Vintage. Very sensible. Very assured. I think I would have liked your mother."

"Of course you would, and she'd have loved you."

"I don't think so! If she had any sense, she'd have warned you off me from the beginning. Any sensible mother would."

"No she wouldn't," Susie said, hating how Fenella sometimes seemed to think so little of herself. "She'd have been in awe, as I am."

"Stop it. Do you have the list?"

"Yep."

"Well, let's go then."

When they pulled into the supermarket parking lot, Fenella put on a pair of shades, even though the day was dull. "Well, go on in. Take my credit card and the bags and see how you find your way around a British food store."

"I've been in a 'food store' before," Susie said. "We even have them in Oregon. We don't go out and shoot racoons for our dinner. But you must tell me why you won't come in. Did the police arrest you for shoplifting the last time you came here?"

Fenella smiled a wonderful, rare, but curving smile that sent Susie's libido soaring.

"No, but it was almost as mortifying. You remember the first day you and I met?"

"Natch. How could I ever forget?" Though she wished she could forget how she'd drooled all over Fenella's lovely suit. "I still dream about how wonderful that first encounter was."

"Stop talking drivel. It wasn't wonderful at all. But somehow, it did upset my sang-froid. Not your fault, but you somehow managed to overstimulate parts of me that didn't need stimulating. My equilibrium went AWOL, and I left my brains in the restaurant. When I returned to Oxford, I realised I hadn't put in my usual grocery online order, so I stopped off here to stock up. But my head was in such a muddle, I wasn't thinking straight. I ended up only buying four bottles of gin and a load of junk food."

Susie raised her eyebrows. "And walked out without paying? Wicked woman! I expect it was my fault. Maybe we're a bad influence on each other."

"Of course I paid. But a zealous woman in a pink cardigan behind me in the line at the till, looked at my purchases and deduced, quite correctly, that I was a terrible mother and a hopeless drunk. She followed me outside to the car and pressed a leaflet into my hand, preaching the dangers of alcoholism and urging me to go to a meeting at her church."

Susie couldn't help laughing. "That's hilarious. People say those sorts of things to me all the time. Someone near Kate's house in Pasadena called out the Neighbourhood Watch about me once. Apparently, they'd seen an 'undesirable element' lurking near the property."

Fenella laughed too. "Why doesn't that surprise me?" she said. "But this wasn't funny at all. The woman hit a raw nerve. I knew I'd been drinking too much, and I felt so humiliated. I haven't touched a drop since. The gin has stayed firmly in the cupboard since you've been on the scene."

"So her intervention worked! You're now in recovery. What a shame though. I'd like to be with you after you've had a few too many."

"I bet you would," Fenella muttered, "but that's not going to happen. I'm only reformed in the booze department though. In other areas, I'm still more trouble than you know."

Susie frowned. "Anyhow, do you really think the same pink jacket woman's going to be here again? I could go on ahead and warn you if there's someone inside the store who looks like her. I never took you for a scaredy cat, Fen."

Fenella frowned and tossed her wonderful dark copper curls. "Go on then. She'd be sixtyish, on the heavy side, with a tight blond bubble perm. She might be lurking near the beers, wine, and spirits hoping to catch more sinners."

Susie jumped out of the car. "I'm onto it. Wait here, and I'll be back in a minute." She strode into the store and canvassed each of the long aisles. She couldn't see anyone wearing pink, nor anyone else who matched Fen's description. She returned to the car. "Nope, there's no one to worry about in there. It's safe. I think you should come in with me, if only to lay the ghost. If you get bored, you can always come back and read your Kindle."

Fenella narrowed her eyes but slowly got out of the car, and they collected a shopping cart. Fenella's entrance turned heads; she was so stylish, with striking good looks and an unconsciously haughty way of striding down the aisles, which Susie adored.

"I think we also need to add something to drink to put into your starter box for college. How about some good sherry? Freshers always had sherry parties when I was a student."

Susie nearly choked. "Sherry? It sounds like something out of a P.G. Wodehouse book. Besides, I can't drink. I'm underage. I am only twenty, Fenny." She batted her eyelashes.

Fenella's eyes bore into her. "So you've told me. You don't need to remind me of that fact again, you little vixen." She smiled. "But you're wrong. Over here in England, whether it's wise or not, everyone's considered an adult at eighteen. So you can legally drink. But don't do as I did and overdo it. And trust me on the sherry. It'll stand you in good stead. Oxford has some funny little ways. When we get home, I'll dig you out a set of Waterford crystal glasses my aunt Mildred gave me as a wedding present. They're still in the original box."

When Fenella added a litre-sized bottle of dry sherry, Susie recognised it as something used in Cajan cooking. Fenella stuck four bottles of Côtes de Rhone in as well. She clearly still liked thinking about liquor and stocking up on it, even if she had quit. Susie took charge of steering the cart, and they made it out of the supermarket without being accosted.

Susie felt brave enough to tease Fenella a little. "Are you okay? Relaxed now? Not too scared to go into a food store anymore?"

Fenella bared her teeth and pretended to growl like a wolf. They parked their cart behind the car, and Fenella pressed a button on her key fob to open the trunk.

"Dear, oh dear! At it again, lovey? I see you haven't taken any of my advice. Still with the drink problem? And here now with your daughter as well? Poor, poor child. What sort of example are you setting her?"

Susie guessed immediately who the voice of doom, in the shape of a strong rural Oxfordshire accent, belonged to. She turned in a flash, feeling Fenella shrink with shame behind her, and a protective fury flared up inside her. Fenella was nobody's lovey but hers. She stepped forward to stand between them. "Go away, you horrible woman. There's no problem here. And I'm not her daughter, I'm her girlfriend. Her *lesbian* girlfriend, and I won't let you talk to her like this!"

"Susannah, please!" Fenella clasped Susie's elbow. She no longer sounded like a wolf, more like a frightened mother rabbit.

But instead of restraining her, it only emboldened Susie further. She grabbed Fenella's hand and raised it to her lips. She kissed Fenella's palm possessively and added a little lick for good measure.

Their assailant stepped back quickly, so shocked she seemed to have lost her previous confidence. "Well! Sorry, but I was only trying to help," she said in a strangled voice and blushed under her permed curls.

"We don't need any help, thanks. We're perfectly fine. Goodbye!"

The woman backed off and trotted hastily away into the store. It was a triumph! But then Susie realised what she'd done. Fenella would be furious, and rightly so. "Me and my big mouth. I'm so sorry!"

Fenella leaned back against her car and muttered between gritted teeth, "Do you realise you've outed me now to all the evangelical alliance born-againers in Oxford?"

"Sorry, Fen. Are you very upset?" Susie sighed. "I didn't like the way she spoke to you and just wanted to help. It came out all wrong."

"No, it didn't." Fenella's eyes softened, and she smiled. "It came out exactly right. And it was something she and I both needed to hear. We're probably equally homophobic."

"So you're saying I truly *am* your lesbian girlfriend? You're owning up to it?"

"I suppose I might be, you little minx. I need to stop hating myself. But I would still consign you to the subjunctive. We might, *might*, one day be lesbian lovers. But it will be a long time in the future, in the narrow space between you growing up and me falling into decrepitude. And neither is about to happen soon."

They emptied the cart, careful not to squash the soft shrimp and all the fruit or break any bottles.

Susie wanted to push the envelope, to turn the subjunctive into the definitive. "That means we have to work through some sort of courtly love scenario, right? Like those knights in medieval times, who wore their ladies' scarves when they went out jousting but were never allowed to kiss them?"

Fenella pushed the last of their bags into the trunk. "I suppose so. Yes." She gave Susie a small grin. "Are you going to be my little Sir Galahad?"

"More like your Lancelot to Queen Guinevere," Susie said and wiggled her eyebrows. "You'll have to give me a pair of your panties to wear, doused in your favourite perfume."

Fenella arched her eyebrow. "You'd try the patience of a saint. I suppose I might find you an old handkerchief. Take the trolley back."

"Sure. We call them carts though. British English is my second language remember."

Fenella looked close to doing something up close and personal but merely pointed to the trolley racks. Susie returned the cart, feeling ace. She was definitely going to get her hands on one of Fenella's retro, lace-trimmed handkerchiefs and tuck it deep inside her bra, next to her heart. That would have to do until she could get her hands on Fenella instead.

Chapter Seventeen

Nate astonished them all on Sunday morning by saying he wanted to go to church. Fenella wasn't sure how to respond, but she couldn't think of any reason to object. "Very nice, darling. Which church are you thinking of?"

"St Helen's, obviously" said Freddy. "It's where Alice Markham's dad is the vicar."

"Is that true, Nate?"

He shrugged, his face flushed fire-engine red, and gave Freddy a death stare.

Fenella patted his hand. "Well, whatever the reason, I think it's a perfectly fine idea. You can say a prayer for us all while you're there. Has Alice invited you?"

"Yeah. And I've got to get there early. She wants to show me the bellringers up in the tower. She thinks I might want to learn how to do it with her."

"That's good," Fenella said. "Their bells are some of the best in the city. It would be quite an honour to be a campanologist there."

"The term's a new one on me," said Susie, peeling king prawns by the sink in prep for her Jambalaya dish. "I don't think I've ever heard live bells being rung in churches, only through tinny electronic loudspeakers. You'll have to tell me how they work, Nate."

But he clearly wasn't about to encourage any more family interest in his potential new venture and said he had to leave straight away. Fenella went to the front door with him and said, "Don't worry about Freddy's nonsense. He's probably a bit jealous you're friends with such a nice girl. You go and enjoy the church service, and here, put this in the collection for me." She pressed a five-pound note into his hand. "But I have some friends coming for lunch, and Susie's cooking special dishes for us all, so make sure you're back by one thirty."

"Thanks, Ma. Okay. Love ya lots."

"Ditto." She pressed the button in the hall to open the electric garage door for him, and he grabbed his bike and cycled away down the street. She loved him so much it almost hurt.

She returned to the kitchen. She and Susie had fought over whether Susie would prepare the entire meal, including dessert, but Fenella had pulled rank and insisted she take care of it. Prepping it was no big deal, as Susie would say. She'd already made a September version of summer pudding, which was defrosting nicely in the fridge, plus she'd prepared two mounds of soft damsons, pears, and stewed quinces, which she would serve with some cinnamon-dusted cream or soya cream. She also had a modest cheese board, with crackers, fresh figs, and a large bunch of black grapes.

Susie had inherited a nose for perfume from her mother, while Fenella had been trained in the basics of French cooking from her maman, a young patisserie chef who had come across the channel in the early 1970s to work in a Michelin-starred restaurant and met her husband one night when he ventured backstage to congratulate her on the strawberry tarts.

Maman had died far too young, but Fenella still had her recipe books and remembered more skills than she normally ever used in her own kitchen. Her husbands had somehow managed to drive away her joy of cooking. They were both always late for meals, often drunk, and generally unappreciative. But she was rediscovering joy in feeding Susie and the boys. Even Freddy was trying out a few more vegetables.

"Tell me about your lunch guests," said Susie, who had moved from deveining langoustines to chopping up onions and red peppers.

She was wrapped up once more in Fenella's cambric chef's apron and looked edible herself. Fenella concentrated on answering her question. "Naimh and Olivia. Olivia Massie runs a publishing house called Barnstorm Books. She and I met in our twenties when we were both editors in the same big publishing company, which doesn't exist anymore. It was taken over, like so many of the traditional firms, having succumbed to the digital revolution. They weren't helped either by the rise of all those amateur independents flooding the market with substandard tosh."

Susie protested. "Ouch! Don't knock digital. I got through all my coursework by reading online, and I devoured dozens of young adult lesbian novels I'd never have found otherwise. Isn't *Perceptions* online now anyway?"

Fenella had the grace to blush. "Yes, but I've had to hand it over to a digital company to do it, and that doubled our operating costs."

"But increased your readership by thousands, no doubt."

Fenella wondered how much Susie had learned from reading all those lesfic romances, and whether she'd practised any of the techniques outlined in them. She probably knew a lot more about making love successfully to a woman than Fenella did, though that wasn't a high bar to reach. "Olivia is very bright, very slick, and smart, but she's also funny, kind, and since she's been married has taken to horse riding of all things."

"Horses? What did she ride before? Motorbikes?"

"Haha. Very funny. But you'll probably immediately hit it off with them if they find out you like horses too. Before they were married, Niamh insisted on bringing her own horse across from Ireland. I think they stable them somewhere in North London and ride together on Hampstead Heath."

"So they're officially married?"

Fenella heard the excitement in Susie's voice. "Yes, still newlyweds. Their wedding was about a year ago."

"You never told me you had all these lesbian mates, Fen!"

Fenella looked around to see if Freddy was listening, but thankfully he'd disappeared back upstairs. "Well, I do. Not that many, but Olivia and Niamh are definitely on my list of favourite people. I have told Olivia a little bit about you, and she wants to meet you."

"Ah, now I get it," Susie said and grinned. "You asked them down to come look me over and advise you on how to get me out of your hair."

"No, not true at all."

"Don't fib, Fenny."

Susie looked her in the eye, sounding as stern as the little schoolteacher she was. Fenella's face heated up. She couldn't deny it a second time. "Well, maybe it was a bad idea I had at first. But now I know they could be valuable friends for you, to warn you off *me*. I'm really not anyone's best idea for a girlfriend."

"Talking crap again," said Susie. "But I like the way you're bringing along reinforcements. I must've really rattled your cage. Good."

Fenella raised her eyebrows. "Rattled my cage? Darling, you've sprung the locks across the whole damn zoo. I thought we've already established that."

Susie grinned. "Now tell me about the other people who are coming. Did you say one of them is a doctor?"

Fenella sighed. Olivia had texted her to let her know that Bel and Bryony would love to come, had told her they were vegan, and sent them Fenella's address. So now there was no getting out of a new encounter with the Wicked Witch of the West. Susie didn't need to know anything about their past history, of course. "Yes, I believe they both have doctorates actually, but Bryony is a medical doctor, a surgeon. Bel Bridgford is an eminent anthropologist who knows more about the effects of climate change on marginal people than anyone else and has written many books on the subject. I believe Bryony works in an Oxford hospital as a surgical registrar."

"And their age-gap?"

"Ooh, I couldn't say. But Bel came up to Somerville College four years before me. Then she transferred to Cambridge to complete her doctorate."

Susie's eyes twinkled. "And their age-gap?"

"Maybe twenty, twenty-five years. I'm not sure."

Susie pumped her fist. "Yes!"

Then she wriggled her behind, and Fenella was sorely tempted to wallop it.

Susie skipped sideways and grinned. "I don't want your friends thinking I'm here to ruin your life. Or poison you all. So I'd better concentrate on cooking. Do you have a heavy-bottomed pan I can use?"

Fenella pulled out one of her favourite Le Creuset wide pans, which could go either on the stove top or into the oven, and Susie seemed happy. The jambalaya started to bubble gently as the flavours melted together, and spicy aromas filled the kitchen.

As sweetcorn was in season, Fenella had thought eight plump yellow cobs would make another good side, along with a tomato salsa and some deep-fried onion rings. It wouldn't be your typical British Sunday lunch, but a transatlantic meeting of recipes. A smaller dish of black bean and squash enchiladas with vegan cheese was bubbling away in the bottom oven.

Freddy bounced downstairs at eleven. "Are we going out for another bike-riding lesson or what?"

"Can I go?" Susie looked at Fenella and started to untie her chef's apron. "For half an hour?"

"Of course. I'm not in charge of you." Fenella watched the two youngsters go off together, happily bickering about nothing, and her heart ached as she watched them. With only six years between them, they could have been brother and sister. What the hell was she thinking, even imagining it could ever be appropriate to be fantasizing about sex with Susie? This was her private purgatory, making her wish she'd accompanied Nathan to church to pray for deliverance from it.

But instead, she concentrated on tidying the house, prepping a tray of alcohol-free, delicious drinks, because at least two of her guests would be driving. She tested her autumn puddings. Those wouldn't let her down. They were no longer frozen and thankfully, not yet mushy. She only hoped she could emulate them and exhibit the same level of crispness.

Susie and Freddy, followed through the door by a very happy looking Nate, returned triumphant soon after one. Susie no longer limped quite so badly as she had before. Fenella had suspected Friday night's prang on the bike had hurt her really quite badly, but she hadn't challenged her. She didn't trust herself with Susie's naked leg needing some close personal attention. This cycling lesson, though, had clearly gone very well.

"I can do it now!" Susie sing-songed.

"She can too," Freddy said. "If I can borrow Nate's wheels, I'll go out with her again when your old lady friends have gone home. We can ride together later this afternoon."

Susie looked happy at the thought, but Fenella had no time to correct Freddy's assumption that four elderly spinsters were about to visit before the doorbell chimed yet again. Olivia and Niamh stood on the doorstep, bearing a large bouquet of flowers and a box of Belgian chocolates. Olivia looked positively glowing, and Niamh, wearing some sort of green-blue caftan, floated in like an Irish princess. They both kissed her warmly.

Fenella introduced them to her two sons, poured them both a glass of elderflower champagne, and took them to the dining room while Susie put the finishing touches to the main course. She'd changed into a simple black top and loose slacks; gamine was the word that came to Fenella's mind. But Susie seemed suddenly shy and reluctant to leave her position by the cooker.

When the doorbell went again, Fenella swallowed her nerves and went to welcome Bel and Bryony. Bel was now one of the most high-profile gay women in London and, despite the twenty-five years since Fenella had seen her and all Fenella's outward confidence and panache, she suspected Bel would still have the power to terrify her.

Chapter Eighteen

Susie heard the doorbell ring from the kitchen and had a mini attack of nerves. When Fenella had outlined their guest list, she'd secretly googled both Olivia and Bel Bridgford, and the latter's cv especially had left her in awe. The woman had worked with remote communities all over the world and in the most extreme places. Her first wife had been an eminent Italian-Ethiopian filmmaker who'd been murdered by criminal people traffickers, and Bel now worked for the United Nations, campaigning and influencing politicians across the world.

Susie felt seriously outclassed. Her cousin's warning, not to upset or embarrass Fenella at all costs, had been branded onto her brain. She tested the heat within the jambalaya and stirred the pot with unnecessary vigour, wanting to stay in the kitchen for the entire meal.

But no such luck.

Fenella came to the kitchen door and beckoned her through. "Susie! Come on out and meet everyone."

Susie wiped her hands on her apron before she removed it and took a deep breath. Oh well, better face them all. She left the kitchen, trying not to do anything to draw attention to herself, but was immediately drawn firmly into an embarrassingly firm group hug. Four good-looking gay women surrounded her and squeezed the life out of her. That was the last thing she'd expected from a group of British strangers. What the heck had Fenella told them about her? The oldest of the group, an astoundingly charismatic woman with beautiful grey eyes, cupped her face and kissed it firmly. Susie's cheek burned with the intensity of it.

"So this is our little classicist from California?" asked Bel, examining her from head to toe.

Susie was worried she was being made fun of, but Bel's eyes were kind, even if there was a hint of melancholy behind them. The legendary Bel Bridgford introduced her to Dr Bryony, her much younger wife. A few inches taller than Isabel, she shook her short corn-coloured locks from her eyes, which were calm and friendly.

"It's lovely to meet you, Susie," Bryony said. "You've come a very long way to study in rainy old England. How did that happen?"

"I came to Oxford because it's the best place to study Latin," Susie said. "And I'm crazy about the Romans for some reason. I've invaded Fenella's life, but she's been so kind. I can't thank her enough. She's even given me her bike to ride."

For some reason, they all giggled.

"Then you have nothing further to worry about," said Olivia. "Fenella's bike knows its way around Oxford better than any other means of transport."

Susie didn't really understand but let it go. She looked back at Fenella. "Maybe we should serve the food soon," she whispered." I don't want it to cook too long and spoil."

"Of course, can we all go straight to the table and tuck in?" Fenella seated everyone around the long table in her dining room. Susie helped her serve the lunch, bringing dish after steaming dish to the table.

"Susie has kindly offered to cook for us today, and you know how lazy I am, Olivia. I simply let her get on with it."

"You don't cook often, Mum, but when you do, it's always great," said Nate, loyally.

"I did my best," said Susie. "I hope it's not too hot for you. My mom used to cook these dishes. She came from the South, originally. Louisiana."

Fenella passed around some large serving spoons and little corncob forks, which were typical of those little tools that had sat in the kitchen drawer all year, only to be used every now and then. Everyone speared a sweetcorn cob, helped themselves to generous portions of jambalaya and enchiladas and dug in.

"Where does the word jambalaya come from?" asked Niamh, turning to Susie, who guessed she was being encouraged to talk.

"I think it's Creole patois, but it means more or less what it says," said Susie. "You know, everything jumbled up together. A one-pot meal that's a mixture of French, African, and American cooking using the local seafood which people had available." It was a good word to describe herself, she decided, as she sat there, barely able to keep her hands off Fenella, even though her nerves jangled in front of all these striking women. Talk about mixed emotions and overheated hot spice. Seeing the other couples so happy together didn't help. Niamh was especially outrageous, fondling Olivia's knee under the table. The boys down the other end of the table didn't notice, but she thought Fenella did.

To Susie's relief though, the main course menu was a huge success, and there were soon clean plates across the table.

"Fantastic! Susie, you're a great chef. Can you come back to London with us and cook for us? We can bribe you with horse-riding on Hampstead Heath." Olivia's eyes crinkled with pleasure as she laid down her cutlery and sat back from the table with a sigh.

"I'd love to, but I start being a student tomorrow," said Susie. "I mean, I did begin a degree in the States, but then I transferred here to study Classical Latin and Greek. I'm pretty up on Latin, but Greek is going to be a struggle. Fenny says I'll have no more time for gallivanting."

"Gallivanting?" Olivia asked and chuckled.

"It's one of Susie's new favourite words," said Fenella. "I keep telling her how hard the work will be, but she doesn't believe me."

"Rightly so," said Olivia. "I wasted too much of my Oxford time by studying and not partying enough. Though I think you did better, Fen. I remember you told me plenty of scandalous stories about your years here. Weren't you dating nine men all at the same time in your final year?"

"Shh!" Fenella clearly didn't want such talk in front of her sons.

"In those days, we all overdid it rather—the social activities, I mean," said Bel. "The trick is to get the balance right. I was very sensible. I always made a point of getting to bed by three. But I confess it wasn't always my own bed."

This was clearly a joke she'd made many times before, and everyone except Fenella laughed. Susie caught Fen's glance across the table towards Bel.

"I'm going out to the kitchen to bring in my autumn puddings," Fen said, turning the conversation rather deftly away from those memories by announcing the second course.

When they arrived, they oozed with golden yumminess, and everyone around the table concentrated on devouring them. Talk of Oxford back before the millennium was then forgotten.

"So tell me about life in California, Susie," Olivia said. "Did you lie on the beach every day?"

"Nah, never. I'm from the woods and hills of Oregon, a thousand miles north of L.A. I spent much of my childhood with horses. But Fen told me you have horses in London? How does that work for you?"

Olivia and Niamh launched into horse talk, showing her gallery shots of their animals from their phones. Susie relaxed. She could discuss horseback-riding and her animals all day, something she unexpectedly had in common with them. "I had to send my horses away when I went off to college, but they're in a great place with a new owner."

"Seriously, you must come to Hampstead when you get the chance, and we'll take you riding on the Heath," said Niamh.

Susie glanced away briefly. "I've only ever ridden western style. I'll probably fall off without a big pommel in front of me."

"Like you did on the bike," said Freddy and laughed.

"No, you won't." Niamh smiled. "It's a question of confidence and balance. And I can see you've plenty of both."

If you only knew.

Chapter Nineteen

Knowing nothing about horses apart from the old equestrian statues of Roman emperors, Fenella was content to let her guests chat amongst themselves. The boys left the table, as usual, to return to their mystery alternative universe upstairs, and she retreated to the kitchen to make coffee. When it had brewed, she carried the tray into the garden room and suggested they all go outside to enjoy the last sunshine of the final September weekend. She had something to show them.

The old, red-bricked villa, an archetypal, double-fronted Oxford house, stood in front of a long garden, where the trees were now beginning to turn a fragile golden brown, and it was warm enough to take a short, guided tour.

"Would I be terribly rude if I lay down on your gorgeous sofa in the lounge for an hour instead and caught up with some sleep?" Bryony asked. "I'm on nights in A&E for the next month, and Saturday nights are always manic. I need to be back there by seven for another long shift, and I haven't been to bed yet today."

"Of course not, you poor darling," said Fenella. "Bel shouldn't have brought you. I wouldn't have expected you here if I'd known." She led Bryony into the lounge and drew the curtains. Bryony lay on the sofa, and Fenella drew the soft velour blanket up over her.

"This is wonderful. Now go back to the others." Bryony sighed deeply. "But I wanted to tell you that I love your houseguest. She's a darling. You should take the plunge and catch her while you can."

Bryony closed her eyes, and Fenella guessed she'd be asleep in minutes. She left the room and closed the door quietly. Now Bel would be alone, so if she wanted to say anything to Fenella about their previous brief encounter, it would be a good time. But Bel seemed not to remember her from those days long ago, and Fenella was determined to be grateful for such a mercy.

She'd been a physical and emotional mess at eighteen and hoped she was unrecognisable now as the fumbling idiot who'd made such a fool of herself. She turned her attention to giving her guests a tour of the back garden. Susie hadn't yet ventured beyond the back door into the long garden, and Fenella was amused at how surprised Susie was by the collection of statuary and how taken she was with the tall trees. Fenella was pleased to show them off. Her ownership of the three ancient pieces of genuine broken Graeco-Roman stone carvings had been made possible by Trevor's deep pockets, and his subsequent lack of interest in claiming them after their divorce.

Her favourite was of a girl carrying a waterpot, her second was a carved, column fragment, and the last was a late Romano-British cast of a young boy, whose weathered face rather resembled Freddy's. They lined a winding path through the shrubs and trees between various other, more modest little statues and reproductions she'd picked up over the years. The result was effective and unusual. Fenella was certainly no gardener, but she liked her little sculpture park.

While her guests carried their coffees to the stone benches at the end, she fetched cushions to soften the seating. Olivia and Bel both drew Susie to one side and immediately began to interview her in greater depth, perhaps in what they thought was a gentle, subtle way. But Fenella knew Susie well enough to know she'd be way ahead of the pair and know quite well what they were doing.

Fenella decided to chat to Niamh, whom she didn't know well yet at all. They sat some way apart from the others and fell into easy conversation. Niamh was heavily into preparing for a Viva exam for a PhD in Irish women painters she was close to completing, through the University of Dublin. Niamh was also a direct descendent of Grace O'Malley, the sixteenth century Irish pirate queen, and she had the looks and wild beauty to match. Hearing her soft Irish accent made Fenella feel uptight, conventional, and stiff in comparison. But her smile was warm and her concern for Fenella's romantic conundrum genuine. Olivia must have filled her in with all the details.

"Livie's told me something of your worries," said Niamh. "I can surely see the attraction. Susie's a force of nature, and such a pretty lass."

Fenella glanced across at Susie. Attraction was hardly a strong enough word. She was mad about the girl, who was so much more than pretty. "She's bright as a button as well, too bright for me to cope with, and scarily direct. I just don't see what I can offer her, why she even likes me. She's highly gifted as well. But intellect and emotional maturity don't often sit easily together. I have no idea why she's attracted to me though."

"Don't you?" Niamh ran her fingers through her untamed hair and twisted it into a rough bun behind her neck. "Might it not be natural good taste?"

"No," Fenella said and straightened a little on her cushion. "She lost her mother to cancer in her early teens and is still scarred by it. I think it's a mother she needs, not a seductress."

"Maybe, maybe not. Love is love, and I believe, given half a chance, it will always find its way through the rocks. I fell for Olivia the day I went to her office in search of a publisher for my late mother's manuscript. And there were big complications. Her sister had also died of cancer, and the whole family was still recovering. We now share a house with her five nieces and nephews and their father, a very head-in-the-air marine biologist."

Fenella gave a little shudder. Coping with two children was challenging enough, but five? "Was it easy, joining them all?"

"Not at first. The elder of the daughters truly hated me. But it's all forgotten now. Our age-gap simply adds an extra dimension. Our blended family straddles three decades, and I can sometimes understand the young ones' point of view better than Livie can. But she's also very patient with me, when I get especially pig-headed and stupid about things. We simply all love each other. That's the secret ingredient."

Niamh almost made Fenella believe in a similar outcome for Susie and her. But she couldn't see it happening. Susie was too young, too brilliant, too fragile. "You're at least five years older than Susie though. She's barely out of her teens and can't even drink alcohol legally in America. I'm the opposite of being the right partner for her."

"Not from where I sit. Livie says that you're the most brilliant woman she knows—after Bel, of course—and she knows everyone. And you've been through the mill of two divorces, you're raising two grand boys on your own, and you can't pretend you don't exude sex appeal in bucketsful."

"Niamh! That's outrageous! Of course I don't!" Fenella laughed at the total Irish blarney. She was far from a wonder woman.

Niamh's eyes twinkled as she wagged her finger. "Oh yes you do. And I speak as a connoisseur of female allure. Believe me, anyone, man or woman, would be proud to have you as their plus one anytime in any place. God, I'd fall for you myself if I hadn't married Olivia!"

Fenella didn't know what to say to that. "So, if you're right, what would you advise? Am I deluded or wicked, to cling on to a tiny glimmer of hope that it might one day work out?"

"You're neither of those things. If you and Susie love each other, I don't see any great obstacles. You can hold off for a while if it makes you feel any better. But I reckon she's tougher than you think. Okay, she's young, but time will cure that soon enough, won't it? If you want my advice, open your arms and let her in. Don't drive her away. Olivia let me in and look how that worked out. She saved me. I can't imagine any other life now other than being madly in love with her. She's the centre of my world."

The passion in Niamh's final words took Fenella aback. She could only nod in response. So what she felt about Susie wasn't an aberration? Other saner women could feel something similar.

"Shall we go in?" she asked when the afternoon grew colder as the damp rose. Fenella carried the coffee tray, Susie gathered up the cushions, and the others followed them back inside the house. Bel went through to the lounge and gently shook Bryony awake. "I'll drive us home, my darling," Fenella heard her say. "You can still snooze all the way back to the cottage." They lived twelve miles from Oxford, near to the A44 past Woodstock, and Bryony commuted back and forth to the hospital. Married bliss. Fenella was surprised to see how Bel had settled down into such mundane happiness. She couldn't believe such a thing would ever be possible for her.

"Unfortunately, we need to hit the road as well," said Olivia a few minutes later. "Traffic down the M40 into London on a late Sunday afternoon can be awful." She hugged Susie tightly, kissed her on the cheek, and whispered something Fenella couldn't hear.

Fenella wondered what their earnest conversation had really been all about. Then they all had a group hug, and their electric cars purred away down the avenue. The motivation for her invitation might have failed, but as an example of two successful gay age-gap marriages, the lunch had proved a shining success. The only trouble was it hadn't solved the problem. She was as much in love as ever, and judging from the way Susie kept eyeing her like fresh meat, her American houseguest had been even more aroused by the examples of lesbian happy endings she'd shown her.

Chapter Twenty

Susie insisted on stacking the dishwasher with all the lunch debris before picking up Freddy's cycle helmet and her jacket and heading for the door. She didn't want Fenella to think of her as a freeloader when it came to helping in the house, but Fenella seemed more concerned about where she and Freddy were off to.

"Don't you remember? We're going out for a proper bike ride, maybe as far as Headington," said Freddy.

"No, don't even think about it now," said Fenella. "It's too late. It will be dusk soon. Susie's next lesson can wait until when her own bike will be available. I must tell the shop to fit lights to it."

"Mum!" Freddy sounded annoyed.

But Susie wasn't too disappointed. She only had one more evening there with Fenella, and it was precious time she wanted to protect. "It's okay, Freddy. Your mom's being sensible. I know you've got homework prep for tomorrow, and I have three double lessons to plan for school, as well as getting ready to move down to the college."

Fenella looked at her and smiled. "Very sensible. Now come with me into the study, please, Susie. I want to talk about tomorrow."

Susie followed Fenella into her book room, where half of one wall was covered in ten years' worth of her monthly magazine. Susie wished there was time for her to start reading it. Every back issue on view would have an editorial article on its opening pages, and she wanted to read all of Fenella's work. It would be the best way to understand her and mine her brain.

When they were alone in the study, Fenella shut the door and leaned back against it. Susie guessed what was coming. "Look, I know you have to be away to work early tomorrow. I can Uber to St Hilary's. You don't have to worry about getting me there."

Fenella shook her head. "No, I'll take you and settle you in. Do you think I'd abandon you to some stranger in a stinky car? I've already told Greta that I won't be there before midday. No, what I want to talk about is something quite different. It's deeper, which is harder to explain." She pointed imperiously to her highbacked wing chair by the fireplace. "So bear with me. Sit down and hear me out."

Susie swallowed hard before she sat on Fenella's command and folded her hands. "Okay," she said and tried to fight the tension in her shoulders. "Listening."

Fenella paced back and forth. "Susie, my sweet… A new phase of your life begins tomorrow, and I wanted to say that you should embrace it with all you've got. Don't think of me, don't look back. Get in there and enjoy it to the full."

"That's what you're being so serious about?" Susie frowned. "How could I not enjoy it?"

"No, listen to me. You've been gifted with an amazingly quick brain and a photographic memory. You love to read, and you love languages. But you've been living dishonestly."

"No, I haven't!"

"I'm sorry, but, yes, you have. It's something I think you've been doing all your life, pretending to be much less complicated than you are."

"Huh?"

"There, it's a case in point. You know quite well what I mean, so don't pretend otherwise. Express yourself as you really want to. You don't have to dumb down your language and talk like a brainless teen anymore. No one here at Oxford will bully you because of your brainpower or your love of words."

Susie's thumbs pricked. Fenella had sussed out her little attempt at camouflage, and she wouldn't have to carefully edit the way she talked anymore. She sighed with profound relief but was ashamed she'd even tried to disguise herself in order to fit in with what she called human beans (after the Borrowers), and she was even more ashamed now to have put Fenella into that category. Fenella openly appreciated scholarship and the love of learning, and maybe the rest of them in St Hilary's and across the university would feel the same way. Could the immense loneliness of being Susannah Webster, the school principal's kid, weirdo nerd and brainbox, finally be a thing of the past? "How did you know I was dumbing down how I talk?"

"By listening to you for a few minutes. You said British English was your second language. But until now, you've been translating your thoughts again into kidspeak when it's obviously not your native language either. You can translate a page of Latin into perfect English, what we used to call Queen's English, but talk like a dumb high school student half the time. You're at least trilingual. And it's such a waste of effort. You say you love me—"

"But I do. You know I do."

"Then show me your real self. From now on, you have to be brave enough to share who you are, as I will have to learn to share as well. If this is going to work, then we need to be honest with each other."

Susie held her breath. Was Fenella actually saying their relationship was going further than her clunking around in armour, while her lady Fenella sat up on the battlements, far above her, out of reach?

"I want to stretch you as far as you can go," Fenella said. "I want to see your limits—if there are any. I think you have a genius inside you, but you've caged her for so long that she's in danger of becoming a shabby tiger."

"For tamed and shabby tigers, and dancing dogs and bears," Susie said, quoting the original poem.

Fenella looked astounded.

"Sorry, it was in an old book my mom had. I didn't know about dancing bears until I read the verse, and when it was explained to me, I couldn't stop crying about them."

Fenella smiled. "There, you've proved me right. You see, ideas and enormous thoughts bubble up all the time in that head of yours. There's no need to hide your love of scholarship here. But I never again want you to pretend to be less intelligent than you are, especially not with me. Now, there's something practical I can do to help you here. I'm going to talk to my friend Dr Stevie Pole in the Classics department and suggest she finds you a tutor who can keep up with you."

"Oh, Fen, no. Please don't. Please don't do that. People have tried it before, and it always backfires. It never works. My dad wrote to my high school once, asking them to let me skip a grade, and it was terrible. The teachers thought I was some precocious attention-seeker, and the other kids all hated me. I told you about it. In the end, I taught myself how to pass the SAT tests when I was sixteen so I could graduate two years early." Stupid tears threatened to sting her eyes.

Fenella gently pulled Susie out of the chair by her elbows. "I'm so sorry. Please don't get upset." She held her close and rocked her in her arms. "I understand how hard it's been. But are you quite sure I can't put in a good word? Paving the way for you could make life easier, at least in the beginning. No one at Oxford should look down on you for being bright, but they might not expect enough from you…coming from America, I mean."

That dried up any threat of tears. Susie leaned back in Fenella's arms and openly laughed. "Hey, Lady Fenella, quit while you're ahead. I know you Brits all think Americans are really dumb," she held up her finger, "I mean, intellectually disadvantaged. See, I can talk like the Oxford Dictionary when I want to. But I can look after myself. I really don't need any special treatment or favours. They already gave me a scholarship, which you say is some big deal—whoops—I mean, an unusual academic mark of achievement. That should be more than enough to single me out above the rest of the poppies." She grinned and squeezed Fenella's hips. "But I like what you said about stretching me though. I'd like that—in bed. You can stretch me there anytime."

Fenella huffed. "Why do you turn every innocent remark into innuendo?"

"Why do I? Hmm. Perhaps because I'm in love with you, and I want to make love to you, and I know from my toes to my head that you feel the same. We're fatally attracted to each other, like magnets. And we only have this last night together. Can't I tiptoe down to your room and keep you warm in bed, please?"

Susie was playing with fire here, but she was deadly serious. Fenella was still holding her in her arms, wasn't she? It would only take one firm grope, one repeat of the garage kiss to seal the deal and pull her in. Her sincere promise to keep her distance now seemed surplus to requirements.

Fenella's body tensed, and she shuddered, as if in pain. "I'm sorry. I'm really, really sorry. But I can't do this. I can't. Because I know how much it will hurt you when I inevitably drop you, or betray you, or say something really hateful when I'm drunk. Please don't ask me again, not if you care at all for me."

Susie frowned. "Why would you do any of those things?" Sure, Fenella could be sharp and bossy, but she would surely never be cruel.

"Because they all happened to me when I was your age, from someone I loved quite as madly as you say you love me. And I won't do this to you. I'm not starting what I know I won't be able to finish. There aren't many happy endings in the real world. Trust me, little friend, I do know."

Fenella's revelation opened up a whole new backstory that raised more questions than answers. She needed to get Fenella to tell her more, but that clearly wasn't going to happen tonight. All the previous talk about being honest and about sharing now made much more sense. They would deal with it when Fenella was ready. But right now, she could tell Fenella's resistance was final. There was to be no last night together tussle under the bedclothes, no chance to see Fenella's divine body naked and be allowed to crawl all over her and wrap her up in love and kisses. "I *do* care for you so much, so I won't ask you again or keep pestering you. But will you grant me one last favour?"

"What?"

"Grant me custody of one of your handkerchiefs, doused in J'Adore."

"I think I might be able to manage one handkerchief." Fenella slowly released her and sighed deeply.

"Then I'll bring it back every week to have it re-perfumed," said Susie, and when Fenella rolled her eyes in mock horror, she kissed her on the ear, and laughed to feel her squirm as it tickled. "You see, I am here to stay. We just have to learn to live with it, Fenny. Now, before I go to my own bed, tell me you love me."

"You know I do."

"That's not enough. Tell me in Latin."

Fenella rolled her eyes. "Amo te magis quam vitam meam,

puella horrenda."

Susie grinned. *I love you more than my life, you horrible girl.* With that definitely backhanded compliment, Susie was quite satisfied, for now.

Chapter Twenty - One

December

Susie blew on her fingers to bring them back to life as she parked her bike in the shed behind the Classics department and pulled her work bag from the basket. It was the last week of the full Michaelmas term, and her last tutorial with Dr Pole was due to start in ten minutes. She couldn't say she was sorry this would be their last session. Next term, she'd be passed onto another mentor, a guy from Worcester College, who specialised in medieval Latin and church archives, a subject which didn't exactly fill her with excitement. But at least she'd heard he was friendly, and he encouraged students to ask questions.

Dr Stephanie Pole had not been an easy tutor. She might have been a best mate of Fenella's back in the day, and the current head of the Latin department, but she was stiff as a flagpole and always formal. She was difficult to read as a person and scarcely less so as an academic writer, even though the subject of her scholarship had intrigued Susie. Dr Pole had made her name through unearthing and interpreting Romano-British epitaph inscriptions, and while they might not seem too enthralling to many, it had opened up a whole new field of interest to Susie.

They had now met for seven weeks, so this would be the eighth time Susie had read aloud the latest three-thousand-word essay she had written for her supervisor. And Susie was determined to crack the hard shell of the woman's mind and get a modicum of praise for her work. She'd never been academically stretched so much, just like Fenella had promised.

But there was always a barrier which Dr Pole refused to drop. While other tutors in the department were friendly and would sometimes chat about their family, or their pet dogs, or ask Susie how she was settling in, this woman kept everything strictly professional and was dryer than dust. Susie's small attempts at humour or any little chat to soften her up had been met with a blank wall, so by the mid-term, she'd given up making any small talk and simply read out her work as required.

Compared to Dr Pole, Fenella had been a pussycat when it came to coping with Susie's Americanisms and quickfire shorthand for correct academic English. The professor had no tolerance for anything less than fully annotated, fully sourced quotations and a pedantic insistence on absolutely correct Latin. In fact, Stephanie Pole had been downright vicious to begin with.

She began by insisting they spoke in Latin during their sessions, which scared the life out of Susie at the first tutorial. But then she realised the woman didn't believe she could really speak or even understand Latin and was trying to catch her out. After fifteen minutes of conversation worthy of the cardinals in the Vatican, Dr Pole grew tired of the game and slipped back into English, where Susie was very happy to follow her.

But paradoxically, the nastier Dr Pole was, the more Susie enjoyed pitting her brain against the challenges she set. It was exactly why she'd come to Oxford, to delve into the most arcane and obscure banks of knowledge and dig out the nuggets of gold nobody else had found. Everywhere she walked in Oxford, there seemed to be echoes of a Roman past, and she'd begun to plan trips outside the city at the end of term. She wanted to visit Roman villas and see the mosaics and artifacts held in other museums besides the Ashmolean. She especially wanted to research into the lives of Romano-British women.

Dr Pole finished deconstructing her final essay of the term. "Beta plus. You've certainly shown some progress over the last eight weeks, and I think we've sorted out the correct way to differentiate between end notes and textual commentary at last."

"Thank you." In America, Susie would have died with shame to get a beta anything, but from Pole, it was like a gold star. "I have a question. Where can I go to see some Roman gravestones in England? I'm especially interested in women's epitaphs."

The professor took off her glasses. "You might start with the Corinium Museum in Cirencester."

"Cirencester?"

"Yes, it's a town in Gloucestershire, forty miles from Oxford. In Latin, its name was Corinium, and it was the biggest garrison town in England after London. But you should know all this by now. Didn't you do any prior reading before coming to Oxford? I suppose getting books in America can't have been easy."

Dr Pole made it sound as though Susie had been raised in a dusty little shack next to a cactus bush, waiting for the stagecoach to come through once a month. The effortless, ignorant arrogance of the old world, as shown through the eyes of some Oxford dons, still amazed Susie. But then she recalled her pure excitement at first stepping into Blackwells bookshop and forgave the woman.

The huge amount of reading Susie had done, plus the newspaper article Fenella had given her, had sparked her imagination. She ignored Dr Pole's snarky question, gathered the printout of her essay, and politely prepared to leave.

The woman could throw cold water over the most enthusiastic student, but Susie was determined not to be daunted. Today was Monday. Only four more days until Friday and her weekly invitation to dinner with Fenella and the boys, which always made her happy. She also could ask Fenella if they could go to Cirencester to search for those gravestones in the museum.

"Before you go wandering off to Cirencester," Dr Pole said, as she headed towards the door, "there's one book you must read."

"Oh, yes? Which one?"

"The one I wrote, of course!" Dr Pole gave Susie the eyeroll to which she'd become accustomed. "It will tell you all you need to know about Romano-British epitaphs. I made my reputation on the subject. Did you not know?"

"Yes, I did, actually." Susie smiled blandly. "Thanks for the heads-up anyway."

"You'll find the book in Blackwells."

"Yes, I know. I bought it back in September. In the week before term began, I read it in preparation for your tutorials."

Dr Pole looked at her over her reading glasses, clearly astonished. Susie realised too late why her tutor might have been so perma-frosty with her all these weeks. She should have said that she'd read her tutor's magnum opus before they even met.

She unlocked Charlotte from the railings and pedalled off through the cold rain, not this time to Fenella's house, a route she and her bike knew by heart, but back down St Giles and around the corner towards the Bodleian library. She had some serious research to do.

Something in Dr Pole's book, especially the middle chapters, had always puzzled her, and now she had done more auxiliary reading, it bothered her even more. She hadn't mentioned anything to Fenella or any of her fellow students. But she needed to check something out, and the stacked bookshelves within the Bodleian would surely hold the answer somewhere.

Chapter Twenty - Two

On Friday afternoon, Fenella looked out at the darkening sky and hoped Susie would be safe on the slippery roads. The weather didn't normally turn this bad so early in December, but there had already been several severe frosts, and the rain was trying to turn to sleet this evening. She now always worked from home Fridays and Mondays, so that she could take the time to prepare a properly balanced evening meal for her children and de-stress herself without the need for reaching for the gin bottle on at least two weeknights.

Tonight, she had a roast chicken in the oven with a potato, onion, and fennel gratin under the grill. For once in her over-busy life, she felt at peace and content. Fridays were always good because that was the night every week Susie came around for dinner. Fenella didn't like to admit how much simple happiness this gave her. As long as the girl was safe on the old bicycle. She must make sure its lights were working before she let her leave this evening to pedal back to her college alone in the dark.

The front door banged open, and her sons came in together, bickering as usual, but not in any alarming way. The thud of their school bags echoed in the hallway, no doubt accompanied by their sports kit and soccer boots. Now there'd probably be mud all over the bright black and white tiles, which Hazel, her weekly cleaning lady, had mopped and polished earlier in the day. She heard Freddy thump straight up the stairs, but Nate came into the kitchen and lingered.

"Hi, Mum, something smells good."

"It's only a roast chicken."

"Because *Susie's* coming around tonight. Good stuff."

Fenella turned to him, her antennae up the moment he mentioned Susie's name. "What do mean? What's Susie coming to dinner got to do with anything?"

"Nothing." He grinned. "Nothing at all. Only that I like roast chicken. Freddie likes roast chicken. Susie loves roast chicken. So we're all going to be happy. Your cooking's definitely improved since you've been hot for her."

"What?"

Embarrassment shot up and down Fenella's spine like mercury.

Nathan laughed. "Sorry, Mum. I know you don't like being teased. But we sussed it out weeks ago: you and Ms Webster. It's as clear as anything. You've got a giant crush on her, and she's sure fallen for you. But aren't you getting a bit old to be a teacher's pet?"

Fenella's brain flapped around like a trapped bird. "What nonsense! How did you— It's not true at all. And of course I'm far too old. Teacher's pet indeed! Really!" She was all indignation and fluster until Nathan came over and put his arms around her shoulders like some kindly uncle.

"Now, Mum. Don't get upset. We're happy for you. We both are. And we like Susie, a lot. All the boys at school do as well. She's super-hot. They'd be mega disappointed if I told them she was gay though."

"You wouldn't dare! Nate!"

"Of course I wouldn't. Don't panic. Whatever's going on between you two is your business. But like I said. I'm always happy when she comes for Friday dinner. I like roast chicken."

"Nate, listen to me. Stop this. Yes, I'll admit that I am quite fond of Susie. But nothing, nothing is going on between us."

He leaned back and looked her straight in the eye. "So you've never kissed her? Not even once?"

Fenella quailed under his inspection. "Well, not quite never, but only once. At the very beginning, that's all. We're good friends. Nothing more." She didn't add that the last two months had been an agony of self-control and frequent use of her little battery-operated friend hidden upstairs in a bedroom drawer.

"Okay, I'm sorry. So you're not having it on with her?"

"No! I wouldn't dream of it." Pure lies, of course.

He moved away slightly and seemed to be weighing up his next words. "It's just…"

"What?"

"Well, we're not blind, and it's clear you really like each other. Like, as in *like*. I think you should get on with it. All I'd ask is, hold off going public until after the GCSEs."

"Why?"

"Because I need Ms Webster to stay as my Latin teacher until after the exams. If she quits, then I bet they'll replace her with some dreadful old bore who can't teach for nuts, and I won't get a nine."

"So what are you saying? That in the hypothetical, most unlikely event she and I might have an affair, then Susie would need to quit teaching?"

"Yes, of course. Don't you think so? Mum, get real, for Freddy's sake if not mine. How would you like the whole world to know your mum was shagging one of your teachers?"

"Where did you get such a horrible word, Nate? But seriously, are you saying that, apart from her being your teacher, Susie and me in a relationship would be all right with you?" That she was even asking him the question made her head spin.

"Yes, sure it'd be okay. It's not the twentieth century, is it? And Susie's a huge improvement on creepy Maurice. You've been so much nicer since she came into the family. It's obvious she makes you happy. *And* you've stopped drinking. That's a major plus. Fred and I were getting worried."

Fenella flinched that he had to say it. "I know, darling, and thank you for noticing it. Knowing you two cared has made me sober, and I feel much better for it." Then she went back to the main issue. "So, me and Susie, okay with you, but what about Freddy? How would he react?"

"Oh, he's cool with anything. Buy him a new sports bike for Christmas, and he'll give you away at the wedding. But seriously, Mum, neither of us will blame you if the love of your life turns out to be Susie. We're not like you, Mum. We weren't brought up to be all homophobic and prejudiced about gays, like you were."

"I'm not!"

"Ha! Got you there, didn't I? Shout up when dinner's ready. I've had double Latin, and my brain is fried. Our teacher is something else," he said and grinned. "She's a real slave driver!"

Laughing at his own not very funny joke, he went away, and Fenella was left standing by her fancy cooking range, trying to make some sense of what had just happened. Had she come out to her sixteen-year-old son? How had he known?

Questions swirled around in her brain so much, she had to sit down. The positive possibilities that their little chat had opened up were too massive to trust right now. She felt naked, exposed. Her emotions seemed to be slipping out of her for all to see.

But then she shivered. Protecting her children from a lesbian mother was no longer going to be a valid excuse. She couldn't hide behind it like it was one of those old Victorian dressing screens. She'd have to deal with the even deeper challenge of allowing herself to be loved for real, for risking herself with Susie. God, what a nightmare that might turn into! She'd never make Susie happy, not permanently, probably not even for a year. Of this, she was convinced. But Nate's revelations had shown up one glaring anomaly. The only person in the household who really disapproved of her loving Susie was her.

Ten minutes later, the object of her affections came rattling in through the back door, unwinding her long, rainbow-coloured scarf and stamping her boots to lose some slushy snow as she entered the kitchen. She hung up her bag on the back of the door and shook raindrops off her shoulders.

"It's horrible out there. It's starting to snow."

Fenella rushed to Susie and swept her up into her arms, wet coat, tousled damp hair, and all, and gave her the biggest bear hug.

"Wow, nice." Susie smiled widely. "What a welcome. But what's brought this on?"

Fenella looked over the top of Susie's head. "Nothing. Nothing at all. I'm pleased to see you weren't thrown under a bus on the Headington road."

"You worry too much. Oh, great, you've made us chicken for dinner! And something with fennel. I can smell it."

"Yes. It'll be ready in half an hour. Now come in and get dry and tell me all about your week."

She helped Susie out of her coat and hung it up on the creel dryer above the cooking range. It was the final week of full term, and Fenella wondered if Susie would now have more time for them to do things together. The school didn't break until the week before Christmas, but lack of lectures and tutorials would give Susie some space in her calendar.

On closer inspection though, Susie's charming face looked tired, well, more like bone-weary. She was still wearing her black school teaching uniform and looked barely older than a sixth-former herself.

"I hear you had Nate in class all afternoon. He's upstairs trying to finish the homework you gave them."

"Got to keep those noses to the grinding wheel. Yep, the school keeps me busy, but it's a break from actual thinking. You were right when you warned me about trying to fit in paid work as well. The longer I'm a student, the more time I want to give to it all, reading and thinking and researching, and I can't believe that term is finished already. I only have eleven more terms to go before they throw me out. It's not nearly long enough."

"No, it isn't." Fenella passed Susie a handful of cutlery, and they began to lay the table for dinner. "But there's no time limit on scholarship. You can always make time for new reading. Unless you stay an academic, the world and its problems, even mundane things like making a living, pushes in. I think, though, that you will stay a student for ever. You're a natural scholar. You should never leave Oxford."

Susie snorted. "Of course I won't, not while you're here. But do you really suppose there's any chance they'll let me stay on here for post-grad work?"

"I do. You're a natural."

"Hm. Your Dr Pole doesn't think so. I've only managed to get one Beta plus out of her in eight essays."

"She's known as a hard marker. Wait until Mods next year; you'll fly through them."

"We'll see. But I want to talk to you about something. Something really serious."

Fenella's heart bounced inside her blue cashmere sweater, hoping for the best, but fearing the worst. "What is it?"

"I've discovered that Dr Pole's a big fat phoney. And her great book—"

"What?"

"It's all based on someone else's work. She's plagiarised it and not acknowledged her sources."

Fenella stared at Susie. "You must be mistaken." What Susie had accused her old friend of was worse than murder in the sacred groves of Oxford academia.

"I'm not. I'm really not. I can prove it."

Fenella couldn't find the right words. Then she remembered the chicken needed taking out of the oven. "Look, let's eat dinner and talk later. I can't believe this of Stephanie though. She's as straight as an arrow."

"So I'm bent? I'm lying?" Susie's voice rose almost an octave, and her eyes flashed.

Fenella had never seen her mood change as fast as this. "No, no. Don't overreact. I'm only saying there must be some logical explanation. Like I said, let's enjoy our dinner and talk this over some more afterwards."

Susie huffed, virtually flinging the plates down on the table. "I need to go wash up. Excuse me."

She disappeared into the cloakroom looking as though she could burst into tears.

Fenella went to the foot of the stairs and called, "Seven o'clock! Food's on the table!"

The boys came, and Susie eventually emerged from the downstairs cloakroom. Yes, she'd definitely been wiping tears away from her cheeks, which were pink with badly controlled fury. They all sat around the kitchen table, but even though she tucked in and made a good meal of it, Susie barely looked at Fenella the entire time and left the talking to the boys and their mother.

Nate or Freddie might think Susie was keen on Fenella, but nothing she said this evening would have endorsed their suspicions. Fenella had one very angry student on her hands, and that was a side to Susie she hadn't seen before. But maybe she shouldn't be too surprised. Besides being a genius, Susie was also a mixed-up kid who probably couldn't cope with a rational adult discussion over some academic disparity.

She wasn't looking forward to their after-dinner chat. But Susie's sulky, cross little face still enchanted her. She decided to pull out some salted caramel ice cream as a topping for the sticky toffee pudding she'd made. She stuck a bowlful down in front of Susie with a spoon. Hopefully, it might cool her little lovebug down and sweeten her up at the same time.

Chapter Twenty - Three

Susie scooped up the last of the ice-cream/ toffee pudding mix and swallowed. Even in December, it hit the spot. But clearly Fenella was intent on neutralising her righteous indignation and smoothing out what she likely assumed was an immature person's over-reaction.

If she hadn't liked the dessert so much, Susie would've refused it. The speed in which her fury had risen to boiling point by Fenella's too easy dismissal of her great discovery had surprised her. But wasn't furious anger a natural thing to feel? Didn't truth and integrity matter at all? If Fenella thought they could have a nice little cosy chat and put her concerns to bed, then she was mistaken.

"Come through and sit with me on the sofa," Fenella said as soon as the boys left them. "We can discuss your worries, but I also have some big news of my own to share, something I think you'll be pleased to hear."

Susie gathered up the dessert dishes and carried them over to the dishwasher. She still didn't trust herself to look at Fenella. This was going to be their first big row, and she needed to control how she reacted if it wasn't all going to end horribly.

"Susie, leave those. Come and sit here."

Susie decided to obey. She sat down next to Fenella on the family room sofa and glared at her. Fenella actually had the temerity to laugh.

"What's so funny?"

"Oh, come on, darling. Lighten up. I'm not your enemy. Did Dr Stephanie ruffle your feathers? Let me smooth them down for you."

Susie clenched her jaw at Fenella's bland expectation that she could take away her anger.

"You don't need to do any smoothing. I'm not a parrot. This is really important, Fen. Please listen to me. Afterwards, we can move on to your news, but this could break my whole career, or Dr Pole's, or both."

Fenella frowned and patted Susie's knee. "Okay, so I'm listening. Talk me through it again, whatever you think you've discovered."

Think? She didn't *think*: she knew. But she decided to treat Fenella like the thirteen-year-old dimwits at St Martin's school and explain the crime in words of one syllable. "You remember back in late September when we went into Blackwells?"

"Yes. Then we moved on to a bun shop and sat by the river, where you covered your face with whipped cream from a millefeuille. I so badly wanted to kiss it off."

"Stop interrupting. This is deadly serious."

"All right? What about the bookshop?"

"I bought Dr. Pole's book, her big one on Roman inscriptions. I read it through in the week while I was staying with you and didn't think much about it. It was very dry, but it gave me a basic understanding of her skills as a researcher. The best things about it were the central chapters that dealt with female gravestones across the Empire, with a special piece on those found here in Britain. In those eighty or so pages, it seemed to come to life."

"Okay, you've read her book." Fenella nodded slowly. "What's the problem?"

"As this term has gone on, and I've seen other things she's written, articles in the *Journal of Classical Studies*, for example, none of them read as though they were by the writer of chapters seven to eleven of her book. I've always found different people's writing styles interesting, and every one's unique. The AI guys have started to exploit that by stealing loads of authors' work and learning their style."

"I know it. I *do* edit a journal that relies on outside contributors," said Fenella. "Long ago we learned to run everything submitted to us through plagiarism detection software."

"So, if you don't trust me, then let me give you a chunk out of your friend's book so you can test it yourself?"

"Of course I trust you. But I find it hard to believe that Stephanie is a cheat. There must be a mistake."

"No!" Susie wanted to stamp her foot like a child, but that would hardly help her case. "There damn well isn't, and I can prove it."

"How?"

"Because this week I've found the original work she lifted. In the depths of the Bodleian Library vaults, I dug out a thesis that was written for a doctorate Dr Pole supervised. The author was a DPhil candidate at Somerville, Marcella Novaroma from the University of Milan. I've spent every spare moment since Monday in the Bodleian, and I found her original work. It was never awarded a DPhil., but it was definitely her thesis. Pole stole it."

"Stole is a very hard word to use, Susie, verging on the cruel. All academics glean from other people's research. Stephanie may have used the chapters, but I'm sure she would have acknowledged all their sources too. The original scholar would have called her out on it if she didn't."

Susie shook her head. "In this case, she couldn't. When I cross-referenced the name online, not only in academia but in the real world, it directed me to the Italian woman's archived Facebook page.

"And? So?"

"Marcella Novaroma never finished her doctorate because she was killed in a plane crash the same year. And I can't find any trace of her anywhere after 2014. Dr Pole must have lifted her unpublished paperwork and used it to pad out her own book. How shitty is that? She didn't even bother to rewrite it."

Fenella went very quiet. "So how come you're the first person in Oxford to discover this anomaly? You're only a first-year undergraduate, barely beginning your academic career, and Dr Pole has had several post-graduate research students helping her, as well as putting her book around the Classics world for peer review."

Susie clenched her jaw, though Fenella's words stung her like a wasp. "I can tell you one reason. Because I reckon I'm the only person who's actually ever managed to plough through the whole of her book. The rest of it is so deadly dull that no normal person could likely get past chapter three. Have *you* even read it? You told me you were her best friend." She glared at Fenella and waited for another question to bat away.

Fenella dropped her eyes and sighed. "Oh Susie, why do you

have to be so clever?" she muttered. "I'm sure you're right, if you say you are. Do you have the book with you, which, no, I haven't yet read? I haven't kept up with Stephanie to much extent, and I agree, her written work was always tedious. Can you show me the chapters?"

Susie went over to her bag hanging behind the kitchen door and pulled out the book. "Here, look for yourself." She pointed to the numerous page markers she'd placed in the central section and handed it across to Fenella. "From page sixty-seven onwards, it starts to flow much more easily, and it deals with more interesting concepts. The writing comes together and has a liveliness about it. I remembered when Pole told me I should visit Cirencester to look at some tombstones in the museum there, and it mentions the very same place. There's something else as well. I don't believe English is this writer's first language. She's most likely translating word for word from the Italian in some places. It flows very musically."

Fenella spent some minutes scanning the plagiarised chapters, then looked in the index and end notes for any mention of Marcella Novaroma. It wasn't a name you'd miss. After an uncomfortably long period, she sighed again and looked up. Susie saw the sadness in her eyes.

"You're absolutely right," Fenella said. "But few people would probably have noticed something amiss. But this isn't simply a careless error in attribution. This has to be deliberate plagiarism, made worse because the person copied is no longer alive to protest."

"Exactly. That's what I told you at the beginning." Susie could hardly contain her anger. "So will you help me?"

"Help you to do what?"

"Confront Dr Pole, of course. Tell her we've found out how she cheated. Then we have to report her to the publishers and expose the fraud."

Fenella put down the book and shook her head. She looked troubled. "But exposing her immediately would ruin her. I can't do it Susie, I can't. We need to talk to her first, and then she can put things right for the second edition. It must be hushed up. If it became common knowledge that she did it all deliberately, she'd lose her job, her career, everything. It's too devastating."

Susie's blood ran cold, as she simultaneously felt the sharp bands of a headache stretch across her skull from ear to ear. She struggled to find any words in response to such blatant hypocrisy, from Fenella of all people.

She loved Fenella, she'd idealised her and put her on some high ethical pedestal, but now her goddess had fallen in a crash of splintered marble right in front of her and was revealed, like her plagiarising friend, to be made of phony plaster of Paris. Susie could see Fenella was about to rationalise her response and might even suggest worse things to tackle the crisis. "You think I should keep quiet about this? Swallow it and let Dr Pole get away with it? You won't back me up if I confront her?"

"No, I'm not saying that, but I'm urging caution, and I want you initially to leave this to me. Let me deal with it in my own way. If you go barging in, then it could end up very bad for you. Stephanie will have an explanation, I'm sure. I'll talk to her and find out what's behind it all first. I've known her a long time, and I expect there's a reason. Perhaps she's been going through a tough time with family problems or health issues. We don't need to expose her so cruelly."

"I can't believe you're making excuses for her." Susie flung her hands up in the air. "What could possibly justify burying this? I feel like all my trust in Oxford scholarship has been broken. I feel like I've been mugged in a back alley, and you're taking the side of the mugger. I'm sorry, Fen, I can't do this anymore." Susie stood up, grabbed back Pole's book and went to leave.

Fenella followed her and grabbed her arm. "Susie, don't rush off and do anything you'll regret. If you try to tackle Stephanie on your own, it won't work, and it'll only lead to more trouble for you as well as her. Please leave this to me."

"And you'll confront her?" Susie hated having to ask this again, but she couldn't trust Fenella.

"Yes, I'll talk to her, and I'll try to leave you out of it as much as possible. You've been at Oxford for barely one term, and she might try to make mincemeat out of you. No one will believe you discovered this plagiarism, and you could end up in hot water yourself. You don't want to end up a victim here."

"So you're saying the whole set-up is corrupt? And that no one will believe the word of some kid from America over a senior professor? "

"Susie, There are no depths to the skullduggery and perfidy of the academic world. Trust me on this one."

"And to think I believed this place was the answer to my dreams. You've got some nice friends." Susie struggled to pull on her boots, trying to keep her tears from falling lest they confirm Fenella's view of her as an over-emotional idiot.

"That's not what I'm saying, sweetie. But everyone is a fallible human being, even here in Oxford, the same as they are in the rest of the world. It's not Mount Olympus or some perfect ivory tower. And people in Oxford can mess up their own lives and other people's as badly as anywhere else. Trust me. Susannah, look at me. Leave the book with me. I will try to get to the bottom of it, and then I'll deal with it!"

"Promise?"

"Yes."

Susie handed Fenella the book again. "I have to go now. Thanks for dinner." She turned her cheek away when Fenella tried to kiss her.

"Don't be like this. Stay for a coffee and let me tell you my good news."

"No, thanks. My dad and Abbie are calling me later, and I need to book a ticket home for Christmas."

"What?" Fenella asked, her eyes wide. "But you never said anything about that before. I presumed you'd be spending Christmas here with us. It's a very long way back to the USA."

Susie stared at her, misery creeping into her heart like ice crawling over a lake. "It is, but maybe I need to put some distance between us. I've been stupid, expecting the moon and putting too much pressure on you. With me out of the way, you can deal with your friend as you see fit, and your nice quiet world will no longer be disrupted by me."

"But you will come back here in January, won't you?" Fenella asked. "You'll come back for next term?"

Could she fling in the towel on the whole Oxford experiment

and run as far away from Fenella as she could? Her brain kicked in, and she shrugged. "Of course I'll be back. I have next term to prepare for, and I need to complete my degree. I don't give up on things I commit to, and I've wanted this for so long. I'm not going to self-sabotage. Going through rehab taught me something."

"And you will come to see me before you leave, won't you?"

Susie could only manage a grunt in reply. She didn't trust herself not to slap Fenella if she stayed any longer, and she couldn't think straight.

"I may not have a chance. With my teaching and you working hard on your journal all the time, we may not see much of each other for a while." She wrapped her long scarf around her neck, still in a fury, and paused by the back door. "Fen, if you care for me at all, please wait until I've gone home before you tackle Pole and her deceit. Don't involve me if you and she are going to cover it all up. I don't want to be any part of that."

Then she marched out of the back door, slammed it behind her, and cycled away into the snowy night. She was in no mood to enjoy the twinkly lights of Christmas that beckoned her all the way back towards Oxford city centre.

Chapter Twenty - Four

Fenella's chest felt the pain before her brain did. She leaned against the kitchen counter, bending over as though a bad-tempered donkey had kicked her between the ribs. She heard the gate click, indicating it was too late to run out and pull Susie back. The shock of what she'd just done temporarily paralysed her. Her breath came in short stabbing thrusts of panic, and for a few seconds, she thought she might be having a heart attack. Then her brain reconnected with her nervous system and told her what her body already knew: that, apart from her children, Susie was the sweetest thing in her life, and Fenella might have destroyed their relationship for good.

"You bloody, fucking idiot!" it raged at her. *"Why did you have to take the opposite side to Susie when you know she's right? Why the hell did you defend Stephanie and make out Susie must be wrong, or misguided, and most condescending of all, too young to understand? All the things that create the unique glory of Susie— her untarnished idealism, her super-sharp intelligence, the fact she is still young enough to see things in stark black and white, the way she doesn't compromise—those are the qualities you most love in her. And you had to trample them all into the mud. You're not even fit to be her friend, let alone a lover."*

Fenella's hand trembled. She needed coffee. And Susie wasn't there to have one with her. She poured a cupful of water into the electric kettle and turned it on. In the old days, Fenella would have reached for the gin bottle and poured herself a stiff one, but she was determined to stick to her new regime. Nate's words from earlier ran through her head. *She makes you happy. And you've stopped drinking. That's a major plus. Fred and I were getting worried.*

They approved of her loving Susie. It was the best Christmas present they could have bought her. But she couldn't share it with the one she loved. Susie would scornfully hand it back. Without

Olivia or anyone else's help, Fenella had singlehandedly achieved what she'd said she needed to do from the start: make the girl stop loving her. The look in Susie's eye had confirmed it more than anything she'd said. Though she *had* been saying a definite goodbye, not only to any future they might share together, but also to the whole delicious, crazy romance. Whatever Fenella did or didn't do about Stephanie's sins of omission, Susie no longer wanted to know. She'd said not to even tell her the outcome. But did this mean their romance was also all over? Kaput before it had hardly begun?

Instead of making real coffee, she wearily pulled down the jar of instant and stirred the hot water over the granules. *You're the cream in my coffee.* The old words came through her mind. Not anymore. Her delicious cream pot had gone. Fenella took her coffee black and cried like a baby into the mug.

It took a while, but she eventually stopped crying and came around to one inescapable truth. She had to call Stephanie Pole and arrange a meeting, urgently. They'd drifted apart in recent years, and she no longer carried Stephanie's current address and number in her phone. But as the woman seemed to almost live and breathe her work, that had never seemed a problem before.

It was too late to ring the Classics department tonight, but she would do it first thing on Monday. Meanwhile, she needed to read the contentious book from cover to cover, so she was well prepared to confront her old friend with some very hard truths. Like the good Catholic she wasn't, maybe she was looking for a miracle to keep both Stephanie and Susie happy. Fenella had never been a people-pleaser but reconciling with Susie was essential if she was ever going to be happy again, and her ties to Stephanie also went very deep. She owed her more than she liked to admit, not least because Stephanie had once saved her life in a dark incident she had never shared with anyone else alive.

She curled up on the sofa, pulled a rug over her knees, and settled down with the book, ready to be bored. Reasons for her twenty-five-year friendship with Stephanie Pole had never included Fenella being overwhelmed by Stevie's sparkling wit or glittering repartee, and her old college buddy still wrote pretty much as she spoke.

As an editor faced with dozens of unsolicited articles on a daily basis, Fenella had perfected the art of speed-reading. But this time, she deliberately slowed down, channelling Susie, who had the ability to immerse herself so deep within a text that she could block out all distractions. She read the first three chapters. It was all so tedious, there was no doubt Stephanie must have been the author…

"Mum! Mum!"

"What?"

"It's way past midnight. It wouldn't be good for you to sleep on the couch all night. You should go to bed."

She groped her way out of sleep and stared up at Nate, who was standing in front of her in his pyjamas.

"I saw the lights were still on, so I came down. I thought maybe Susie was still here."

"No, no, she left straight after dinner. I was just reading a textbook written by a friend of mine."

He glanced over at it and grinned. "Can't have been much of a page-turner then."

Fenella looked down to where her finger was still caught on page one of chapter four. "No, it isn't, to be honest." She threw off her rug and stood up. "Thanks for waking me. Let's go to bed." She followed him upstairs, doing her best to hide the truth about the damned book, and the way it had exploded like a grenade straight through her sweet romance.

Three days later, she was even more frustrated. She so wanted to keep her promise to Susie, but it had proved much harder to get hold of Stevie Pole than she'd imagined. When she called the Classics department first thing on Monday morning, the receptionist was unhelpful to the point of being obdurate.

"Dr Pole is unavailable. She's currently away from Oxford."

"Can you tell me when she'll be back?"

"No, I can't say."

"This week, next week, any time before Christmas?"

"I don't have that information."

"Can you give me her phone number then?"

"No, we do not disclose academic staff's personal phone

numbers."

Fenella bit her tongue. Stupid jobsworth woman. "Well, how about an email address? I'm an old friend, and this is very important."

"You may contact her via the department. But we do not expect her back before the start of next term."

"That will be January. I need to speak to her within the week, not in a month's time."

"I'm sorry, she is currently out of Oxford and cannot be contacted."

They were now circling the airport with no hope of landing. Fenella decided to give it up. She'd have to try another way. Someone must know where Stephanie had gone. She wasn't working for MI5, after all. She called Susie to give her an update and try to make up from their painful parting on Friday.

Susie always picked up quickly, usually before the second brrr. Fenella needed to tell her she was trying to get hold of Stephanie, how she'd ploughed through the whole book over the weekend, a task that made the Sunday evening routine of ironing ten of her sons' school shirts seem positively fascinating by comparison. And yes, Susie was indisputably right. Stephanie had lifted whole chapters of someone else's work, and there were no acknowledgments or attribution at all.

Fenella had carelessly dismissed Susie far too quickly, underestimated her commitment to the truth. But surely Susie could forgive her an initial wobble, questioning her evidence rather than her judgement. She only needed to talk to her. "Pick up, pick up, pick up!"

"The number you are calling is currently unobtainable."

Susie must have switched off her phone, something she never did unless she was in a lecture, a tutorial, or a lesson she was giving at the school, or when she was with Fenella. And Monday morning wasn't one of Susie's teaching slots. So where was she?

Fenella had become so used to the certainty of Susie's undivided devotion for her that she had almost begun taking it for granted. Over the last three months, it had grown into a warm muffler around her restless heart, and she'd settled into the routine of repeatedly saying no to hanky-panky, while letting the girl cuddle up to her and share in the warmth of their mutual affection.

She realized how complacent she'd been, how stupid not to realize this wasn't a game she could win. She needed Susie to love her. She couldn't do without it. She phoned her on the hour, every hour, for the rest of the day. Nothing. In the end, she got into the car and drove the mile to St Hilary's College.

"Hi, Ms Carlton, how are you doing?"

She'd popped in so often to see Susie that Roy, the Head Porter, treated her like family. "Fine, can you tell me if Susie Webster is in?"

He glanced over his shoulder up at the ranks of little wooden boxes, all numbered by room. He knew them by heart. "Hm. No, sorry. She's left her keys with us, so she must be out."

"Oh." Fenella's heart fell down to her Italian boots. "I can't raise her on her phone, and I need to talk to her urgently."

"We haven't seen her all weekend. Perhaps she's gone away with friends now full term's over. Maybe send her a text?"

Fenella nodded. "Yes. Sensible suggestion. I'll text her and drop her an email as well." She didn't like to say that Susie didn't have masses of friends in Oxford her own age. Fenella had rather dominated her social life. But perhaps she'd gone to London to stay with Carla. That would make sense. Standing outside the porter's lodge, under the light of the college lamps, she fumbled on her phone to find Madeleine Farlane's number. They were still in regular contact over the ongoing revamping project, with Fenella gradually coming to terms with purple and black triangles. She hoped Madeleine would give her a number for Carla, and then Carla would help her reconnect with Susie.

At least Madeleine picked up, thank God. Fenella asked for Carla, trying not to sound like some desperate idiot.

"Sure I can give you Carla's number. I'll text it through now. And Fenella, I'm so happy you called. Can we fix up a face-to-face this week? We've finished the revised mock-ups, and I'd like to show you them in person."

"Yes, we can do. Arrange a time with Greta on Wednesday or Thursday. I don't suppose you know if Susie's with Carla at the moment, do you?"

"Sorry, I don't, but I doubt it. Carla's away in Falmouth for a few days, staying with her guy. But her number should be coming through to you now."

Fenella mumbled a thanks and called Carla. The dark and wet December evening seemed to close in around her. She could see her breath coming out in the frosty cold under the lamplight and shivered with anxiety..

Carla picked up after five rings.

"Hi, Carla, it's Fenella Carlton. I'm trying to reach Susie and wondered if she was with you."

"Hello, Fenella, great to hear from you. No, sorry, the last time I talked to Susie was more than a week ago. I'm in Cornwall for a mini pre-Christmas break. I thought she was staying with you for the next few days. Wasn't that the plan?"

Fenella could hardly think straight, let alone respond to questions. "Yes, it was, but for now, I've lost her. If you can get hold of her, please ask her to contact me, urgently."

"Sure, of course. Bye."

Fenella would have to confront Susie at St Martin's school tomorrow. She had lessons on Tuesday afternoons there, and she took her teaching commitments seriously. She wouldn't let them down. Fenella normally worked in the London office on Tuesdays, but not this week, as nothing was as important as reconnecting with Susie. And of course she would text her little sprite, a message so loving and conciliatory that Susie couldn't fail to respond.

The misery and the mystery deepened on Tuesday. She'd still had no response from Susie, even though Fenella spent a ridiculously long time composing the sweetest love letter ever sent by SMS. At three p.m., just as Susie's last lesson of the day would be finishing, Fenella drove through the gates of her sons' school and pulled up in the visitors' carpark. After bypassing the reception, she marched straight down the corridor to the language labs and headed for the classroom where Susie normally taught. A flustered and irritated deputy head, John Collins, confronted her.

"Ah, Mrs Carlton, this is a right to-do. No word, no apology, no reason. Do you know where Ms Webster has disappeared to? I've had to cover the classes myself, and frankly, I'm disappointed. I thought your young friend would have given us sufficient notice if she had to let us down like this."

Fenella shivered even more inside her warm winter coat. This was news she'd been dreading. "That's why I'm here, to find out where she is. No one has seen her since last Friday evening. I'm very worried about her. And I can assure you, she wouldn't have simply failed to turn up. She takes her teaching work at St Martin's very seriously."

He didn't look convinced. "I suppose we need to remember she's very young, and unqualified, of course. Students today don't know the meaning of the word *reliable* or *commitment.* She's been very popular with our pupils, but we will be re-advertising for a qualified and more dependable Latin teacher from next term."

"I assure you, Mr Collins, there will be a cast iron reason for Susie Webster's absence, and I won't rest until I find it. In turn, please call my home number if you hear anything, and please don't advertise her position before we know the circumstances of her absence."

They walked down the corridor together when Fenella heard a noise behind her and turned to see Freddy barging along a few feet behind her.

"Hi, Mum, why are you here and not in London? Is it about Susie? Everyone's talking."

She let Mr Collins move on and stopped. "I'm so worried. No one knows where she is, and she's not answering any of my messages." Shameful tears start to prick the backs of her eyes. "Do you or any of the boys here know anything?"

"No, but it's all around the school how she's bunked off. She's the brightest spark around here, the only cool teacher, and the guys are all wondering what set it off. Do you have any idea?"

Fenella feared *she'd* been the one to set it off. God, she hoped Susie hadn't done something stupid to herself because of their encounter on Friday evening. She knew the fragility of Susie's little spirit after learning all about the abyss into which she'd sunk as a teenager. Maybe she should call the police and report her as a missing person. "Come on, do you want a lift home with me?"

"No, thanks, I've got my bike. I'll see you later," he said and disappeared into the crowds of other tall young men, all in navy blazers and long grey trousers.

These days, Nate spent nearly every early evening over at his girlfriend Alice's home, so Fenella would be returning to an empty house. She ran to her car and jumped in before she started to weep. Then she drove straight home to dissolve into a puddle of despair.

Chapter Twenty - Five

Susie regretted the door slam the moment it happened, which wasn't only down to her. A gust of wind had caught it behind her as she'd gone out into the winter night. But she knew it would make her look childish and petulant rather than outraged and broken-hearted.

Fenella had cooked her a perfect chicken dinner, with the scrumptious date toffee pudding to follow, and she'd barely thanked her for all the trouble. But Fenella wasn't in her shoes. She didn't know how much Susie had been struggling with what she'd discovered, nor how she'd already sought any possible excuse or explanation. She'd wanted to share it with other students in her faculty but had kept it bottled up inside until she told Fenella. Fenella, whom she still loved, of course. But Susie couldn't respect her anymore. Fenella had said she'd deal with it. Cover it up, more like! Susie's mind was in turmoil, her heart was bruised, and her hands were freezing. She mounted her bike and started pedalling towards the city centre.

The weather was nasty, with temperatures not yet frosty enough to make the branches become white but barely hovering around freezing. The rain had turned to sleety snow, which hit her straight in the face as she pedalled doggedly away into the darkness. At the roundabout at the edge of the town centre, below Christchurch meadows, she slowed down and pulled off the road to try to adjust her flickering front lamp.

The traffic swirled around her. She still mistrusted the British circular roundabouts where cars and trucks never stopped. It was like leaping onto a deadly carousel that kept spinning, and she felt completely vulnerable on her little bike and in her long black coat. She needed to get a safety vest.

Anyway, she needed to get back to college to Facetime with her dad and Abbie and then try to recover from her first real bust up with Fenella. She fumbled in the bike's front wicker basket for her phone, only to remember that she'd left her whole bag hanging on the back of Fenella's kitchen door. God damn it! Now she couldn't call anyone until Saturday.

She'd also wanted to catch up with Kate and Catriona to find out how they were doing. Fires were raging all across their part of Los Angeles. Politics back home had also become so toxic since the presidential election, and Susie worried about them. Kate was at the forefront of the opposition to all things MAGA, and every day brought forth new horrors.

Everyone Susie knew in America, who had any sense of decency, dreaded the day the elected president would assume office in January. It had taken four years to repair the chaos and damage caused by his last administration, and now he had the backing of that strange car weirdo and a whole heap of other billionaires.

With those thoughts swirling inside her head, and the evening traffic doing the same outside it, she put her foot on the right pedal and headed out into the turmoil. Whether she failed to notice the car joining from the left, or the car driver didn't see her in the dark, she never knew, but she felt Charlotte, with her aboard, being hit full on and then they were both airborne, narrowly missing being crushed by a double-decker bus coming in from the right. She glimpsed the horror in the bus driver's eyes as he swerved, knowing only his skill and quick reaction could save her life, and the bulk of the great vehicle blocked the roundabout as the scream of its tires on the wet road pierced the air. It was the last thing Susie heard in the second before the world went black, and she fell into a pit of pain. Then nothing.

Being a patient in the emergency room is an appropriate description. But for Susie, all throughout her first long Friday night in hospital, it was a virtue she didn't need to possess. The crack on the head she'd received was sufficient to fracture her cycling helmet and had knocked her out cold.

It was late Sunday afternoon before consciousness returned in the shape of pain everywhere, and to begin with, all she knew was that her whole body hurt like hell, and her mind seemed to be floating in some strange no man's land. She recognised nothing and remembered nothing.

Her mind was blank, so all she could do was lie and wait, in something approaching agony. The blankness soon became unbearable, so she tried to take stock, forcing information into her brain, which at present seemed to have gone completely on strike.

The five senses came into play one by one. She could only look up, as turning her head or trying to lift her neck hurt too much. The ceiling above her was tiled with some sort of white polystyrene squares. She tried to count them but couldn't make sense of their patterns.

She felt with tentative fingers and thought she must be lying in a hospital bed, with tight white sheets pinning her down and a monitor behind her steadily bleeping. Other sounds came through the mists, other monitors beeping steadily around distant beds, but as her eyes flickered right and left, she could see she was in a cubicle on her own.

Then she felt the weight of heavy plaster cast on her left leg and another on her right arm, and a large bandage wrapped around her head. Wires and cannulas were in her arms, and she realized she'd been catheterized.

She felt nauseous. So this must be a hospital, and it looked like she'd been in some really bad accident. She tried to make more sense of the whole nightmare, but nothing else came to mind, not even her name. Whatever disaster had brought her here, she had no way of knowing. Her memory was wiped, and she was alone.

It was a horrible, horrible feeling, and to avoid screaming out in panic, Susie took what seemed to be her only option: to escape back into the peaceful neutrality of sleep. "Hello, darkness, my old friend." The words of a song came into her head, but she was asleep before she could remember the tune.

Sunday night, Monday, Tuesday, all came and went as Susie slept. At times she heard and felt people talking around her, bathing her, moving her, taking her temperature, her blood pressure. But they were all too far away to call out to, and it all made no sense. She was also frightened of rising up again into the pain-filled misery of being awake and so stayed snugly down inside her rabbit hole. She didn't feel ready to climb back above ground.

But one morning, her eyes opened naturally, and she stared at a female health care assistant who was adjusting her hanging drip bag of nutrients. "Hi," she said cautiously.

"Hello!" The woman smiled at her. "I'll call a staff nurse and tell them you've come round."

She looked nice and reassuringly human. At least Susie hadn't been abducted by aliens. She croaked, her voice hoarse. It was painful to speak with her mouth feeling so dry. "Don't go. Where am I?"

"The JR trauma unit. You took a nasty knock or two. I believe it was an RTA."

Maybe this was an alternative universe after all. Did everyone speak in acronyms? Susie didn't understand the initials but liked that she knew what an acronym was. Her head felt like an eggshell being hit by a teaspoon, a particularly nasty and violent teaspoon. "How long have I been here?"

"You were brought up here to the ICU early on Saturday morning from A&E. I saw you when I came on shift at eight a.m. and they'd just moved you up in here from the operating theatre then. You'd been in there all night from Friday evening."

"What day is it today?"

"It's Wednesday morning. Your consultant will be coming to do her rounds soon, and then you can ask lots more questions."

Susie slowly and methodically did a calculation on her fingers. It was like wading through treacle. "Friday, Saturday, Sunday, Monday, Tuesday, Wednesday… That means I've been in here five days?"

"Yes, right. You sound American. Are you American?"

"Am I? Maybe. I don't know. I might be."

The woman smiled again. "We haven't been able to identify you yet. It's good you're awake now so we can clear up the mystery of who you are. I expect your family are anxious about you. Now lie back and rest, and I'll tell the nurses you're awake."

She did as she was told. What was her alternative? So all this pain was the result of an accident. How had it happened? She hated not remembering. She hated not even knowing her own name. The attendant had spoken with a British accent, so maybe she was in

England. She tried to make sense of it all, but thinking only gave her an even worse headache than before.

Things improved. Within a short time, a small team of white-coated doctors arrived, walking behind a woman who seemed to be their boss.

"Good morning! I'm Gillian Davis, head of orthopaedic surgery here at the John Radcliffe Infirmary. I'm happy to meet you at last. You've been in an induced coma for a few days to help your brain heal. But everything is going according to plan. You will recover, don't worry."

"Why am I in plaster? What have I broken?"

"You have a badly fractured left femur, something we call a compound fracture, because it broke through the surface of your leg and nicked your femoral artery. But the paramedics did a great job and brought you here in time for us to stem the flow and give you a blood transfusion. But you've also broken your left ulna in two places, that's your bigger arm bone, and I'm afraid you have a few cracked ribs. But you're young. The fractures will heal in time, and you'll eventually be as good as new."

She realised she must be American, because the fear of what all this medical treatment must be costing made her shiver almost as much as the pain. She didn't know if she even had any medical insurance.

"You suffered swelling on the brain and some severe concussion," Dr Gillian said, "which is why your memory is probably a bit slow at the moment."

Slow? More like non-existent. "Sorry, I don't remember anything. I don't even know my name."

Dr Gillian smiled. "Don't worry, we'll send along someone who can help you work it out. Unfortunately, there was no ID with you when you were brought in, but I expect you might be a student at one of the colleges."

She frowned. "Colleges? What colleges? Where's here?"

"This is Oxford, England. I think you're probably studying at Oxford University."

"What? England! Do I have medical insurance?"

"If you're an international student, then it will have formed part of your entry visa. There is a flat fee of about £750 a year."

She liked the idea of all that care for around one thousand dollars. "I hope you're right. I think I always wanted to come to study at Oxford, but I've got no idea how I got here."

"A psychologist is scheduled to see you soon," said Dr Gillian, "and she can help you recall everything gently. Temporary amnesia like this is quite common after a head injury, so don't worry too much. I'm sure things will come back to you in a few days. Physically, you're doing well. All the vital signs are good, and your fever has dropped. There's no serious organ damage, which is very lucky. We'll move you out of the ICU tomorrow. You've been on NBM, but do you think you could manage a light lunch and maybe start drinking water?"

She didn't feel very lucky, but she figured these people *had* saved her life.

"NBM is nil by mouth," whispered one of the younger doctors, clearly seeing her bewilderment.

"Oh, yeah. Lunch, yes, thank you." She suddenly felt thirsty and hungry. She couldn't remember her last meal, but then a memory jumped into her head. "Sticky toffee pudding and caramel ice cream!"

Dr Gillian laughed. "I don't think the canteen can rise to such splendour."

"No! It was the last thing I ate." She licked her lips as though it was still there. "I can remember the taste and the smell of it."

"And can you remember where you ate this, or who gave it to you?" Dr Gillian asked.

She closed her eyes, but nothing came. "Sorry, it's all a blank."

"Well, hang on to the memory of the pudding. That's a good start."

The consultant moved on, presumably to other bashed-up accident victims. Some of the younger doctors stayed by her bedside, talking about her above her head and making more notes, but eventually they all departed and abandoned her too.

She was left with the health care assistant, whom she discovered was called Sharon, and then an older nurse in a dark blue uniform arrived, whose name badge said she was Hazel. Sharon brought in a little tray of chicken soup and a soft white bread bun, both of which tasted of cardboard, but she finished the meal, and hoped they'd soon let her eat and drink normally.

Her incarceration was likely to be a long one. She had no idea where she lived or what she did outside these four walls, but worrying only hurt her head more. So with fresh pain killers coming through the drip, she did what they told her and rested. After drinking the soup, nothing else happened, and she drifted asleep to the ticking of the wall clock and the beeping of the monitor, hoping that she might wake with all her memories intact.

Chapter Twenty - Six

For Fenella, Wednesday turned out to be an even worse day than the four preceding ones, if that was possible. She couldn't avoid going to the office to tackle the pile of work needed to get March's edition of *Perceptions* ready for the printers. She'd neglected her day job for far too long and reminded herself she loved her work, was totally committed to it, and, for the last fifteen years, it had been like her third child.

But when she looked at her calendar, the day's appointments included one with the Farlane designers. Seeing them booked in took her straight back to the day in September when her whole emotional world had been upended: the day Susie had walked into her life.

This time though, there was to be no Carluccio's lunch, no slut's spaghetti. The pair from Farlane were coming to her office instead, where Greta would organise a light buffet lunch, and they would finalise a contract with them to set up the new designs. These were for a root and branch makeover, not only for the print version but also for the online magazine, their website, social media outlets, and even the office décor.

Before Susie, Fenella had an impeccable grasp of her own brand, knew her own mind, and always dressed stylishly, but now she felt like a hopeless mass of indecision. She was losing focus, she could feel it, and it was bringing out all her inner insecurities. None of her clothes looked good this morning. She was surprised she'd even put on matching shoes, she'd felt so distracted as she'd dressed for work.

"Tell Sal and Gary to join us," she said to Greta before the meeting, wanting to involve two young staffers who ran the social media, techy end of *Perceptions'* business operations. "They'll know much more than I do about what will excite the great British public."

"That's a good idea. It's not the great British public we need to attract though," said Greta. "It's the bright, inquisitive, literate under-thirties. Our old fogey set of readers are already secure. We need new blood, younger readers. Like your little buddy, Susie, the one you keep talking about. How is she by the way? Coming to you for Christmas?"

Fenella' eyes filled with tears. "I don't…I don't know yet. It's all up in the air right now."

Greta frowned. "Well, I expect Carla will know more about her plans. Now, can you look through their folder for one last time? They've made a lot of adjustments to fit in with your requests. Let's finally get this project put to bed."

Fenella grabbed the folder and looked down at it, shielding her eyes from any further inspection. She wished she could locate Susie and put her to bed, then climb right in with her. But Greta had no need to know all the details of her boss's fantasies.

What Fenella yearned for above all else was to be told Susie was safe. But deep down, she bitterly regretted not acting like the predatory shark she'd once been known as. She should have captured Susie, body and soul, and swept her into bed. Then Susie wouldn't have disappeared over one silly argument. She'd be tucked up tight against Fenella's heart and never be able to escape.

When Madeleine and Carla arrived at noon, they spent an intense hour working together with the magazine's team on the redesign, The two younger members of staff and the commercial director in charge of advertising all talked together around the table and were excited by the new look. Greta steered the process. She expertly covered up for Fenella's lack of focus and for her habit of staring out of the window, twisting a cotton handkerchief back and forth between her fingers.

Fenella let them all talk and agreed to everything they suggested. When Madeleine handed her the contract, she signed without any more hesitation. *Perceptions* was moving on. Maybe it would do better in the future without her as a useless editor holding it back.

"The caterers have set up in the next room," Greta said. "Let's go through."

"I'm sorry I couldn't be more helpful when you called on

Monday," Carla said to Fenella as they walked through. "I only came back to London yesterday afternoon, but I can't contact Susie either. Have you managed to find her yet?"

Fenella shook her head. "No, and now I'm so anxious," she said, having summoned up the courage to speak about her worst fear. "When I return to Oxford tonight, I'm contacting the police. I'm sure something must have happened to her. She missed her Latin teaching lessons yesterday, and that's unheard of."

"Well, it isn't the first time she's done something like this," Carla said. "According to her dad, she's often disappeared before. When she was sixteen, she vanished for three months before anybody found her. They tracked her all the way down to Louisiana in the end. So I wouldn't worry too much."

"I can't help it," Fenella said. "Maybe you should contact her family. This can't carry on. If it does, I shall go mad."

"You really like her, don't you?"

"She makes the sun rise for me," Fenella said and clutched her chest. "I adore her. I don't think I can live without her. We had a bitter argument though on Friday, and I think I'm to blame that she's missing."

Carla's eyes widened, clearly taking stock of Fenella's true feelings. "Okay, then let's find her. I'll call her dad tonight. I said I'd take care of her over here, so she's my responsibility as well. Don't worry, Fenella. We'll all work together on it. You aren't alone here."

Fenella grasped onto the most caring and hopeful words she'd heard all week.

Carla looked her over. " I think you should head back home as soon as you can before the rush hour. You look exhausted. Greta and Madeleine can iron out any further wrinkles, and you've got a good team working for you here. I think you need to take care of yourself. Call me tonight, okay?"

Fenella looked at her and caught a faint glimpse of Susie in her. "I will. I will."

Fenella couldn't face any food and fled the room. Everyone at work would know soon enough she was mad about the girl, a walking mid-life crisis before their eyes. But she didn't care.

Nothing mattered apart from finding Susie alive and confirming she was okay. Not her business nor her reputation. Nothing but Susie mattered. She missed the four o' clock train by minutes, so it was after six when she arrived in Oxford and collected her car from the station.

When she got home, her car needed recharging, so she entered by the garage, and then put her key into the back door instead of the front. It seemed more resistant than usual, a little heavier on the hinges, so she looked behind it. Had Nate hung his hockey kit bag from the coat hook?

But then she looked under her old garden anorak and gasped. Susie's book bag—her everything bag, a large cotton tote with St Hilary's crest on it, in which Susie carried around all her worldly wealth and daily possessions—was hanging from the hook. It had been there all this time. Susie had clearly forgotten to take it when she'd left five days before. Fenella pulled it down and scrabbled inside it. Tucked down under some books was Susie's phone, switched off from the moment she'd walked through Fenella's door on Friday evening, like she did whenever they were together.

"Being with you is so precious, I don't want any interruptions…" Fenella remembered those words from a much earlier Friday evening, when she had thought it was sweet and silly but had secretly cherished confirmation of the special place she commanded in Susie's affections.

Now it meant all those frantic phone calls and texts had gone unanswered for a chilling reason. Susie hadn't been ignoring her. She'd simply never received any of her messages, nor had she returned for her phone, which meant she *must* have definitely suffered a catastrophe.

She walked through to the main house phone to dial 999. Her hand was poised on the receiver when the front doorbell rang hard and urgently, as if someone was putting their whole weight against the button. Was it Susie? Fenella ran to open it and stepped back as Bryony nearly fell into the hallway on top of her. "Bryony? Oh my God!"

"I decided to come around in person. You won't know yet—"

Bile rose up in Fenella's throat, and she clung to the door jamb, sure she was about to faint. She knew exactly what was coming. "Susie's dead. I sent her to her death."

"No, no! She's not dead." Bryony clasped Fenella's forearm. "But she *is* with us at the JR. She was knocked off her bike at the end of Headington Road on Friday evening. I discovered her when I came back from leave today. She has some nasty fractures, and she looks like she's survived five rounds with Mike Tyson. But she'll be okay. She's alive. My colleagues have done a great job on her injuries."

"Oh, thank God! Come in. Tell me everything you know." Fenella walked slowly, unsteady on her feet. Maybe it was with relief instead of dread and foreboding, but she thought she might rush to the cloakroom to throw up. "I've just discovered her book bag hanging on my back door. That's why she couldn't call me or let anyone know."

"That isn't the only reason," said Bryony. "And that's why I'm here. I want to take you to see her right now. She's in intensive care, badly concussed, but she has a damn good excuse why she couldn't let anyone know what was going on. None of my colleagues knew who she was. Susie didn't have any ID, and she's lost her memory, even her name. We all hope and expect it to be temporary, but—"

"Oh, my lamb, my poor lamb."

Bryony reached out to her with a hug, and her strength and beaming positivity helped Fenella through the shock. They stayed together until Fenella drew back and said, "Sorry. Sometimes, good news can be as much of a shock as bad. I'll just write a note for my boys before we go."

She wrote the note and stuck it onto the fridge door with a magnet, then she flung on her outdoor coat. "Thanks so much, Bryony. But let's go now."

As they stepped outside, Bryony said, "Bel will want to visit Susie as soon as possible. Did you know, she and I first met six years ago when I was her assistant, after she had a similar accident to Susie's? There's nothing Bel doesn't know about recovering from multiple fractures, dealing with pain, and a head injury."

Fenella *did* know that, and she didn't care to hear it again. Her entire focus was Susie. "So Susie won't know me," she said, battling with the connotations of that fact and what it meant for their fledgling relationship. "She's forgotten everything?" She slipped into the passenger seat of Bryony's car.

"Not quite," Bryony said, "she remembered one thing, which confirmed you were the first and right person for me to take to her. You can bring her memory back. Do you know the only thing she can remember?"

"What?" Fenella's voice trembled with panic. Had their foolish quarrel, had her behaviour, caused the accident? Was it everything to do with her? Or nothing?

"That her last meal ended with a bowl of sticky toffee pudding with ice cream." Bryony smiled. "When I heard that, I knew she had to be talking about you."

Bryony started the car and set off towards Oxford's renowned hospital, located five miles northeast of the city in Headington. As the seriousness of the situation settled into her mind, Fenella could no longer hold her emotions in check, and she sobbed into her handkerchief.

Chapter Twenty - Seven

There was only one window at the end of the ICU, and her cubicle was nowhere near it. Hers was lit instead by overhead tubular lighting and the flashing of her bank of monitors, so when she woke, it could have been midnight or noon. Every time she did manage to drag herself into consciousness, disorientation kicked in, and she had to push her poor brain out of stand-by mode and into some kind of functioning organ.

She blinked slowly and wiped at her eyes to make sure she wasn't seeing things. Someone new was standing by her bed. She slowly tried to work her visitor out. Dark blue scrubs, pulling a cap off a shock of blond hair, nice eyes, the cool touch of a hand picking up her left wrist. Someone rather younger than the head of surgery who had come before. Someone she felt she should know but couldn't place.

"Hello, Susie."

The statement opened a tiny door of hope leading beyond the miasmic fuzz inside her head. "You know who I am?"

"I do indeed. You're Susie. Susannah Webster. You came all the way from Portland, Oregon in the US to study here at St Hilary's College, Oxford, and we first met when I came to lunch with your good friend Fenella Carlton, back in early September."

"Oh, wow. I'm sorry, I don't remember any of that. So who are you?"

"I'm Bryony Bridgford. I'm a surgical registrar here at the John Radcliffe Infirmary. I've come up from theatre to check on your progress, and I recognised you at once. As soon as I'm free this evening, I'm going to bring Fenella here to see you, and I'll arrange to tell your family in America what's happened. We have a great team of neurologists here who can help you regain your memory. But one thing you should know is that you have someone here in Oxford who loves you very much, and she'll be overjoyed to know

"

you're alive."

"Are you sure?" Susie blinked back tears. "Maybe you've got the wrong person. Maybe I'm not the person you think I am. I know I must look terrible, and I'm a mass of bandages and bruising. Is there really a family and people here who know and love me?"

"I'm 100% sure. Susie, you can't wriggle out of being the amazing, lovely, and brilliant person you are. So many of us love you, but Fenella loves you the most."

"Fenella? That's a nice name, but I don't remember ever hearing it before. The other doctor thought I might be a student. But what's my major?"

"See! Proof you're from the States. We don't have 'majors' over here. You're at Oxford reading Classics, specifically Latin and Greek. It's a four-year course, and you've just completed your first term."

She seemed so confident, Susie began to believe her, but how crazy was the idea of her studying such strange subjects?

"Latin and Greek? I don't know any Latin or Greek."

"I think you do. Your brain is recovering, so the section taking care of memory still needs to wake up. But we'll help it come back. Give it time. Where there's life, there's hope."

"Ubi vita, ibi spes," Susie said without any idea where the words had come from. "What the heck? Why did I say that?"

"At a guess, because it's a Latin translation for what I said before. You'll be okay, Susie, trust me. And I'll be coming back to see you very soon. I'll leave you with Sharon now who has a little something for your tea."

Then Dr Bryony, a vision in scrubs, disappeared, and left her to Sharon, who was equally as kind. Sharon was carrying something beige on a tray. She placed the food on a table, which she scooted forward on wheels to fit over the bed. It was some sort of mashed potato pie thing, next to an apple pie slice with tinned custard, and cutlery wrapped in a brown paper napkin.

"I've been told my name's Susie Webster."

"That's a nice name," said Sharon.

"I suppose it is. At least it's not something awful like Brunhilda Stottlemyer."

"You're funny, aren't you?"

Sharon raised up the head of her bed so she could sit up enough to eat, Susie chased the food around the plate with her one good hand and enjoyed the mediocrity of the meal. It brought her back down to reality. Because what Dr Bryony just told her had been almost too exciting to believe. She was a student at Oxford University, halfway across the world in England, studying classical languages? What kind of crazy idea was that?

But the notion there was someone here who loved her very much was an even wilder one. Susie still didn't know who she was, but she had a gut feeling that she'd been in love, in a special way that makes one's heart race and the ground unsteady under one's feet. She wondered if she was still a virgin, or whether she'd even ever been pregnant. She didn't expect so, but without a memory, how was she supposed to know? She might be the mother of twins.

It was a bummer not to know anything about oneself, even one's own body. But now she'd remembered two things about herself. She knew a little Latin, and she liked sweet puddings. And she had a name. Susie sounded rather girly though. It wasn't much to go on, but it was a start. The good-looking Doctor Bryony could be her lifeline back to normality. She let the healthcare people come and go, filling and emptying bags, and taking her readings virtually every hour, while she patiently waited for Bryony to return.

When Bryony did return two hours later, she brought with her the most strikingly attractive woman Susie could have imagined. She wasn't a stereotypical, blue-eyed blond with a curvy figure and rosebud lips, but she was totally divine. Tall and angularly elegant, the woman had huge dark eyes under a shock of almost cherry-coloured dark curls. But Susie also noticed her slightly ravaged, pain-filled face.

This lovely woman, probably in her late forties, had clearly had adventures. She'd been through something, maybe quite a few somethings over the years. Her eyes were wet with tears, and her clothes hung on her, like she could use a good meal.

Susie wanted to reach out and comfort her. If she could've moved, she would have crawled all over her. If she dared, she wondered if she could even hold one of those slim, ring-covered hands and kiss her palm. Could this woman, this vision of all she might worship, be the good friend Fenella, whom Dr Bryony had told her about?

"My God, Susie, what have you done to yourself?"

A low voice with a highbrow British accent came out of her visitor's mouth, almost impatiently, as though Susie had done something to irritate her. It was thrilling but also scary to hear her speak.

"I'm so sorry," Susie said and looked up at her, feeling very small and definitely inadequate to be a friend of this person. "They tell me I fell off my bike. A car knocked me over, rather. I didn't fall off. I don't remember even learning how to ride a bike. I don't know who I am. I don't know anybody. I'm so sorry, I don't even know who you are."

Susie's voice dropped to a whisper and then broke. Tears rolled down her face. "Are you very cross with me? Are you the person who Bryony told me loves me? Are you Fenella?"

Fenella stared into her eyes, leaning over her with far more pain than irritation. "Oh, my precious darling, yes, of course I am. And how could I ever be cross with you? I've nearly died with worry over being frightened I'd lost you, but it's all been entirely my fault. I should never have let you go off into the night on your bicycle. I should've driven you safely back to college myself. It wasn't even a new bike; it was a thirty-year-old one in my shed, one I rode as a student. And when Bryony told me you were alive, that you were here, in the very good care of her and her colleagues, it was the biggest joy in the world for me."

This sounded so kind, so loving, that Susie snivelled a little and tried to wipe her tears with her left hand.

"Here, let me." Fenella pulled out a damp cotton handkerchief from her cuff and tenderly wiped the tears from Susie's cheeks.

"Kiss me," whispered Susie, staring up into those glorious, dark, troubled eyes. "Please kiss me, if you can bear to. I know I must be all black and blue and look like shit."

"I'll leave you two together," said Bryony quietly, "to get reacquainted, and I'll tell the nurses not to disturb you. It's the best thing you can do for her, Fen. Stay as long as you like."

Fenella sat down on the edge of Susie's bed and leaned in. Susie felt the touch of her lips like a butterfly landing. It was soft and exciting, but far, far too gentle. "More, more." She groaned into the next kiss that made it clear Fenella must love her very, very much. The following kisses were certainly not those of a chance acquaintance.

When Fenella's mouth released hers, Susie bit her lip. "I'm afraid the bike was smashed up. They told me a bus narrowly missed me, but it got the bike good and hard. If I have any money, I'll replace it for you."

Fenella shuddered and closed her eyes. She took Susie's right hand and kissed it. "Don't be an idiot."

They sat holding hands together without talking anymore, until Susie fell asleep, and when she next woke, all the lights were out, and Fenella was sleeping in the chair by her bed.

Susie began to believe what the medics had told her: everything would eventually fall into place, and she knew that even if it didn't, she would still be all right. She had Fenella, and this wonderful stranger, for whatever reason, truly loved her. That was enough. And it really felt like it would always be enough.

Chapter Twenty - Eight

Fenella woke with a crick in her neck when the ward lights flickered to signify it was six o'clock, and wakey-wakey time for the patients. She stretched and looked across to check Susie was still in the hospital bed beside her, and it hadn't been a dream that she was alive. Yes. Thank God the little patient was there, asleep on her back, as any other position was pretty impossible.

She looked so frail, so beaten-up, that Fenella wanted to cry. Why had such an awful thing happened to Susie? Irrational thoughts flooded in. It was her fault for giving her the old bike. Perhaps it had skidded, or the brakes had failed. But she'd sent it to be serviced, and it had new tires and new brake pads. Then she should have driven her home by car. She should have bought her a bright yellow high-viz jacket to wear. She shouldn't have upset Susie by doubting her word, making her flee into the darkness of night.

If she kept blaming herself, she could find herself buried in guilt and self-reproach. She was simply indulging in self-flagellation, and it had to stop. There were better ways to help her young friend. Fenella laid a hand on Susie's forehead and was pleased to find it cool and dry. The fever had abated, which meant her brain's inflammation must be reducing. Susie's face was still raw and swollen in several places, but she hopefully wouldn't be scarred, her two black eyes would fade, and she might be in a fit state to look at herself in the mirror within a few days.

Susie's eyes opened, almost as though she could hear Fenella's thoughts. "Hey, you're still here. Thanks for staying."

"Nowhere in the world I'd rather be," whispered Fenella. "But I do have to leave you for a while. My boys are home alone, and I need to get back and give them breakfast before they go to school."

"You do have boys, don't you? I can see them… Nice faces. Curly dark hair. But I can't remember their names."

"Nate and Freddy. I'll bring them in this evening to visit you, if you could cope with seeing them."

"I'll like that."

Fenella straightened up and pulled on her coat. "I also need to call your family. I have your phone in a bag at home, but I don't suppose you remember the passcode for it. If you don't, it's not a problem. I'll call your cousin Carla and get her to give me your father's number.

Fenella pressed the electric bed hoist button to raise the head end, so Susie could sit up a little.

"Sorry, no, my passcode. Think, think, think!" Susie tugged at her hair.

"Don't try too hard."

"Wait, wait. It's not numbers. It's a shape. Something that means a lot to me. A letter shape."

"S?"

"No." Susie looked at Fenella and grinned. "Try F."

Fenella raised her eyebrows.

"I love it when you do that, all exasperated like."

Fenella lowered her eyebrows and smiled. "I haven't been exasperated with you for months."

Susie reached out for her hand. "Then I must be remembering previous times. I hope I haven't been a pain in the butt. I have no idea how we even know each other. But I'll get there. They say I'll slowly remember everything."

Fenella guessed she would, but worried that the last harsh words they'd had would be the first to return.

"Have we had much sex yet?"

"No, none, and such nonsense should be the last thing for you to worry about. I'm here to take great care of you and get you well again. That's all that matters."

"I don't think so. I know how I feel, and I can see the way you look at me. But I'm glad it hasn't happened yet. I would've hated for us to have already done it and not remember."

Fenella had to laugh in spite of the situation. Susie was irrepressible. "Ridiculous girl. Nothing has happened apart from some kissing and hugging, and me making a fool of myself."

"Not even groping? I hope there might at least have been some groping."

"Shh. Yes, I'll admit there might have been a certain amount of touching and the odd grope. I do adore you after all. But you've been wonderful at respecting my boundaries. I've been worried about how my sons would feel—" She wondered if now was the right time to go into all her hesitations and unconvincing excuses. But she needed to be clear about them no longer being obstacles.

"What are they called again?"

"Nate and Freddy."

"And they don't yet understand, about us?"

"No. But I think they're going to be fine with this—you and me, I mean. Nate said as much. Your father, on the other hand, will probably be appalled. But at least I can tell him you're going to be okay."

Then a nurse arrived, and Fenella dropped a light kiss on Susie's forehead. "I need to go. But I will be back on the dot of two, when official visiting hours start, and I'll bring your phone. I'll also call St Martin's school and explain why you missed classes."

"I'm still at high school? Bryony said I was a student at Oxford University."

"You are. But, sweetheart, you've also been teaching Latin in a high school, the same one my boys attend."

"No way. Teaching? Then I must have some nerve."

"Indeed you do." Fenella smiled and left Susie with the nurse. She went down to the main entrance to book a taxi home. It was six-thirty on a cold, dark December morning. But the underlying joy in her heart made it feel more like midsummer.

Susie was alive, and even the frightening memory loss gave them one blessing: she'd totally forgotten how angry she was with Fenella, which gave Fenella time to put things right before Susie's brain clicked back into action. She rang for an Uber, and when she got home, the house was still quiet and the blinds were drawn. A note on the fridge door from Nate read *It's eleven, so we're going on to bed. Hope Susie is okay. Don't worry if you need to stay out all night. I'll set my alarm and get Fred up for school. xxx*

Fenella smiled at her sweet boy's missive. She turned on the kettle, in desperate need of hot tea, and then took Susie's phone from her bag. It needed charging, so she plugged it in and called Carla.

"Hi, Fenella," Carla said. "Thanks so much for your text last night. So Susie really is going to be all right? Thank God. I rang her folks last night to say we'd found her."

Fenella put Carla on speaker while she made her tea. "It'll be after ten last night on the American West Coast. Should I call her father now, or will you?"

"I'll call Chris and give him your number, then he can get back to you. I know they've been as frantic as you were."

"I'll keep my phone on me all the time," said Fenella and ended the call before getting milk from the fridge. She tried to calm down by doing some small domestic duties, like setting the breakfast table, as if Nate and Freddy normally ever took the time for a sit-down meal before they left in the mornings.

Between sips of tea, she laid out place mats, cutlery, and dishes. She decided to make some old-fashioned porridge on the top of the stove, instead of pushing it into the microwave. She found stirring things oddly comforting, and it centred her mind, which was still flashing and flaring like glass shards within a kaleidoscope. When the porridge was ready, she moved the pan to the back of the hotplate and then sat down at the table. It wasn't long before her phone buzzed.

"Hi, you don't know me, but I'm Chris Webster, Susie's father. Can you update me with how she is? Has she been in a traffic accident?"

"Hi, Mr Webster, yes, I can reassure you. She was knocked off her bike in Oxford last Friday, but don't worry. She's in a good hospital and will be well looked after," said Fenella. She relayed the story as Bryony had told it to her but didn't want to alarm him too much. "She's broken some bones and has internal bruising, as well as some temporary memory loss."

"My poor girl! We want to come over but I think it will have to be next week, when my high school breaks here for Christmas. I can't leave before without a load of hassle. Could you cope until then? I know it's a huge imposition."

"No, it isn't, not at all." Fenella had mixed feelings about the idea of Susie's people coming. Of course Susie would want to see her parents, but selfishly, Fenella cherished the idea of holding and caring for her alone. She hated herself for having such a base desire but had to admit it, if only secretly. Chris Webster clearly had no idea of their relationship.

"I'll go look at hotels and Airbnb options around Oxford, somewhere self-contained where we can take her while she recovers," he said. "We were trying to persuade her to come home for the holidays, but as that's now out of the question, we'll share Christmas with her over there."

"No, please don't worry about Airbnb," Fenella said, trying not to sound too desperate. "I have two large ensuite guest rooms. Come here and stay as long as you like. We'd love to have you both. Susie knows my house very well and is settled here. It will be easier for her here to remember what happened."

"That's very kind, but you must be one busy lady with enough to do without coping with our daughter. But what did you mean by the last thing you said? How bad is her memory loss? Can't she remember much right now?"

"Right now?" Fenella wondered how to put it. Better be honest and tell him the truth. "Nothing much. Her amnesia is pretty total, I'm afraid. Everything before the accident is wiped out. She didn't know who she was, to begin with. But a friend who is a doctor in the hospital recognised her, and now she's making great progress."

"Can you give me a number for the hospital? I need to talk to her doctors at once."

Fenella bridled a little. Didn't he trust her? But of course he would want to know. He was Susie's father after all, and he might learn far more from the medics than she could. She had no connection on paper to Susie at all, and that simple truth made her feel very insecure. The family in America could take Susie back into their fold, not only to somewhere else around Oxford, but also maybe take her home to Oregon as soon as she was deemed fit to travel. Away from Fenella, away from everything they had together. Fenella's morning mood stopped being quite so optimistic.

She found the main switchboard number for the hospital on her iPad and read it to him. "Please, do take my invitation to stay at my house completely seriously. I would love to have you and your wife here, and I know Susie would prefer to stay. She's very fond of…my boys."

He brushed the offer politely to one side. "Thanks, Ms Carlton, but let me try to talk to Susie myself before we arrange anything definite. May I call you again later?"

"Anytime, day or night. I have to work this morning, but I will be seeing Susie at two p.m., and I'll tell her to expect a call from you."

"Good idea, but I need to contact the hospital before then. I'll call them now."

"Goodbye then." Fenella ended the call. It took another cup of tea to calm her nerves before she went upstairs to rouse the boys. They agreed to eat porridge with her, as long as it was laced with golden syrup and didn't have any of the 'yucky' healthy options she wanted to add. They battered her with questions about Susie's health, and she realised just how much she meant to them.

After they had left for school, she called Greta to explain why she was working from home on a Thursday, and then she wrote an email to Stephanie, the true cause of everything bad that had happened to Susie. Whatever the difficulties, she had to find and confront her with the plagiarism issue. Stevie Pole might risk losing her career and her reputation for untainted scholarship, but Susie had damn well nearly lost her life. There was no comparison.

Chapter Twenty - Nine

The mysterious interactions within a large teaching hospital like John Radcliffe were beyond Susie's range of knowledge as she lay in her high electric-powered bed and tried to make a connection with her former self. But from the moment Fenella left, everything began to move quickly, and she kept meeting new faces and learn new names.

Fenella had only been gone five minutes when Sharon's replacement, a health assistant whose lanyard name tag said she was called Tanzi, carried in a tray of food. Susie had ticked the boxes to choose her breakfast preferences the night before but couldn't recall ordering cornflakes and a synthetic-tasting peach yoghurt or cold, floppy white toast and marmalade. She'd ticked on the list of options for a soft-boiled egg, brown toast with Marmite, and melon. But she made the best of it and ate what she was offered, while Tanzi adjusted the bed, checked her fluids, and changed the catheter bag.

"Hi, Tanzi, Are you from around here?" she asked, trying to get some compass points in her head.

"It depends," said Tanzi. "I'm originally from Zimbabwe, but I live in Cowley now."

Susie wanted to find out more, but Tanzi didn't have long to chat.

"Don't you worry now. They're going to move you out of here later, because you're doing so well. They need to get you up and walking again."

A tall nurse, called Khalid, then came into her cubicle. "You're doing so well, you don't need to be in the ICU any longer. When there's a bed available in MAU, we'll send you down there."

"Is it far?" asked Susie. "I'm not sure I can walk very well yet with a broken arm, ribs, and leg."

Khalid laughed loudly. "You won't need to walk. The porters

will take you and your whole bed down in the lift."

"You mean an elevator?"

"Yes. How is the memory this morning?"

Susie couldn't bear to talk about it and simply gave him the thumbs down sign.

"Don't you worry though. They will give you lots of support in the MAU to get you up and about."

"Everybody keeps telling me not to worry," she said, "but I'm panicking here. How can I live when my entire life before I came here is a blank?"

"You took a bang to the head, and you were under general anaesthetic for over six hours. Try to be patient and hopeful. You are doing okay, and in the MAU, they will get you off the drips and catheters and back to going to the toilet yourself. Then the physios can help with exercises to help you regain mobility."

Another nurse came through the curtain and whispered to Khalid.

He turned to Susie. "Hey, it seems your father is on the phone right now from America. Would you like to talk to him?"

"Of course!"

"Then we'll bring in a portable handset, so you can use it. Wait a minute, please."

Susie gulped. She was about to talk to her own father, and she couldn't even remember his name or what he looked like. The nurse brought her a phone, and she gingerly put it to her ear with her right hand. "Hi?"

"Oh my God, Susie, honey. We've been so worried, but your friend Fenella Carlton gave me the number for the hospital. How are you? How are you doing?"

"Much better now. They're moving me out of Intensive Care later." She recognised the voice on the phone. It was a warm, very American voice, one she must have heard thousands of times before. She tried hard but couldn't put a face to it. "The medics keep telling me not to worry. They say I'll be fine. But tell me how things are at home. Tell me everything." She hoped he wouldn't pick up that she was searching for clues that she couldn't remember what her own dad looked like, what home was like, what family she had.

"Well, since we last talked, we've had the first snow, enough to block the road up to town, and to Deirdre and Bernard's. Abbie went up there to visit with them but came back before the storm. Reggie, Bob and Catto are okay. Mandy is laying again and Fletch is annoying everyone as usual."

Susie couldn't keep up and had no idea who her dad was talking about. "Fletch, yeah, he's so annoying." she said. "What a guy!"

"Fletch is your crazy rooster, pickle," he said, sounding confused. "The one you raised from an egg. You don't remember him, do you?"

"Dad." Susie felt her insides crumple and confessed. "Daddy, I don't remember anything. I can't remember what you look like, or who any of those people are you've just talked about." She burst into tears. "Can you come? I need help to relearn everything. Fenella is lovely, but she doesn't know any of you guys, or what my life was in the States."

"Honey, Abbie and I will come over to the UK right away. We'll be on the first flight we can get. We'll be there by tomorrow night if I have to hire a private jet to get there. Just hang in there, and don't worry."

Susie managed to stop crying. She clutched onto the kind, cowboy-like twang in his voice, the Western drawl. Then a face floated through her mind. "Dad, do you have a beard and dark eyes? And wear glasses?"

"Yes, pickle."

"And your name's Chris?"

"It was the last time I signed a check."

"Oh, Dad! I do remember you!"

"That's great, honey! Now I need to make some arrangements. You get some rest, and I'll be back in touch when I know about our flight."

"Fenella's bringing me my phone when she comes back this afternoon. Then we can talk face to face. I think there's a hospital Wi-Fi I can join. They're going to move me somewhere where I can talk. But here in the ICU, everyone's supposed to be quiet and very ill, so they don't like a load of noise."

They finished the call, and the nurse took the phone away. Susie sat back on her pillows and thought deeply about her dad.

She sensed they'd been through a lot together. But where was her mom? He hadn't mentioned her at all. Tears threatened again as she sensed a huge feeling of loss. Maybe Fenella would know.

Two porters pushed her and her bed with all its connected apparatus out of the ICU and then took her on a bewildering journey through corridors and inside a huge elevator. As it went up, she saw the guys pushing and pulling her were called Ahmed and Gary. Susie was developing an appetite for collecting people's names. It helped endorse her own fragile grip on reality and her own sense of self. She asked Ahmed what MAU stood for.

"Medical Assessment Unit."

Oh, good. At least it wasn't short for Memory AWOL. They left her there in the care of Maria from Manila and a tall person from Latvia called Sonya, who must be someone special because she was dressed in a sweater and slacks instead of a hospital uniform.

"Let's take off your head bandage and inspect the damage. Then we can get you all lovely and clean for the day ahead," Maria said.

All of that took most of the morning, and then the ward rounds happened again.

"Now we'll have to get you up and about," Dr Gillian said, appearing from nowhere. "No more lying in bed all day."

"I'm up for it," said Susie. "But where's Dr Bridgford today? She's my friend. She knows me, even if I don't."

"She'll be coming on shift after lunch. You can see her then."

"How soon will I be able to leave hospital?"

Gillian Davis turned to her little posse of medical students and juniors. "See, this is a good sign. The quality of the hospital food works wonders for rehabilitation."

She turned back to Susie as the team laughed obediently. "If things keep improving, I hope to see the back of you by next weekend—if you have people who can look after you at home."

"I do, I do. Dr Davis, sorry, but where do you live? I'm collecting place names."

"I drive in from Cirencester. It's a town forty miles from here, in Gloucestershire."

A bell rang in Susie's head. "I've heard the name before. I think it's important."

Gillian Davis smiled. "Well, maybe not so much now, but in 200 A.D. it was the second biggest Roman garrison town in England after London. There's a nice museum there you should visit if you're interested, when you're up and about again."

Susie looked at the doctor. "Corinium."

"That's right," she said and looked impressed. "Cirencester was once called Corinium. So you *are* the Latin scholar Bryony told me you were."

Dr Davis bustled away with her little flock, leaving Susie clinging to the straw of that one little word: *Corinium.* She liked it. But it also troubled her. It had some meaning she couldn't remember.

Sonya returned shortly after and sat beside her. "It says on your notes you're a student studying Latin, and you also teach in a local school. Do you remember anything in Latin at the moment?"

"One or two odd phrases popped into my mind, but that's all."

Sonya smiled and nodded. "It may help if you can read something in Latin to stimulate the language section of your brain. Can someone bring you in a book or two?"

"I'm sure my friend Fenella can when she comes. I hope to see her very soon, but I can't tell her to bring books until she's here. I wish I could call her, but she has my phone."

"Well, when she visits, give her a list of everything you want. But for now, take this," Sonya handed her a clipboard and pen, "and start to write down what you want and then anything you think of on the paper. Let the words come through your mind and jot them down. I'll come back later, and we can look at the results."

"A literal brainstorm?"

"That's the ticket. I can see your use of English hasn't deserted you."

"Fenella said that before I even started Latin, I was trilingual, in US English, proper British English, and US kidspeak slang."

"When did she say this?"

"Months ago, when we first met... Hey! It was before the accident. How did I know?"

"Everything that's ever happened to you is tucked away inside your brain, which is healing in its own good time. Gentle stimulus will help, but stress won't, so try to avoid worrying."

Susie sighed and rolled her eyes. "That's what everyone keeps telling me."

"And they're right."

Latvian Sonya went away, and a whole series of other people bustled in and out, helping her stand and hop from bed onto a wheelchair and then be pushed to a toilet where she could sit in privacy and do her stuff. Amazing what she'd achieved in the twenty-four hours since she'd woken from the coma.

Chapter Thirty

Fenella's email to Stephanie Pole went against all her avowed rules of grammar and style. She repeated herself three times, used the word imperative twice in one line, and ended it with at least four repeated exclamation marks. The title of the email read, "I must see you. Urgent. Urgent. Urgent." If that didn't raise the old stick, nothing would.

Wherever Stevie was hiding, Fenella received a reply within thirty minutes. Why she hadn't circumvented the stroppy receptionist in the first place and done this obvious thing, she wasn't sure. Being in love with Susie was annihilating her own common sense, that was why.

What's so urgent? I'm staying in Whitney, pet sitting for my cousins' cats and catching up with some reading. If you want to see me, come over. I'm in all morning.

Tell me the address and I'll be there. Fenella wasn't about to give Stevie any forewarning about the reason for her visit.

Whitney, thirteen miles west of Oxford, was a pretty market-town with good schools, and was a favourite dormitory for academics who couldn't afford Oxford prices. She found the house tucked into a corner of a sprawling estate of more than a hundred houses. It was a maze, appropriately called The Warren. Stephanie was staying at 124, and Fenella needed her sat nav's help to find it. She squeezed her car in between people's front gates and walked up the path, briefcase under her arm.

When Stevie opened the door, Fenella had to stop her mouth from falling open. Stevie had gone grey since they'd last met, and her hair fell in a straight, uncompromising line down each side of her face. She wore a shapeless, grey knit dress, with a grey cardigan on top. With her fair complexion and grey eyes, she looked like a ghost. An outfit that might have looked stylish on a teenage model in Vogue made her look twenty years older than she was, and worse, made her appear defeated. She certainly wasn't a poster girl for Classical Studies.

"Hello, come on through," Stevie said. "I expect you'd like a coffee. It's only instant."

"Don't go to the trouble," said Fenella. I haven't got very long, as I must get back to Oxford by two. But I need to talk to you about your latest book. I've been reading it."

"Oh? Then come through to the sitting room." Stevie shooed away three cats who had come to see if their owners were at the door. Disappointed, they faded away into a back room, and she and Fenella took a seat.

"How are you doing, Fen? Got over what's-his-name doing a bunk yet?"

"Fine. It wasn't difficult. Old news now."

Stevie had never married and seemed to regard Fenella's three failed attempts to build a happy family with great suspicion. Fenella decided to get straight to the point. "Stevie, why did you use someone else's writing and research in this book and give them no mention, not even a footnote, nor any credit for all their research and scholarship?"

Stevie abruptly stood up, a flash of temper crossing her face. Fenella thought for one moment she might even be struck by her old friend, but she merely paced across the room and stood looking out of the window, hiding her face from Fenella. The ensuing silence was painful.

"Don't tell me you didn't. Because I've read the whole thing, and the middle chapters aren't by you at all. In fact, I've sourced the whole eighty-page section, and it was written by an Italian DPhil student called Marcella Novaroma who was killed ten years ago in a plane crash."

"How did you find that out?"

Fenella wasn't going to mention Susie and have her possibly scape-goated. She wasn't sure how vindictive Stevie might be. "I write and read for a living, remember? And with the help of AI it was easy to—"

"Oh, AI! Yes, of course! I might have known, of all people, you'd know how to dig up the dirt on someone. What are you going to do? Set up a smear campaign?"

Fenella frowned. "Isn't the essence of a smear that it's untrue or exaggerated? And why assume I'm on some sort of vendetta? We've known each other twenty-five years. No, this is all about you, Stevie. How has it come to this, you being so stupid? So lazy! What's happened to you?"

Stevie wearily resumed her seat. "I've no excuse. No terminal illness dragging me down and no demented old mother I need to care for. I'm just totally, utterly pissed off with Latin. I wasted half my life on the Romans, but not anymore. I hate the bunch of fools in the Classics department, the archaic nonsense of this pompous university, and everything else in my life." She turned back towards Fenella, who was concerned by the bleakness in her eye. "I couldn't be arsed to finish the book by the publishers' deadline, not that any more than fifty people will ever think of buying it. So I took a shortcut and crammed Marcella's work in the middle to pad it all out. No one but you has even noticed. And Marcella made me angry, back in 2014, when I supervised her. I suppose I wanted to take my revenge."

Fenella shook her head slowly, not quite believing the drivel she was hearing. "But why? What had she done wrong to hurt you?"

"She was everything I once might have dreamed of being and wasn't. Young, idealistic, sincere, and excited by everything. She was also very pretty and wrote well, far better than I can write. I tried to be her friend, to mentor her. I even suggested we went out for a drink together. But I could tell she wasn't interested."

The slight inference that Stevie might have fancied Marcella surprised Fenella. She'd always seemed impervious to same-sex attraction. "So? Did that really matter?"

"No, but one day, I overheard her mimicking me in the corridor to some other students. That hurt. Really hurt. When her plane crashed, I was devastated. But then my heart closed down, and I buried everything. It was only when I started to write about tombstone inscriptions that I remembered her thesis and thought, 'What the hell? What have I got to lose?'"

"Your job and your reputation? How about that for starters?"

"To be honest, I don't care about either." Stevie shrugged. "I hate my job, and I couldn't care less about my reputation."

"But you can't let it lie," Fenella said. "You have to put it right."

"I know. It's only a matter of time before someone else as bright as you picks up on it. In fact, last week I had an idea someone already had."

"Who?"

"Oh, no one you'd know. An annoyingly precocious little American first-year who wears her brains and love of Latin on her sleeve like a shiny badge. She reminded me somewhat of Marcella, and I know she wanted to talk about the book, but I managed to send her packing. I can't bear the enthusiasm of bright students anymore. The brighter they are, the harder they'll fall. They all need to be discouraged from thinking scholarship is fun or worthwhile."

Fenella closed her eyes briefly, stunned by Stevie's cynicism, by the depth of her nihilism, and her obvious depression. "So what will you do about this?"

"What I've already almost decided to do," Stevie said quietly, her expression blank and cold. "Resign my fellowship and the professorship, withdraw the book, and go far away from Oxford to do something else with the rest of my life, something I've always wanted to do."

"What?" Fenella leaned forward to hear her better.

"Move to Fiji and learn to carve ocean-going canoes."

"What? You must be joking." This was bizarre, even funny. Stevie had the muscle tone of over-cooked spaghetti.

"Not at all. I saw a documentary on *National Geographic*. There's a place there where you can train. That's what I want to do—what I'm going to do. If you expose me, it will be a big favour. It will be easier for people to understand, and it'll let me escape. When I've carved a canoe, I'm setting out on a voyage of discovery in it, across a limitless ocean."

Fenella moved closer and took her arm. "If you mean what you say, then I won't need to expose you. But Stevie, I'm serious. If you don't end the fraud yourself, I *will* do it for you. And before you go off travelling to the end of the earth, I think you need to see a doctor and get some anti-depression medication, and you should see a therapist. I feel guilty for letting it get this bad and not keeping in touch. But I always assumed you had your dream job, that you were fulfilled and happy teaching in Oxford."

"Ha! Maybe we're both good at hiding depression. But I've never been suicidal, like you were over that Bridgford woman. I never wanted to take my life, although I've been pretty near it at times."

Fenella wrapped her arms around Stevie's thin shoulders and hugged her. "I'm so sorry. I'll never forget how you saved my life. If you hadn't found me after the overdose and called an ambulance, I wouldn't be here now. Thank you for never telling anyone. You helped me recover, and I'm so grateful that no one else ever knew how I almost died."

"It was your first big love affair," Stevie said. "She seduced you, took you to bed, and then dumped you when the next pretty face turned her head. She was a heartless bitch, and I hope she's had her just rewards."

Fenella shook her head. "Bel has changed profoundly since her twenties. I saw her not long ago. In fact, she and her wife came to lunch with some mutual friends, and I don't think she even remembered me from our time in college. She slept with so many women in those days. But since then, she's had her own disasters and heartbreak. Her first wife was murdered by sex-traffickers she was investigating, and then Bel nearly died in a road crash. She still walks with a slight limp."

"Well, I'm glad. God, how I hate the bitch."

"Don't say that."

"You don't still carry a torch for her, do you?"

"No, I don't. But there is someone—"

"Tell me about it some other time. I have to write letters to the faculty board and my publishers, and I want to get them in the post this afternoon. You know how terrible the service is right now, and I need my resignation to reach them before Christmas."

"Christmas! It's only ten days away now. So, I suppose it's goodbye, my friend, and good luck. Send me a card from Fiji."

And Fenella fled the house, and the smell of cats, and Stevie's black mood. But she knew now she could tell Susie the truth about their last time together, and she could have real hope that the outcome would satisfy her. She headed towards Oxford and put her foot down, desperate to not miss a second of the hospital afternoon visiting time.

Chapter Thirty-One

Fenella came sailing around the corner of Susie's new ward on the stroke of two p.m. looking stunning. Fresh stylish clothes, clattering high heels, perfect make-up, and smoothed down copper-coloured curls. Something had changed in her mood, since she'd staggered away from the hospital at six a.m. Susie hoped it was mostly relief that she was on the mend, and they could resume whatever their relationship was before.

Fenella dropped two interesting-looking bags onto the bed. "Good to see your head's out of the bandage. How does it feel now?"

"Better." Susie couldn't help a smile of pleasure, even though any movement in her face hurt. "The little man with the road drill has gone to lunch. I thought you might not find me tucked away in this new ward."

"It's actually easier to find than the ICU, once I asked at the front desk. This hospital is the size of a small town."

"But you found me. I so hoped you would."

"You still know who I am, I suppose?"

"Of course; you're my humongous giant crush."

"And I go by the name of?"

"Fenella."

Fenella smiled. "Second name?"

"Don't push it. What does that matter? We're definitely on first name terms."

Fenella sat down on the edge of the bed and let Susie pull her in for a long kiss. She smelled of something wonderful. Susie held her in close with her left arm and remembered the perfume. She couldn't quite grasp its name, but its importance was obvious. "You smell amazing." She nibbled on her bottom lip. "I think I have something with the same scent. They've given me a bag of my clothes from the ambulance, and there was a little handkerchief inside it. Can you pull it out of my locker?"

Fenella retrieved a large plastic bag. She screwed her eyes shut in apparent horror at the bloodstains on the ruined skirt and tights.

Susie pulled her arm. "Okay, don't look too much. You can throw the whole bag away if you like. But grab that little cotton hanky on top. It means something very special. It smells of your perfume. They said they found it stuffed inside my bra."

Fenella lifted out the tiny white square and stared down at it for so long, seeming to find it fascinating. Then she sniffed it and made a strange little noise, clearly trying not to cry.

"What's the matter? "What have I done?" Susie was alarmed. The last thing she wanted was to make Fenella sad.

Fenella looked back at Susie with tear-filled eyes. "I knew you'd be nothing but trouble, the first time we met. I knew I was lost for good."

Susie reached over and took the scrap of cloth from Fenella's hand. "So tell me the story of this handkerchief."

"We were together in my house in late September, for our last evening together before you took up your place at St Hilary's. You begged me to let you stay the night, to take you up to bed with me, and I so badly wanted to."

"So why didn't you? Before I looked exactly like a car wreck. I don't know how you can possibly want me anywhere near you now." Susie could have cried just thinking how gross she must look to Fenella.

But Fenella leaned over and laid a finger against her lips. "Shh. Because I had some nonsensical idea about not exploiting you and making you unhappy, so I wouldn't listen to my feelings. Then you'd obviously been reading too much Chaucer, because you came back at me with a silly notion of medieval courtly love."

"What? Did I?" Fenella stared into her eyes and held Susie's gaze.

"Yes, for a joke to begin with. You said if you were going to be a knight hanging around outside my castle and I was a lady looking down from on high, you needed a token of affection, a favour as they used to call it, and you asked for… Well, let's not go there, but I gave you this handkerchief."

Susie frowned. "That's so weird. I don't think I've ever seen a woman's cotton handkerchief before. Certainly, we don't go in for them in America."

Fenella narrowed her eyes slightly. "How would you know? Do you remember? Anyway, every Friday since, when you've come for dinner, you've made me douse it afresh in a scent called J'adore, and I've indulged you. You then tucked it into your bra, flashing your breasts at me while you did it, of course."

Susie was happy. It was such a fun story. "Sounds as though it was quite a party. But do I still need an excuse to flash my boobs? Wear your love token instead of experiencing it first hand? Are you going to stay up in your castle for ever?"

"It was never much of a castle." Fenella smiled and ran her fingers along Susie's cheek. "And I have no more battlements left in place against loving you. I've knocked them all down myself. I'm completely vulnerable. I think it's up to you whether you break my heart or not, and in return, I'll try not to break yours. Could you possibly love me, Susie? How I need to be loved?"

Susie was so close to her, she could feel Fenella's breath on her face. "And how is that?" she whispered.

"Madly, deeply, the whole caboose. I want you with me for ever. I want to marry you one fine day, if you'll agree to such a crazy idea."

Susie swallowed, hard. She had no words. Was Fenella proposing to her before they'd even had sex? She felt totally inadequate. She didn't know, but she might still be a virgin. How could she ever make someone as experienced and wonderful as Fenella satisfied in bed?

"I know my track record is disastrous," Fenella said and then kissed Susie's knuckles, "and that I'm probably older than your father. He's bound to be horrified and will rightly hate me on sight."

This thought jolted Susie's mind onto another track. "Well, we'll find out soon enough," she said. "He's arriving late tomorrow."

Fenella gasped. "Is he? When we last spoke, he mentioned having to wait until the holidays."

"He called me after he talked to you, and he changed his mind on that idea pretty fast when he realised I couldn't even remember his name and I thought Fletch, our rooster, was a guy."

Fenella released her hand. "In that case, everything changes. Forget what I've said. Family comes first. I'll wait until you've completely recovered before—"

"Hey! Wait one frigging minute! You can't declare undying love to a person and then say, 'Whoops, sorry. Didn't mean it if your dad's turning up.'"

Fenella had the grace to look ashamed and took Susie's hands again. "Sorry, I panicked. I have very little moral courage. But if it was just the two of us involved here, what would you say to my clumsy proposal?"

Susie knew Fenella was completely sincere, and this was a most wonderful offer, but she needed to be equally truthful, and as brave herself. "If I was fit, I mean, like with functioning arms and legs and a brain that works, I'd say, bring it on. You've loved me before, for whatever mad reason, and I'm crazy in love with you. But I don't think you know what you're offering, Fenella. You can't be shackled to someone without a brain, someone who can't even remember where you live, or the names of your children. Supposing my memory never comes back? Supposing I stay like this for ever?" She couldn't let Fenella sacrifice her whole life to nursing and caring for someone with total amnesia.

"You won't stay like this," said Fenella firmly. "Losing your memory is not unlike losing your luggage on a transcontinental flight. It may take a little time, but eventually, it will come back to you. But anyway, in the extremely remote possibility of that not being the case, we will just set to and create new memories together. You'll still be the same exasperating, adorable little genius. We need to trust in the Universe."

Susie wondered how to express her adoration. Physically, that was a problem right now. She decided she'd try to deflect the heaviness of the moment, because the underlying reality of her amnesia weighed down on her more heavily than her plaster casts. "Sonya, the hospital psychologist, suggested I should try to read some Latin. She told me it might help trigger my memory centres. I don't suppose there are any Latin books in the bags you've brought, are there?"

Fenella opened the first one. "Let's find out. At least I've brought you some fruit and snacks, the sort I know you like. "

Susie looked inside and saw grapes, easy peel oranges, dates, and liquorice toffees. Fenella clearly had a care for the workings of her digestive tract. Then she looked at the second bag, a large cotton tote with a college crest on it.

"This is your bag," Fenella said, "the one you always carry over your shoulder. It has your phone inside." She carefully placed the tote on Susie's bed. "I've charged it up for you. And you also have some Latin schoolbooks in here, the ones you were using to teach teenage boys, including my sons."

"Oh shit, did I miss any classes?" Susie's heart thumped with anxiety about missing her unknown professional commitments.

"Don't worry about that. I've sorted it with St Martin's. They know all about your accident now. And the school closes this week for the Christmas break, so you can decide in January if you want to return."

"Doctor Gillian said they might let me out in a few days. Can I come home with you?"

"Of course. When I talked to your father, I invited him and Abbie to stay with us as well, but he was talking about getting an Airbnb or some such nonsense. I need to convince him we'll all be happier in Lavington Road."

Susie saw the property in her mind and squeaked. "Number thirty-eight! I can remember it. It has a blue front door and gables."

"Good Lord, that's right! See, I'm sure everything will come back to you before long. Now read me some Latin, and I'll test you on the translation."

Susie pushed the book aside and grabbed her wrist. "Not now, I have something much more urgent to ask you. I need to know what happened to my mother. Dad didn't mention her when he called. And who's Abbie? Have I told you stuff about my family? Can you fill me in, so I don't look too stupid when they get here?"

Fenella set down the Latin primer she'd taken from the bag. "Okay, if you think you're ready for it," she caressed Susie's thumb gently, "I'll tell you what I know, what you told me."

Susie listened carefully to Fenella tell her the story of her mother's death, her own subsequent unhappiness and years of drug abuse and self-harm, and her father's second marriage. It was a hard tale to hear, especially as it was all true. Fenella wouldn't make anything up. "Jeez, I sound a total headcase and a hellish brat. How could you, or anyone, possibly love me?"

"Silly heart," Fenella said. "You were young, and you were in pain. Of course you acted out."

Then Fenella gathered her in and hugged her hard, rocking away the pain. Susie relaxed into the embrace, needing Fenella like the beat of her own heart. Whatever it took, however long the struggle, she would get fit again and be worthy of Fenella, the amazing and gorgeous woman who lived at 38 Lavington Road, the big redbrick house with the blue front door, and the woman who clearly adored her.

Chapter Thirty-Two

On Friday morning, Fenella climbed the stairs to the guest rooms for the third time since breakfast. Hazel, her weekly cleaner, had made up the beds and left the ensuite bathrooms gleaming, but Fenella still double-checked all the drawers and closets, refolded the towels, positioned some Molton Brown bottles of shower gel and hand cream in the shower, and twitched the window curtains to make sure there were no hibernating little bugs behind them. She was being ridiculous, but Susie's father and her stepmother had finally accepted her invitation to stay with her, and she was as nervous as a twenty-something youngster wanting not to offend the in-laws.

Fenella had already ordered a single bed to be put into the back snug for Susie in anticipation of her return, so she wouldn't have to hop up and down two flights of stairs on her crutches. That meant Chris and Abbie could have the top floor all to themselves and enjoy some privacy. Fenella didn't think Chris would appreciate a busman's holiday, sharing space with two noisy teenage gamers all Christmas.

Their flight from Oregon was due into Heathrow around one, where Carla was meeting them with a hired car booked to drive them to Oxford, so they should arrive before the winter afternoon became too dark. Fenella turned up the thermostat for the central heating and went downstairs. She had an hour or two to herself before visiting Susie, and she collapsed on the sofa with a coffee and put her feet up. She was about to grab her iPad to check for emails when the front doorbell rang.

"Who on earth is that?" She wasn't expecting anybody and reluctantly went to answer the door. She pulled back the heavy winter curtain and clicked open the lock.

A person she last expected to see, Bel Bridgford, stood on the step, muffled up against the cold, her large grey eyes peeping out from under a fake Russian fur hat. Fenella couldn't hide her surprise.

Bel said, "I know. I should've phoned first, but I bottled out. Can I come in? I need to talk to you."

Fenella found her voice, finally. "Then yes, come on in. How are you, Bel?"

"Fair to middling."

Fenella led her into the lounge. She hadn't seen Bel since the lunch party back in September. After Stevie's diatribe, she wondered whether she should be angrier with Bel than she felt. It was ironic that Stevie still loathed the woman after a quarter of a century, while Fenella…well, she didn't feel anything at all. "Coffee? Tea?"

"No, thanks."

"Take a seat then and tell me what brings you here."

Bel perched on the edge of a chair. "I visited Susie last night, after you'd gone home. I went to collect Bryony a little early, so I could find her ward before they kicked out visitors. Poor kid, she's had a tough call."

"I know," said Fenella, her chest tightening at the memory of Susie in the sterile, hospital bed, alone and hurting. She didn't need any lessons in anxiety.

"But she's dealing with it much better than I did when I broke pretty much the same number of bones seven years ago. I was horrible to everyone, and to myself. For weeks I wanted to die, and it was only Bryony flying into my life like a good angel who saved me."

"Yes, I heard you went through a terrible crash, after losing your wife." Where on earth was this going?

"But Susie will be all right. Much better than me. Not only because she's a much kinder, nicer, less judgemental person than I was, but because she has you. I came to tell you, Fen, that Susie really, really loves you, and I'm sure that she'll make you very, very happy."

This wasn't Bel's place to judge. Fenella felt more than irritated to be instructed on Susie's feelings for her. How dare she presume to give her advice?

"I know she loves me, and I hope I can make her happy. That's my only worry. But why visit me in person to say this?"

"Because I have a huge burden of guilt on my heart, one that I've carried for years already, and I wanted to make sure you're all right." Bel took off her hat and suddenly looked smaller and more vulnerable. Her mouth trembled. "I need to know what I did to you all those years ago hasn't destroyed your confidence or made you doubt the wisdom of loving a woman. I was a selfish, rapacious bitch then, and I treated you like shit. You were so lovely, and young, and trusting, and you never deserved the tiniest bit of what I did to you."

Fenella couldn't hide her astonishment, but if Bel wanted to clear the air, then she'd gladly participate. "You're right, I didn't deserve it. I see that clearly now. I'd never even kissed a girl before you, and you took my virginity. You showed me what ecstasy could feel like, but then you threw me away. I have never felt so bad, before or after. And when you came to lunch here in September, you acted like you didn't remember me. That made me feel like I was forgettable and worthless and simply one of so many, another notch on your bedpost."

"Oh, Fen, don't think that," Bel said. "Of course I remembered you. No one could ever forget you. I was so nervous before your lunch, about meeting you again, that I nearly didn't come. You weren't merely a passing fancy for me. With you, I might have made it, but I didn't have the guts to try. I knew it had to be all or nothing, and that you'd never settle for a casual fling, but I was too scared of commitment. So I ran away to Cambridge and pretended it hadn't been as important a relationship as it was. But something happened last night that's shaken me to my bones."

"What?"

"Stephanie Pole called me late, quite out of the blue. She told me you tackled her on plagiarism and for stealing a student's research to pass off as her own. She says her life here is over, and she intends to head off to Tonga or somewhere."

Fenella nodded. "I did. I went to see her yesterday and confronted her. But it wasn't me who actually discovered the fraud; it was Susie. I didn't want Stephanie to know that though. She's so negative and full of self-loathing, she might do anything. She says she hates Oxford and all it stands for.”

“Well, she certainly hates me, and she decided to make amends to you by telling me a few home truths.”

“Oh no!”

“Oh yes, she told me everything that happened after I left, and it shocked me to the core. I never had a clue that you felt so bad. I would’ve come straight back to Oxford if I’d known. I’m truly, deeply sorry that I made you so unhappy you swallowed a whole bottle of aspirin and tried to end your life.”

Fenella listened to the words, and now, a quarter of a century later, could hardly believe it of herself. “Thank God Stephanie found you in time! I know you won’t ever forgive me, but I wanted to tell you, I’m completely penitent. Life has kicked me in the teeth a few times since, and my oldest friend, Jane, made it plain that if I ever hurt Bryony like I hurt you, she won’t be responsible for her actions.”

Fenella shrugged. She’d worshipped Bel once, but looking at her now hardly raised her heartbeat at all. “It all happened a long time ago. We’ve both kicked a few barrels down the road since. I’ve hurt people too, mainly men. After you, I tried to hide my sexuality and join the mainstream, but it never worked. It satisfied neither me nor them. The truth of who we are has an annoying habit of surfacing sooner or later. But Bel, believe me. I forgive you, completely. I’m over it, and you need to know that. Don’t worry about it anymore.”

“Can you really forgive me, after what I did, for such a cowardly reason?” Bel gripped her hat and twisted it in her hands.

Fenella stood up. She was taller than Bel by at least three inches and felt it was time she took charge of the conversation. “I can, and I do. Dumping someone when you’re twenty-something isn’t a capital offence. If I hadn’t lost my mother and hadn’t been all at sea emotionally before I even met you, it probably wouldn’t have got to me so much. They say to love someone inevitably leads to hurt, but I also think it means you can so easily hurt others as well.”

“Well, that’s true.” Bel stood up herself and met Fenella’s eye. “Why do we do it to ourselves and each other?”

Fenella shrugged. “It’s a form of madness. It’s why I’ve tried to be so careful with Susie. She’s the same age I was when I met you, and she's had very similar issues to mine, growing up. But with you, I can honestly say, taking that overdose and enduring its painful aftermath shocked me out of loving you. I'm no longer unhappy, and I'm not in the least bitter. I genuinely admire all you've done with your life, your cleverness, and your candour, and I hope we can move towards being friends in future."

Bel's eyes fell, and she seemed doubtful. "I'd like it too, very much, if you'll let us. My wife wants it, I know. Bryony thinks you and Susie are both wonderful, and she longs to know you better. She has great taste."

"Bryony is a darling. I can't think how she copes with you!" Fenella let the conversation finish on a lighter note. "Now, if we're done, I must throw you out as I have someone else to worry about. Susie's father is arriving shortly from America, and I'm as nervous as a teenager wanting to date his daughter."

Bel moved to leave. "He'll be very lucky to have you. So you and Susie? Have you bought her a ring yet?"

"No, but I have clumsily asked her to marry me when she's better, although she's worrying about her memory loss now and being a burden. I need to show her how much it doesn't matter. And I will. Olivia will tell you how head over heels in love I am with her, more now even than I was in September."

"We've both seen the best and worst of love, haven't we? These days, I'm so grateful for every moment I have Bryony in my life. With the world in such chaos, she keeps me centred."

"The old truth. It makes the world go around. Thanks for coming, Bel. I know it took courage, and I appreciate it."

As Fenella opened the front door, Bel pulled her hat back on and wound her scarf around her neck. "Let's see some more of each other in future. After the holidays, you and Susie should come out to Woodstock to visit us. I have several friends in Oxfordshire and Gloucestershire she should meet too. And there are so many Roman remains to visit as well. The Cotswolds are packed with them."

"We will, we certainly will." Fenella ushered Bel off and waved her goodbye. The encounter gave her much to think about, and perhaps Stevie pole-axing Bel with hard truths would mark a turning point in their unfinished business. The air was finally cleared between them, and some new kind of friendship had been made less implausible.

But now Susie was waiting for her in hospital, and all Fenella's thoughts turned back to her. Susie still hadn't answered her proposal, and Fenella was terrified that every hour apart would make her less likely to agree to it.

Chapter Thirty-Three

Bel's surprise visit the previous evening had encouraged Susie that she'd regain her memory, but more importantly, it had strengthened her understanding of Fenella. Bel had to introduce herself to begin with, but the longer they talked, the more certain Susie was she knew her, and that they'd met before at Fenella's. "You're vegetarian, aren't you? Didn't I once cook a meal for you and Dr Bryony."

"You did, and it was delicious," Bel said. "You're a great cook. Bryony, who is also a superb chef and does most of the cooking in our home, copied the vegan recipe you made especially for us at the lunch party Fenella held. We've eaten it several times since."

"What was it?"

"You tell me. See if it comes back to you."

Susie had screwed up her face and shut her eyes. She could visualise removing a large serving dish from the oven. "Black bean enchiladas!"

"Spot on."

"I remember their smell and the taste of the sauce. The psychologist told me smells can be the first thing we remember. Smelling Fenella's lovely perfume helped me too. And the very first memory I had after the road crash was of sticky toffee pudding and caramel ice cream. I could remember the smell and the taste of it without any prompting. But why is everything so random?"

"Don't worry if your head is all over the place," Bel said. "The immediate aftermath of a road traffic accident can be traumatic."

Bel told her the story of how she and Bryony met, and what a monster she'd been to begin with. "Brain-damaged, bruised, broken, and furious, I was the worst patient in the world," she'd said. She'd been in hospital for six weeks before she hired Bryony as part nurse, part assistant. "I was completely off my head for half of the time in hospital."

"So I'm not doing too badly?" Susie asked.

"I should say not," said Bel. "You're doing brilliantly. Your brain simply needs more time to heal, as long as your external bruises might take. Probably longer. But when you're back with Fenella and out of these institutional surroundings, I'm sure your memory will improve more quickly. She's a wonderful person and very kind under all that glamour and style."

"I'm so worried that I won't get my memory back enough to be back to my old self, to be independent. I couldn't bear to be a burden to Fen."

Bel shook her head. "Don't tell her that. It will only hurt her. I pushed Bryony away because I didn't want to lumber her with me, but it simply made us both miserable. I think you'll bring huge joy into Fenella's life, and I want her to find the happiness she deserves."

"Have you known her a long time?"

Bel hesitated and looked uncomfortable. "I knew her when she was a freshman student in the college where I was a junior research fellow. But our paths divided then for many years, until our mutual friend Olivia invited me to join them for lunch. But you don't need to hear our old history. I wanted you to know there are a whole group of friends around Fenella wishing you well, and we're all here to encourage and support your recovery."

"Is there a big age-gap between you and Dr Bryony?" Susie asked.

Bel shrugged. "I would think it's about the same as between Fenella and you."

"And it works? You don't find her too young and annoying?"

Bel laughed. "Quite the opposite! Bryony is the sensible one in our marriage. I rely on her for nearly everything, and I bask in the warmth of her glowing reputation. She's going to be a brilliant surgeon, and loving her is my greatest privilege. She is the breath in my lungs. She keeps me alive. And sane."

They chatted some more, and then Bel kissed Susie's cheek before she slipped away into the labyrinth of the hospital to wait for Bryony. Susie had thought about their conversation for the rest of the evening and had come around to firmly deciding she shouldn't hesitate in accepting Fenella's proposal. She wouldn't keep Fenella waiting. When she came at visiting time, she would definitely say yes to marriage, if Fenella really wanted her, bruises, crazy brain, and all.

She didn't know what the alternatives were and didn't care. They were in a void right now, like floating on a cloud, with Susie having no conscious past and no fixed plans for her future, but it didn't matter. She would take Fenella in both hands and trust she knew what was best for them both.

While she waited for Fenella to arrive, Susie sat on a chair with her fractured leg supported on a footstool. She had started to read one of the school's Latin grammar books and found that she understood most of the words on the page and could automatically translate them.

When Fenella did come clattering down the corridor, turning heads, she carried another bag of goodies. "You like these," she said, offering up more grapes and liquorice toffees. "And you can do the super fiendish sudokus in the *Times* in less than ten minutes." She laid out the paper and a little book of puzzles on Susie's table.

"Can I?" Susie grinned and held out her good arm for a hug. "I reckon I must have a few brains then."

"Just a few." Fenella kissed her mouth gently. "I'm pleased to see your face is healing. Your dad is due in Oxford later, and we don't want to upset him too much, do we?"

"No, but I think he might not only be upset by what a mess I look, but also when I tell him I'm going to marry you and live here in England with you for ever."

"Are you?" Fenella looked relieved. "What brought you around to this crazy idea?"

"Bel. She came to see me last night and told me it would be mean not to marry you and let you take care of me."

Fenella chuckled. "Did she now? Well, Bel came to see me as well this morning, and we became reacquainted. She's been a very busy woman."

"But she was right. I love you from your heels to the top of your head, Fenella, and I vow that when I'm fit again, I will do all I can to make you happy. Please be patient with me."

Susie didn't say more, frightened she already sounded pathetic, but her mood kept swinging from optimism back to despair. Her biggest fear was of disappointing Fenella, who deserved a girlfriend with the sharpest wit and highest degree of mental acuity.

"Of course, though you already make me more than happy. But let's keep our long-term plans quiet for now? We don't want to upset Daddy so soon, and I need to have a talk with my boys to prepare the way before we make any big announcement."

"Naturally. Your time frame. Tell me what to say or not say. You told me before that your boys were coming to visit me tonight. Nathan and Freddy. Is that right?"

"Yes, but I think now they can wait until tomorrow. It's more important your dad and stepmom have time with you to themselves this evening. They've agreed to come back home with me, and I hope they'll stay with us until after Christmas. Carla, your cousin, is meeting them at Heathrow and driving them to Oxford. She'll be with them this evening."

Fenella hadn't noticed, but Susie had lost her halfway through this conversation. She was forced to ask, "Carla? I'm not sure I know her."

"Oh, yes, you 'll remember her when you see her. You stayed with her in London. Carla introduced you to me."

"Then I love her already!"

Susie picked up the Sudoku magazine. She didn't even remember the word. "Now, what am I supposed to do with this puzzle book?"

"Give it to me, and I'll show you. It is full of logic puzzles, of various levels."

Fenella showed her how sudoku worked, and Susie discovered something else her battered brain could enjoy. At three, Fenella dashed away again, but when she returned to the hospital at seven, she came with three people in tow, two of whom Susie instantly recognised, which was a giant relief.

"Daddy! Abbie! How could I forget? And Abbie, all your purple braids! I love them. Oh, and you're Carla! How could I forget you? How's Richie doing?" It took Susie a few minutes to calm down enough for anyone else to get a word in.

Her dad looked tired, but so like himself she could have cried.

He kissed her forehead and held her hand. "Slow down, pickle. Take a breath and tell us the whole story. How are you, really? I want to hear it straight from you."

Susie's first impulse was to declare herself fit and well. But that'd be a stupid lie, and she'd promised in rehab never to pretend she felt better than she was. "I've been told I'm on the mend. Everything aches right now and my face is sore, and I've probably got lots of internal bruising, but the most frightening thing is not being able to remember or recognise anybody. Although that horror is lifting in little patches, like the sun peeping through the clouds. There seems no pattern to it. But smells, and tastes, and reading Latin passages all seem to help. And I recognised you the moment you walked in. So that's amazing."

Abbie put her hand over Chris's. "We can help you rebuild the jigsaw, and I'm sticking around here for as long as it takes. Your dad may need to get back to work in the new year, but I can stay for weeks, even months, if Fenella will put up with me."

Susie stared up at Fenella, standing a little to one side, and couldn't resist blowing her a kiss. "Oh, I'm sure Fenella will do that. She's a totally lovely person."

She wasn't going to push their relationship in her dad's face, but she wasn't going to pretend Fenella was simply some randomly kind woman who'd taken her in either. She grinned when Fenella's cheeks coloured. "Now I've embarrassed her. I only want you to know she's an ace human being."

"We know that already," said her dad. "She's shown us our rooms, and the house is beautiful and so warm and welcoming. We couldn't be better looked after."

"It's a pleasure to have you stay," said Fenella, moving forward. "Now I'm going to leave you three here with Susie while I go home to prepare supper and see my sons. Can you find the way back, Carla?"

"Good old satnav took me to your house, and I'm sure it'll lead us back there."

"Then I'll see you all later."

Fenella reached around the Americans and kissed Susie on the lips. "Goodnight, darling. Sleep well, and I'll see you tomorrow.

Maybe they'll let us know then when we can take you home."

So Fenella wasn't going to be too embarrassed to admit they loved each other after all. Susie was relieved. After Fenella left, she enjoyed another hour of memory building and reminiscence together with her folks. Susie couldn't recall everything, but the pieces of the jigsaw puzzle were beginning to fit together, and one thing she knew for sure was that her dad and Abbie loved her a lot.

"Kate and Catriona also send their best love," said Abbie. "Kate's having a terrible time with the new political situation, but she's determined not to be cowed by all the threats and bluster."

"Tell me about it," said Susie. "Just remind me who Kate and Catriona are?"

So then Abbie launched into another huge catch-up about Susie's American extended family, and who exactly was who, in the life she'd left behind three months earlier. Susie hid from her visitors how much the conversation exhausted her, but she didn't care about that so much. She was slowly sliding back inside her own brain. She understood most of what Abbie was telling her, which was like a miracle. She knew she still had miles to go, but this was a start. The nightmare of the last few days was beginning to release its grip, and best of all, Fenella hadn't walked away. Whatever her future held, she knew Fenella would be in it.

Chapter Thirty-Four

Rebuilding memory is never easy, and there were so many moments over the next ten days when Fenella shed secret tears and bouts of empathetic weeping as she watched Susie's struggles. She ached for Susie and longed to see her regain the sparky joy she had when rushing off to classes so happily only three months earlier.

Chris and Abbie were allowed extended visiting hours, so between them they kept Susie company most of the time. Her progress was patchy however, and when she visited, Fenella often found her sunk in depression and spitting with frustration. Susie was also soon desperately bored with hospital life, and having finished the Sudoku book in record time, vowed she never wanted to see another nine-by-nine square as long as she lived. But Bryony also visited every day and brought in Bel's latest book for her to read, only its doomsday analysis of the effects of climate change made for such alarming reading that Susie reverted back to Mary Beard's history of Rome for light relief.

"Your Latin seems pretty intact," said Fenella one afternoon, seeing Susie's textbooks open on the bed.

"Yes, I think my brain is in recovery. But I've forgotten all the classical Greek I learned this term," said Susie. "I really don't see how I'm going to retrieve that knowledge."

Chris and Abbie sat by Susie's side for as long as possible each day, while Fenella commuted on the train back and forth to London. She needed to still go to work: *Perceptions* wasn't going to edit itself, and the branding relaunch was set for early January.

But the last week before Christmas was always frenetic, and catering for houseguests, however considerate they were, was stressful. However, the final days before Christmas finally tumbled away though, and Susie was finally declared fit enough to leave hospital.

She could now hop up and down the corridors and manage the stairs on crutches. Her cabin fever was terminal, and she made everyone aware how desperate she was to get back into the real world. Chris and Abbie brought her home on the last Friday afternoon before the holiday, and when Fenella heard their hired car draw up outside, she opened the front door wide to welcome them in.

Susie swung down from the car, holding the crutch in her stronger arm and waving her plastered one in its sling. "Oh God, I've missed you!" she said dramatically as she tried to stand upright.

Fenella ran forward and grabbed her as she threatened to slide sideways on the front path's wet paving. She clutched Susie fiercely to her body, and Susie leaned in with all her weight. Still encumbered by her two casts, she carried rather more than her normal sylph-like poundage, and Fenella revelled in the substance of her.

"Idiot!" she said, before she kissed her mouth, her earlobe, and then the little dimple on her cheek. "You only saw me last night."

"It's not the same, in the hospital." Susie looked up at the floodlights on the front lawn projecting giant snowflakes onto the brickwork and all the silly Christmas decorations including a plastic reindeer that Fenella had let Chris and her boys hang from the gables. "Hey, you've put lights up all around the front of the house, just like at home."

"Your father persuaded me to send for them, and he supervised putting them up."

Susie grinned. "I bet you hated the very idea."

"At first, but now they're up, I'm quite enjoying them. I'm not such an old stick-in-the-mud."

Fenella didn't elaborate, but every day she was finding herself liking American extravaganza and ebullience more and more. She knew that the superiority complex she'd enjoyed over all things USA was nonsensical, especially as the love of her life turned out to be one of its brightest sparks.

"I'd say not! Now lift me over the threshold."

"I'm not carrying you!"

"Oh, shame. But I'll make you do it one day. You and I both

belong here, at No 38, with its lovely blue front door. We'll not be the Ladies of Llangollen, but the Ladies of Lavington Road!"

"I'm glad you still think so," Fenella said, trying to hide her whole collection of misgivings and fears. She was still afraid that, once Susie was released from incarceration in the hospital, she still might rightly come to her senses, or be persuaded by her parents to think again. She would surely see that a future tied to Fenella was not a sensible way to proceed. Her only comfort was that Susie could never be called sensible.

Chris and Abbie had been so tactful and forbearing as they'd watched Susie fling herself all over Fenella that it had been impossible to find the right way to tackle them or talk about some hard truths. But while they had never criticised, her visitors had also remained silent on the elephant in the room throughout the last week. There had been not a word of congratulations on any engagement, or endorsement for any physical show of affection. They'd simply smiled blandly and acted as though nothing had happened. Fenella assumed they didn't want to address the relationship, while Susie was so vulnerable and her recovery still in doubt. She'd be the same in their shoes, she supposed. But their reticence still scared her.

"Anyway, do come in. It's too cold out here." Fenella ushered them all inside, and the warm glow from an open fire greeted them. Freddy and Nate had already broken up for the holidays and had been useful. They'd also brought in a Christmas tree that stood five feet high in the window of the sitting room. It was wedged a little precariously inside a red bucket, and the boxes of decorations still lay on the table. "I thought we might all dress it together this evening."

"Great idea," said Chris. "I'll stabilise the tree and pack it into its stand."

"While you make it safe, I'll take your daughter through to her new bedroom."

"You mean the snug?" Susie grinned.

"Yes. Now then, Hop-along, follow me."

Susie swivelled on her crutches and hopped after Fenella across the corridor into the warm and bright little room which now held a single bed, a desk, and a closet.

"I love it. It reminds me of my college room. But the bed is only single. This won't fit us both. Where did you get it from?"

"I ordered it new for *you*, not us. I hope the mattress is the right firmness."

"I can just about manage stairs now. Why can't I sleep with you?" Susie looked less than joyful at Fenella's gift.

"Because you're still a bundle of broken bones, and I don't want to roll over and crush you in the night. Also, I'm going to have enough trouble relaxing enough to show you my body without worrying about your dad and Abbie listening to bed squeaks from above, and your inevitable shrieks of laughter from my room."

"You're saying I'll find you funny?"

"That's my best hope. I have serious fears that if I ever strip off for you, you'll break even more bones running away."

"Fenny, stop talking crap and sit on the bed!"

"What?"

"Just do it!"

Fenella did as she was instructed, and Susie sat down beside her. She leaned over Fenella and slowly unbuttoned her shirt. Fenella shivered as Susie's fingers brushed against her breastbone, and as Susie's mouth followed them, dropping kisses down her throat to the edge of her bra. Susie then lifted Fenella's breast and pulled it out of its cup. A sweet kiss enveloped her nipple, and she moaned as Susie's hungry mouth tugged on it and licked it.

"Oh my God, how I've wanted to do this for so long."

The sensation travelled directly from her nipple down to Fenella's core, the contact quietly driving her mad, and for some long minutes, she was powerless. She let Susie undo her bra, release her breasts, and smother them both with kisses. But eventually, Fenella put up her arms to hold her back. "Oh, please, please!"

"You want me to stop, or do you want more?"

"More, more, I obviously want more. But we have a house full of people. And you're in no fit state—"

"Here we go again." Susie snorted and dropped her hands. "You're just a big tease, Carlton. You drive me mad with desire and then act so damned sensible. But okay. For now, I'll cool it down.

I'm dead serious about how I feel though. I just wanted to convince you, if you still need convincing."

"I don't need convincing," Fenella whispered, trying to catch her breath.

"Then will you let me make love to you properly on Christmas day, as my Christmas present to you?"

Fenella sighed. "I will. I was hoping for a more sensible present though. You probably don't even remember our first big clinch."

"Oh, I do. It was in the garage, up against the shelf with the paint cans."

"Ah, so your memory *is* returning. That's great. But, seriously, my darling, do you really remember everything? If so, something not so good happened on the Friday of your accident that I must talk to you about."

Susie patted her away and shrugged. "I think I know what that is, but it can wait for now, can't it? Let's go back to the others. I want to talk to your boys and find out how Nate's big thing with Alice Markham is going."

"So you remember Alice as well!" Fenella was happily surprised by this. "That's fantastic. Nate will doubtless tell you a lot more about her than he tells me, I'm sure. But he's joined the bellringers at her father's church, so he's seen a great deal of her. They're ringing on Christmas Day and doing a triple peal to bring in the New Year."

Fenella then demurely refastened her bra, helped Susie to her feet, and went back with her to join the others. Susie had pretty swiftly changed the subject from their terrible falling out and the spectre of Stephanie Pole, and Fenella wondered how much she had remembered, and why she didn't want to talk about it. And what did that mean for their relationship? It was something they had to clear up before much longer.

Chapter Thirty-Five

Susie knew, even as she lived through it, that Christmas 2024 would be one of the best she'd ever experienced. The joy was enhanced because, deep inside, she knew how very close she'd been to not being alive after the crash. In that scenario, she could only have been here in Fenella's house as some sad little ghost floating above the merry crowd, looking on at the festivities. Though she guessed that if she had died, Fenella wouldn't have been cheerful at all, and there wouldn't have been much festivity in the house.

She was still encumbered by an arm and a leg fracture, three cracked ribs, and a whole range of bruises, but the love that flowed to her from Fenella and the whole household bathed her in a happy glow. Everywhere in the house was warm and cosy against the British winter weather outside. Her dad and Abbie had never spent so long in her company, and while they built up her memory banks together, sharing pictures from their phones, she felt closer to them than she guessed she'd been in years.

But what had put the cherry on top of the cake was something he'd said in the car driving home from the hospital. "She's maybe not the person I would've expected you to choose, but I can see Fenella's right for you. You love each other. And I trust her to look after you. Completely." That had warmed Susie's heart more than she could say.

She'd puzzled over what presents to buy Fenella and the boys on such short notice, but online shopping came to her aid. By interviewing Nate and Freddy separately, she learned what new video game the other wanted, and Amazon came through with the goods overnight.

From hospital, she'd ordered a hand-knitted fisherman's sweater from the Outer Hebrides for her father, and now she sat snugly on the sofa by the sitting room fire while she made more purchases through her tablet. For Abbie, she bought a set of the best gouache chalks and a large sketch book with top quality art paper. Then she scoured the internet to secure something special for Fenella. She knew what she wanted and had seen it somewhere online, but she couldn't quite remember where.

Fenella seemed to enjoy cooking for a crowd and kept herself frenetically busy in the kitchen most of the time. Abbie, who had spent more than twenty years cooking on a tiny trailer hotplate, asked if she could be Fenella's sous chef in her expansive kitchen. She seemed very happy creating her own vegan nut roast and stuffed squash alternative dishes for the menu.

Susie perched on a stool beside her on Christmas Eve while they made up a batch of spiced cinnamon cookies, snickerdoodles, and English mince pies. Then they both learned from Fenella how to ice a heavy fruitcake, which came delivered to the house, along with a large turkey, vegetables, and a whole package of trimmings. Fenella clearly wasn't going to risk a third encounter with the pink lady by going back to the supermarket in person.

"Marzipan *and* white icing? Do you want me to get fat?" asked Susie, already cutting herself a slice of the former.

When the icing had set, Fenella pulled out an old tin of little plaster characters and a collection of miniature fir trees from a kitchen drawer. "Here you are. You can both decorate the Christmas cake. Recreate your Oregon forests with these."

"How will we possibly have room for this after the big dinner you're planning?" asked Abbie.

"We'll save the cake for Boxing Day, the day after Christmas," said Fenella. "I thought it would be nice to invite a few friends around."

"So we can all start fighting each other?" asked Susie, and Fenella laughed at her.

"No, darling, Boxing Day is for visiting friends with boxes of gifts and handing out presents. I know you haven't fully recovered, but I thought you might enjoy seeing some people again, including the ones you met in September. They're all keen to see how you are and to meet your folks."

"Are Bryony and Bel coming?"

"Yes, they are. And Olivia's bringing her whole family out from

London: all five youngsters and a brother-in-law, as well as Niamh, of course."

"Wow! What a houseful. Fantastic. I think I might begin to enjoy parties for the first time."

"That's not all. Carla and her fiancé, Richie, are coming too. We have so much to celebrate this year. Last year's Christmas was pretty wretched for us here with just Nate, Freddy, and me, and Maurice turning up drunk and causing a scene. Like I said before, I'm in the business of making new memories, not just for you, but also for us all."

Later on the evening of Christmas Eve, there was much surreptitious rustling of paper and missing scissors all over the house, and the pile of presents under the tree grew into a satisfying collection of mystery objects. Chris, Abbie, and the boys had decorated not just the tree but also the whole downstairs with fairy lights, and Abbie had painted cardboard angels that flew along golden ribbons in lines across the whole of the ground floor.

Susie realised she was a sucker for Christmas schmaltz, and she enjoyed seeing how Fenella's normally immaculate and carefully designed interior had been transformed into a magical kingdom full of silliness. Stars, animated bears, votive candles, and even Santa-themed napkins quite destroyed her idea of Fenella as the queen of cool. But Susie had a cunning plan to make Christmas even more special.

Early on Christmas morning, well before dawn broke, she braved the stairs and slowly hitched herself step by step up to Fenella's room like a secret Santa. She pushed open the door with her crutch and limped over to the large bed, which was covered in grey chenille. Fenella lay motionless in the centre, her shock of copper curls emerging from under the duvet, and the room still lay in darkness. Susie placed a parcel at the end of the bed and then slid into bed next to her. "Move over, darling. I need some space here."

"Hm?" Fenella stirred but didn't wake.

Susie slipped out of her dressing gown, snuggled down as best she could, and wrapped her less painful right side around Fenella's body. Satin pyjamas were smooth and silky under her hand, and she quietly began to walk her fingers under the jacket and across

Fenella's gorgeous body. She must've been deeply asleep because Susie took quite a little hike as far south as the flat plane of Fenella's belly and under the waistband of her pyjama bottoms before her exploration was detected.

Fenella squeaked, "What the fuck?" Her hand gripped Susie's and held it tightly, stopping its progress.

"Merry Christmas to you too, darlin'," Susie whispered.

"I thought I was dreaming." Fenella didn't seem angry or outraged. She turned towards Susie and quietly undid her own pyjama buttons, allowing her in.

"I came bearing a gift, and to collect the one you promised me," murmured Susie, her head resting against Fenella's wonderful breasts as she traced her hand across the contours of her body.

"Here it is for you then, such as it is," Fenella said, her voice muffled with sleep. "It's a poor gift for such a wonderful person. There's a better present for you under the tree downstairs."

"Shh, everything I want is right here. Are you going to let me make love to you at last? Let me taste you, feel you, see you? Can we turn on the light?"

Fenella touched her bedside lamp once to give a faint glow. "That's as bright as I'll go. I'm a crumpled old thing."

"Au contraire. You're a goddess. And I'm coming to worship at the temple."

Fenella stretched like a sleepy cat against the pillows, and Susie knew at long last she'd been given a straight home run, with no barriers against her desires beyond her own awkward physical limitations. She replaced her fingers and began to make love with enough pent-up energy to ignite a volcano. She might only have one functioning hand, but she had her lips, teeth, and tongue. She could lick, kiss, and caress to her heart's content. While the rest of the house slept, Susie set out to prove how much she'd fallen for Fenella. The clock beside the bed had said six a.m. when she'd crept under the covers, and it was past nine before they finally surfaced.

As daylight finally crept around the edges of the window blinds, Fenella lay back and stared at the ceiling, her body seemingly turned to syrup. "I can hardly move," she whispered, her eyes huge in a face flushed with post-coital exhaustion.

Susie, who had an energy bank in her charged enough to keep going much longer, laughed with pure joy. "Was that a nice present? Well, here's another one."

Sitting up a little, she reached across the bed and passed Fenella a ten-inch square box covered in Christmas wrap and tied with a large red ribbon.

"What is it?" Fenella pulled herself up against the pillows and shook it. "It's not as heavy as it looks."

"Open it. I hope you like it." Susie helped her undo the bow and shed the wrapping. Fenella used her manicured thumb nail to slit open the tape, and she pulled out copious amounts of tissue paper to reveal the contents.

"What? Oh! She's lovely! Is this Diana?"

"Yep. She's a replica of a first century Romano British figurine. She's pulling out an arrow from her quiver, about to fire it at someone or something."

"Look, she has quite modern dress, and little boots, and her bag is just like yours," Fenella said, clearly delighted. "In fact, she looks just like you, full of mischief. How did you find her?"

"In the Corinium museum shop in Cirencester—online, of course. But I hope we can go to visit the original soon. I thought you might like her as part of your garden collection."

Fenella shook her head. "Oh no, she's far too precious to sit outside in all weathers. I'm putting her on her little plinth here in my bedroom." Then she got out of bed and stretched, naked and confident, all false modesty forgotten. "Let's shake a leg. People will wonder where we've both got to."

Susie wanted to make quite sure that she'd sealed the deal though. "So I've climbed the battlements. Can I sleep with you in here from now on?"

"You can, and you may. In fact, if you don't, I shall be seriously upset. This will be *our* bedroom from now on."

But then, as Susie prepared to join her, Fenella pushed her back and sat naked on the bed next to her. "There's one thing more we have to clear up first. Please hear me out. Don't argue or push it to one side."

"Okay." Susie guessed what was coming. She'd done her own

research.

"I know I hurt you badly when I initially dismissed your worries about Stevie Pole's plagiarism, and I can never undo that. But I regretted it immediately, and I want you to know it's been properly dealt with. I went to visit her and confronted her. She's withdrawn the book, resigned her position, and has left Oxford for good. It's all over. In fact, she mentioned you. She guessed you'd sussed her out, that you were too bright for your own good."

Susie looked up into those beautiful dark eyes and took Fenella's hand. "Not so bright. I thought I was being clever. But I was a self-righteous little brat, and I'm sorry I was so quick to judge. If we fall out again, I will always assume it's my fault, and just ask you to kiss us better."

Fenella pushed her back against the pillows and kissed her on the mouth. "Like this?"

"Hmm. Lovely…"

Then Fenella pulled back and said brightly, "So now that's settled, let's go downstairs and see what other presents are under the tree."

Nobody else noticed when Susie came down the stairs rather than from her own room, and the morning went by in a happy chaos of present-exchanging and coffee-drinking, with Bucks Fizz, cream cheese and smoked salmon bagels, and Classic FM playing carols on the radio.

Fenella passed Susie a tiny box, no bigger than a pack of cards. "This is for you."

"What is it?" Susie guessed it wasn't a ring. It was too soon. "A bicycle bell?"

"No fear. This will hopefully keep you out of the bike lane for good."

Susie slowly opened the box and then the inner little casket within. It must be a pendent, but when she looked inside, she saw a car key on a fob with the Mini logo embossed on it. "You haven't! A car? That would be amazing! Won't the insurance be phenomenal?"

"I bought the car, and your father has purchased the insurance. We agreed it was the best thing to keep you safe when you are back at university."

"When can I see it?"

Fenella smiled like Alice's Cheshire Cat. "Look outside. It's at the front of the house now."

The whole household rushed out to look. The little car sat on the street, in dazzlingly sapphire blue with leather seats. Susie positively salivated at its total gorgeousness. "It's far too much. It's too generous. Fenella, honey, I can't accept it."

"Yes, you can, and don't fret about the price. Nate's father runs a group of motor retail outlets. He owed me some big favours, and I got it well below cost price. So once you've recovered, you can put your name down for a parking space at St Hilary's."

"I'm going out to sit in it now!" Susie swung herself outside and spent the next half hour sitting in her first ever car, while imagining driving Fenella all over so they could visit Roman remains together and have sex in hayfields across the counties of southern England.

Chapter Thirty-Six

The rest of Christmas Day went by in a happy dream, and on
Boxing Day, the house was invaded by hordes of people,
including some of Bel's friends from Gloucestershire, who were
another lesbian couple called Jane and Jennie. Susie picked up
Jennie's accent as French Canadian and asked, "Are you from
across the pond too then?"

"Guilty as charged," said Jennie, "by way of thirty years in
Africa."

"She used to be a nun," said Jane, putting her arms around the
older woman. "But I'm gradually re-educating her."

"I need to know more." Susie laughed, responding to their happy
faces, and then Fenella introduced them all to her close neighbours
who were Africans. The Mugabi family were African doctors
from Kenya, and their children knew Nate and Freddy. They made
friends with the other gang of kids from London easily enough.
Everyone under eighteen migrated to the top floor, while the rest
stayed below to eat, drink, and get rather merry.

After lunch, Fenella, Abbie, and Chris seemed to have a private
conversation in the corner.

Susie's father, proudly wearing his new sweater, looked
repeatedly at his phone and then nodded. "In less than an hour,"
he said.

Susie wondered what that meant, but her brain didn't register
it as significant until the front doorbell rang, and a buzz went
through the party. Everyone other than her seemed to know what
was happening.

Fenella opened the door, and Susie gulped as the unmistakeable
figure of Kate Konrad strode in with Abbie's daughter, Cat Sinclair,
and their three teenage daughters coming just behind her. The bright
variety of American accents and large personalities burst into the
room.

Susie wanted to cry, she was so moved. She hopped forward and was swept up into Kate's and Cat's arms. "Oh my God! You came all this way from LA just for me?"

"Chris and Abbie have told us you're going to be living with Fenella here in Oxford for good, so we thought we'd come to check up on our little sister here," Kate said. "But you may be seeing a lot more of us all in the future. The fires across Los Angeles are still raging, but they're nothing to the clouds of fascism gathering over Washington. Anyone who loves America and respects its constitution is in for a very rough ride. Just watch out. Next year is going to see things so bad, you won't believe it. I've decided I need to have a safe place ready where my children can live if we're forced to flee. So I'm planning to buy a house here in Oxford."

"Will it come to that?" asked Fenella. "Will things be so bad?"

"Just wait and see. But for now, can you show me the way to a bathroom? It's been a long drive from the airport, and I'm desperate."

Kate and Fenella left the room together, and Susie could see they would soon be fast friends. She knew she was surrounded by people she loved and who loved her, and that her dad clearly accepted Fenella as her partner and one of their family.

No longer the oddball, no longer lonely, and weird, and misunderstood, Susie had not only travelled five thousand miles to fall for Fenella, but she had also found her true home. Love, like Latin, might be a hard and mysterious language to learn, but with Fenella being such a brilliant teacher, she reckoned she was well on the way to learning it by heart.

~ THE END ~

Author's note

Would you like to know more about Susie's American family, and how she came to Oxford, and also what happens next to Kate and Catriona? Then look out for the final book in my *Behind the Camera* series. It's called *Faultlines* and will be published in the spring of 2026.

And finally…

If you've enjoyed this book, please leave a rating on Amazon, and a review if possible. This makes such a difference to where the book is placed and encourages others to read it.

About the author

Maggie McIntyre is an award-winning author living in rural Lancashire. Maggie believes in the power of storytelling to inspire, break down barriers, and help people discover their true selves. A lover of spring flowers, warm animals, and the smell of rain, Maggie finds joy in laughter and the connections she's built with friends around the world.

Other books by Maggie McIntyre

SERIES ONE: ISABEL AND FRIENDS

Isabel's Healing
A devastating road accident leaves climate-change campaigner Bel Bridgford broken and bitter, but when a young assistant steps into her life, can she learn to live again?
Lesfic Bard Award winner for Best New Writer category 2020

A Girl on the Plane
Isabel's project manager, Steph Miller, fears the worst when a terrified young girl approaches her on a plane from Kinshasa, as she flies home for Christmas. In this passionate and emotional sequel to Isabel's Healing, Steph and her partner Alana struggle to save both the girl, and their own future together.

Into the Rough
Restless Canadian nun, Jenni Argent, finds new friendships working for Isabel's development agency, but meets open hostility from Isabel's best friend, sportswoman and golf fanatic Jane Walkley, who fears and distrusts all religions, and especially nuns. Will they ever make friends? A warm and humorous look at a most unlikely love affair, on and off the golf-course.

Love Under Lockdown
Isabel, Bryony, their friends, Jane, Jenni, Steph and Alana are locked down in England as COVID rages across the country. The three couples each take different pathways through the pandemic, but sustain their love, friendship and hope for the future. An uplifting novel about the power of love.
Runner-up in the 2022 Lesfic Bard award for romantic fiction.

SERIES TWO: BEHIND THE CAMERA

Heatwave
Katherine Konrad, self-made millionaire and head of Montpellier Media, is a force to be reckoned with in television, but she meets her match in Catriona Sinclair, straight out of the Oregon backwoods and fiercely ambitious for a career in filmmaking. It's hot in the city, and the heat also runs through the pages of this fast-moving

and passionate story set in present-day California.

Wildfire
Cat Sinclair takes her lover Kat Konrad home to meet her eccentric family. But this turns out to be the least of their worries, as they are swept up in devastating wildfires which ravage the rural Oregon community. Will they and their loved ones even escape alive?
Runner up in 2021 Lesfic Bard Award Category Action and Adventure.

Love and Money
More adventures and another challenge face Kat and Cat as they face a hostile takeover of Montpellier Media, and discover something rather strange is going on in an elder-care home in suburban Orange County.

Blaze Away
Oscar-winning actress Blaze Bentley heads to Ireland for a film, but danger from her past resurfaces. As threats close in, she calls her best friend Kat for help. Can they survive the shadows that haunt Blaze?

FANTASY ADVENTURE NOVELLAS
Series: High Queens of Hesperia
Vol 1.   The Woman at the Gate
Isolated and in fear of a despotic emperor, Princess Alessandra waits for the moment she can take revenge. Then a strange, older woman is dropped at her gate, half dead, and her life changes for ever.

Vol 2.   Golden Boy
Alessandra and her two female companions set out on a perilous winter journey to rescue her son. Will they succeed? Page-turning action and heart-stopping romance provide the answer.

Vol 3. Powerful Magic – coming soon.

STAND ALONE FICTION
Up the Garden Path
When international celebrity Cait mistakes Maisie for an insolent waitress, their relationship sours before it even begins. But Maisie

and Cait soon find themselves drawn closer together. This is a delicious romantic comedy set in an English summer garden, as both women discover that love can be found in the most unexpected places.

For Love of Thunder
Ten years have passed since her riding mistress, Tara Morris, broke Ricky Gates' tender sixteen-year-old heart. Now, through one scorching summer, she has agreed to accompany her old teacher on an epic road trip across America to sell her beloved horse, Thunder. Can they get through the journey without hurting each other again, or will love blossom along those dusty highways?

What's Your Story?

Global Wordsmiths, CIC, provides an all-encompassing service for all writers, ranging from basic proofreading and cover design to development editing, typesetting, and eBook services. We specialise in helping self-published authors get their books into the world but also help authors find a traditional publisher or agent.

Another part of our work is charity and community focused, delivering writing projects to under-served and under-represented groups across Nottinghamshire, giving voice to the voiceless and visibility to the unseen.

To learn more about what we offer, visit: www.globalwords.co.uk

A selection of books by Global Words Press:

Desire, Love, Identity: with the National Justice Museum
Aventuras en México: Farmilo Primary School
Times Past: with The Workhouse, National Trust
Young at Heart with AGE UK
In Different Shoes: Stories of Trans Lives
Our Pride: with Nottinghamshire Healthcare Trust

Self-published authors working with us:

Max Beeken
Ramona Black
Dee Griffiths
Troy Jenkinson
Meg Marlow
Maggie McIntyre
Simon Smalley
Kit Stone
Adam Rainford
Louise Wilding

www.ingramcontent.com/pod-product-compliance
Lightning Source LLC
Chambersburg PA
CBHW070939190726
48292CB00004B/1242